SORCERERS

ALSO BY JACOB NEEDLEMAN

The Essential Marcus Aurelius
What Is God?
Money and the Meaning of Life
Lost Christianity
The Heart of Philosophy
The American Soul: Rediscovering the Wisdom of the Founders
A Sense of the Cosmos: Scientific Knowledge and Spiritual Truth
Why Can't We Be Good?
The New Religions

Sorcerers

A Novel

Jacob Needleman

Monkfish Book Publishing Company
Rhinebeck, New York

Printed in the United States of America

First published in the USA by Mercury House, Inc., 1986
Published in Great Britain by Arkana, 1989

Library of Congress Cataloging-in-Publication Data

Needleman, Jacob.
Sorcerers, A Novel / by Jacob Needleman.
    p. cm.
Paperback ISBN: 978-1-939681-47-8
eBook ISBN: 978-1-939681-48-5
                    2010005893

Monkfish Book Publishing Company
22 East Market Street, Suite 304
Rhinebeck, New York 12572
USA 845-876-4861
www.monkfishpublishing.com

Contents

Part 1

PHILADELPHIA

Shadows on the Door

Some people say that Philadelphia is a place where nothing ever really happens. Life just grinds on there. People get up, work, go to bed, live in little row houses, eat the same meals every day, and eventually disappear without a trace. Perhaps this is no longer true of Philadelphia, and probably it was never really true. Or, perhaps all of us live in this dull city that seems permanently off-limits to the magical possibilities of life. In any case, it is just there that this tale of magic takes place—at the start of the 1950s, a decade when to some people, the whole world seemed a little like Philadelphia. . . .

* * *

A wet and cold November night. Eliot Appleman, age fifteen, wearing a chocolate brown shirt, a pale green coat, and a yellow necktie, drifted into a cobbled back alley off Walnut Street in downtown Philadelphia and entered a run-down brick building called Pennypack Hall, where for seventy-five cents he witnessed a spectacle that turned his life around. He watched young men his own age seemingly defy the laws of nature and the human mind. Flowers and live animals appeared out of nowhere. Balls floated in the air. Bodies were penetrated with steel knives which were then harmlessly withdrawn. Hypnotic spells were cast and the privacy of thought telepathically invaded. It was the Fourth Annual Show of the Sorcerer's Apprentices.

During the intermission, Eliot approached a glossy-skinned young usher and breathlessly asked how he himself could share in these phenomenal doings. The young man looked him over very carefully and, when the show was over, whispered to him about a certain meeting the following week at a certain address.

*

That certain address was not far from that particular building, and was also ill-heated, run-down, and drab. An antique elevator pinched Eliot's fingers before its gate clicked shut and its agonized, vibrating motor raised him to the second, third, fourth, and finally to the fifth level. There, with a thud, it stopped, as though forever. Its metal door slid open with alarming speed and threatened to close just as quickly. Eliot leaped out and found himself in a dark, tiled corridor. His footsteps echoed as he walked down the corridor and paused before room 515. From the other side of the door he heard laughter and talk. On the frosted glass he saw the shadows of people moving about in a manner heavy with purpose. He knocked on the rattling glass. A shadow grew large in front of him and opened the door.

A man—long wavy hair, unusually complex lips, tall, scented with cologne—stood in the open door. Behind him was a small, brightly lit room, young men, some with their jackets off, one carefully knotting the end of a crimson scarf....

"I'm Eliot Appleman...."

"Yes," the man said, musically, "please come in." He closed the door behind them and introduced himself as Stephen Blake, extending a hand with a large gold ring upon it. He wore a dark, subtly patterned suit, a Windsor-knotted maroon necktie held in place by a gleaming silver clasp, and exposed French cuffs linked with the silver masks of tragedy and comedy.

There were fewer people in the room than the shadows on the door suggested. One of them was the usher Eliot had spoken to the week before; the others had all been performers in the magic show. Eliot recognized the man before him as the one magician who had been in costume—a long, saffron robe, bejeweled white turban, face whitened, lips rouged to a sharply cleaved smile. His had been the concluding act; spectacular, oriental, bizarre; apparatus with exotic designs.

He led Eliot to some flimsy folding chairs placed by the wall and sat down next to him, crossed his legs and propped his elbow on his knee. His arm stayed rigid as he spoke, but he gestured luxuriantly with his fingers. Eliot admitted to the meagerness of his magical experience, a few cheap twenty-five cent tricks such as the Bottle Imp, the Nickels to Dimes, one or two elementary sleights with coins, and some awkward, mechanical card tricks. Blake assured him that his past experience was of no importance; all that mattered was the sincere desire to learn magic. Eliot, in turn, assured Blake of his sincerity. Blake answered that time would tell. He would be admitted as a prospective member and, after six weeks, be voted in or out.

Blake then proceeded to outline the goals of the club. As he did so, the room began to fill up with other members. They entered usually in twos, some carrying painted boxes, or metal tubes, or bulging paper bags. Several started setting up tables with holes cut in the center. One removed from his bag a small metal contraption, a foot-high silver rod resting on a tiny silver base. He then blew up a yellow balloon and attached it to the top of the rod. Another brought out half a dozen pastel silk scarves and began knotting them together. Then, a cadaverous young man dressed in a black suit entered, accompanied by a ludicrously tall, scrofulous fellow groaning under the weight of some oddly-shaped object covered with burlap and tied with frazzled white twine. The cadaverous young man quietly directed the other to set his load at a particular place in a corner of the room and to remove the wrappings. The other, with much mumbled chatter, obeyed, but needed help untying the knots. The cadaverous one produced a monster jackknife and sawed through the twine; the scrofulous one whipped off the burlap and revealed a man-sized, orange and red lacquered guillotine.

"Five years ago," Blake was saying, "the club was founded by an extraordinary woman named Irene Angel. She wanted this club to be patterned exactly after adult magical societies, except for one thing: no adult society will accept you unless you already have developed an act. That is as it should be, but young and inexperienced people like you are forced to waste time practicing without a teacher, ferreting out secrets from dated old books, growing into styles that don't suit their personalities. But here, my friend, you'll learn the right things from more experienced magicians, like myself or like some of the older members, and you'll have to submit what you learn—as you learn it—to the criticism of the others. They won't be easy on you, they won't applaud you like a doting family, and they won't make light of your errors. But I promise that you'll learn what magic is, just as Irene taught us."

Eliot nodded. He sensed in Blake's words that this Irene was no longer living and he refrained from asking about her. He hardly knew how much was allowed him, and this man Blake was unlike anyone he had ever met. Eliot guessed him to be in his twenties, but he was so eloquent, fine, and self-assured that Eliot felt the distance between them as infinite. It was hard to believe that such people lived, after all, in Philadelphia.

Blake then stood up and called to a short, slender young man wearing rimless spectacles. With a gentle pressure on the shoulder, Blake kept Eliot from rising. "Eliot Appleman, this is Wally Pound. You'll be in his charge until the voting. Wally, you'll answer his questions, take him to Templeton's, and . . . well, you know." With that, Blake left their company and went to the long table at the head of the room. The bespectacled boy sat down next to Eliot and offered him a cigarette, which Eliot accepted. The cigarette rose spontaneously from the pack. Wally Pound smiled with clenched teeth as Eliot's eyes widened.

"I'll show it to you after the meeting."

Blake pulled his chair to the side of the table, sat down, and gracefully folded his hands upon his crossed legs. Three young men then came to the tables; one remained standing. There were now about fifteen people present in the room. The others had left their various apparatus at the rear and had taken their places before the long table.

The young man standing at the center of the table rapped his gavel. As he did, one last Sorcerer quietly entered—a strikingly and almost menacingly handsome young man with silky blond hair and luminous blue eyes. Moving like a cat, he took a seat apart from all the others.

"The meeting will please come to order," said the president in a subdued, gravelly voice. "If there is no objection, we will dispense with the reading of the minutes of the last meeting and proceed with the Treasurer's report."

The boy seated to the left of the president rose. He was fat and wore a thick orange sweater under his suit jacket. Smiling, he inhaled two quick, childlike sips of air and began reading from a black loose-leaf folder.

"The Fourth Annual Show was held on November 15, 1950, in Pennypack Hall. Paid attendance was 160 which, minus costs for hall rental and printing of tickets and advertising, left a net profit of eighty-six dollars. A donation of twenty-five dollars from Max Falkoner, manager of Templeton's Magic Shop, was gratefully received, as were four donations of ten dollars apiece from the parents of president Stillman Clipper and members Sandy Hyman, Terry Laken, and Kim Vogel. The treasury now stands at one hundred fifty-one dollars. The outstanding debt is three months' back rent for the meeting room, forty-two dollars. The treasurer has been informed by the owner of this building, Mr. Baum, that as of January first, monthly rental will be increased from fourteen to fifteen dollars."

The treasurer took his seat and closed his loose-leaf folder. The president—short, black-haired, dressed in Ivy League clothes—rapped the gavel again.

"Old business is now in order, but if there is no objection, we will suspend the rules of order so that we may listen immediately to Steve Blake's comments on our performances in the Annual Show."

Blake remained seated and reflected for a moment, tapping his fingers together. "Yes. In general, the level of presentation was not too good. But let's start from the beginning. . . . Sandy?"

Eliot listened with little comprehension but intense interest as Blake criticized the performances. As each boy rose and listened obediently to what Blake said, Eliot vividly recalled the particular act in question. He could not believe there was as much wrong with them as Blake seemed to be saying. They had all done magic. One had read minds, one had produced bouquets of flowers from an empty box, one had changed a gallon of milk into two white doves, one had impaled his own hand with a dozen long needles, one had caused solid steel rings to pass through each other. The last had especially enthralled Eliot. But now Blake was indicating how these tricks had actually failed; he spoke of "faulty misdirection," "talking body loads," and "uncoordinated patter." And the members all meekly acquiesced.

"Now," said Blake in conclusion, "as I pointed out all through the rehearsals, these technical errors almost always come about because you're not sure of your central style. You can't simply get up on a stage and do magic, plain and simple. Magic is not just 'showing tricks.' *You* must be the one who is doing something. If you're doing a silent routine, then *you're* the medium through which magic is passing into the objects you use. If it's a comedy routine, then perhaps you're magical in spite of yourself. You can't just handle things like ordinary people; strange things happen every time you take a step or make a move. If you're doing mentalism, like Ronnie, you've got to be the person for whom ordinary material barriers don't exist—you've got to feel yourself into the part. You are actors; you're playing a role and you can't step out of it. You can't rely on the apparatus, even with the mechanical tricks. The moment you start relying on the *tricks,* they'll start being *mere* tricks, and your audience will try to *figure them out.* The audience will become your enemy. But if you really enter the role of a magician, you'll give them what they paid for— magic, the impossible. I've said it a thousand times: everybody in the audience—except for the hecklers—comes prepared to see the impossible. While you're on stage, if you don't act completely as though you are able to do just that—the impossible—if you don't seem completely sure of your own magical powers, they'll jump on you with both feet. But to do that, you've got to have your *own* style. All right, enough. It wasn't such a bad show—we'll make it better next year."

When the formal part of the meeting was over, Wally Pound introduced Eliot to some of the other members. They were all extremely friendly to him, quite likeable; in fact, they actually seemed ordinary, not unlike his classmates at school, though most were a little older. But this did not ease Eliot's sense of being an outsider. Their ordinariness merely indicated to Eliot that they were extraordinary in a subtle and hidden way, and though Blake had tried to reassure him, he began to grow afraid that they would read in his very eyes the lack of any gift for magic. Blake, at least, had the appearance of a magician; he *looked* like he was cut from a different cloth.

The second part of the meeting was about to begin. The large table was moved to the side, and the two odd persons with the guillotine took the stage. Eliot had not met these two during the intermission, and he was comforted to perceive that, without a single doubt, they were specimens of the Creep class. The cadaverous one was a cadaverous creep, the scrofulous one a scrofulous creep. Their names were Edgar Wick and Gordon Bunche. The former looked like an emaciated version of Peter Lorre, with half-closed eyelids, deathly pale skin, and milky blue eyes that seemed glazed over in a hypnotic trance. The latter, next to Edgar Wick, had to suggest a bumptious version of Bela Lugosi. All the color that had been drained from Edgar Wick's face seemed to have wound up in a ridiculous disarray on the blotchy, pimply, scaly face of Gordon Bunche. The fellow seemed everywhere overburdened by a surfeit of blood; his jumping eyes were red, the end of his fingers were orange, with fingernails bitten down and sprinkled with tiny flecks of clotted blood. They made quite a pair. Wick was slow, mechanical, deliberate; his voice was a flat monotone. Bunche was nervous and jerky; he spoke in a jumble of squeaks and growls with a voice that seemed at one moment to emanate directly from his bulbous nose and at another from his paunchy belly. Wick was quite short, sleekly dressed; Bunche was enormously tall, and a slob.

Bunche lugged the guillotine to the center of the floor and sat down in the front row of chairs. Then Wick took the stage, carrying a straw handbasket containing a cabbage and some carrots. He set the basket on the stand next to the guillotine, placed his hands behind his back, and then turned to the audience. With his shiny black shoes touching, his shoulders stooped, and his eyes staring straight forward, he droned out his memorized speech.

"Ladies and gentlemen, we may date the birth of democracy from the onset of the French Revolution in 1789. Until that time, death by decapitation was a privilege reserved only for the nobles of the European nations. Lower classes had to endure grotesque and tortuously slow and painful executions. They were burned, drowned, drawn and quartered, crushed, gibbeted and garroted. But in the year 1791, the great Jesuit physician, Joseph Ignace Guillotin, persuaded the Constituent Assembly that men of all walks of life deserved the deliciously swift and painless exit from this vale of tears provided by the instrument you see standing to my left, the very name of which has lent immortality to the good doctor, *la guillotine.* We are all familiar with its workings. . . ."

Wick took the cabbage and one of the carrots from the basket and set the basket on the floor directly under the opening for the head. "The blade," he said, stroking it with the carrot, which was instantly sliced in two, "must be finely honed. The victim's head is placed in this large aperture—" as he said this, he inserted the cabbage "—and locked in place." He pointed to a heavy padlock. Then he walked behind the apparatus and gripped the upper handles. "With one stroke—" he grimaced and shoved the blade down with a loud crash. The cabbage split in half, and one of the pieces fell into the basket. "—the job is done. Mercifully, beautifully. But for years the question was much debated as to whether or not death by the guillotine was instantaneous, and in support of the negative side, the case of Charlotte Corday was adduced. Her countenance, it is said, blushed with indignation when the executioner, holding up the head to the public gaze, struck it with his fist. It is my firm opinion, ladies and gentlemen, that this is mere fabrication. And with your kind assistance, I should like to establish the case for the guillotine once and for all. For my experiment I shall need the help of someone from the audience. What? No one comes forth? Surely there must be one among you despairing of the sorrows of life who, seeking the gentle hand of death, would be grateful at the same time to advance the cause of scientific research. Ah! There I see a man with sorrow written on his very brow. You, sir, . . . would you please come forward?"

Wick moved toward Gordon Bunche, grabbed his hand, and began pulling him out of his chair toward the guillotine. "No, No!" cried Gordon Bunche, "Not me! I'm too young to die!" Bunche pretended to struggle against Wick's grip—a bit too strenuously at one point, where he nearly knocked Wick off his feet. But the magician succeeded in "forcing" him to the guillotine and inserted his head into the opening. He clamped shut the stocks and turned the key in the padlock. Above and below the opening for the head were two smaller apertures. Wick placed a carrot in each, so that when the blade came down they would be convincingly sliced in two. Bunche rolled his eyes in horror. He squealed and shrieked, while Wick adjusted the basket beneath the head and again went to the rear of the apparatus and clutched the crossbeam handle.

"And now, ladies and gentlemen, proof positive! *Vive la guillotine!*" Wick started to push down the blade, but then paused. "Sir," he said, "would you mind turning your head a little to the left."

"No! No! Let me out! Help! Help!"

"Good," said Wick, addressing the audience from his post behind the guillotine, "he is now actively alarmed, and we shall see beyond a shadow of a doubt that no trace of life remains when the blade does its work." And this time Wick did shove the handle down, apparently with all his strength. The upper carrot snapped in half. But something obviously went wrong, for at that very instant Bunche let out an extremely convincing, ear-piercing "Yeeow!" and wriggled frantically for a moment, rattling the wooden frame and the locks.

At that, Eliot let out a bellowing laugh, but was quickly silenced by a poke in the ribs from Wally Pound and a sour, sullen glance from Edgar Wick. No, it was not a comedy routine. Yes, something had backfired, and yes, Bunche was squealing from pain, though his head was clearly still attached to his shoulders. Once again, Edgar Wick raised the handle high and brought the thing down full force. Bunche clenched his fists, closed his eyes, and contracted his brow. This time it worked; the blade sailed through the fellow's belabored neck, chopped the lower carrot, and stopped with a nicely resounding thud. Edgar Wick bowed, the audience applauded, and Bunche was set free. He straightened up and proffered the back of his bruised neck to his partner, who disdained to examine it until the applause was done with.

"Edgar, you'd better get that angle-latch oiled," someone said.

"I'm very sorry," said Edgar Wick to the audience. "That never happened before. But how did you like the patter?"

"A little gruesome, isn't it?"

"That's the whole idea!"

"Yeah, but I mean it's a little . . . , like that bit about the head after it's chopped off. Someone could lose his dinner on that one."

"See, that's what I told him," said Gordon Bunche, still rubbing the welt on the back of his neck. Wick froze his partner with another sour look.

"Edgar," said another, "I think the patter's okay, but you don't build up enough after Gordon's head is locked in. You went too fast there. If I were you, I'd do some more byplay with him."

Eliot watched Edgar Wick retain his composure as criticisms began falling out of everyone's mouth. It was always Bunche who nodded in agreement, while Wick stoutly maintained his vision of the general effect. Nothing seemed to fluster him, while everything flustered Bunche. To Eliot, something about them suggested man and wife, or puppet and puppeteer, or mind and heart, or some two things that should be in one person, rather than two. Creeps. Demi-creeps.

But how the hell did that guillotine work? Nothing anybody said made it clear. In all fairness, he did want to speak out and say, "But it *fooled* me!"

Before the meeting was over, three more members presented tricks, but Eliot could not get his mind off the guillotine. He kept imagining the damned blade as actually passing through Bunche's neck. This worried him, that somehow, somewhere in him he was perfectly ready to believe—not exactly that it was real magic, but that some strange device enabled a blade to pass through a person's neck without hurting him.

When they adjourned, some of the members grouped together, and Eliot was invited to join them. It was another cold, drizzling night, but this time the emptiness of the streets and the vague, watery outlines around the lamps did not oppress him. And when they crossed Market Street, the gaudy jellies of neon for once sat well with him and didn't press him into himself and make him fear the dim green subway ride back home or the hollow wait at the corner of Germantown and Chelten for the E bus, with its silent Negro driver.

They turned on Chestnut Street; Eliot and Wally Pound brought up the rear of the procession. Up front, Blake was laughing with the president, whose name he now knew to be "Clip." Blake's laughter was interspersed with speech. Eliot had never heard a person able to talk in the middle of laughter like that, without disrupting the laughter. But then the laughter itself was so like speech—from the lips, articulated, thinly turned. To watch Blake's back one could never tell he was laughing. He walked with his hands clasped behind him, his beautiful duck's ass haircut sailing forth smoothly like a yacht, his fine camel's hair coat, $125 at Jacob Reed, shedding the droplets like the expensive grand thing it was—whereas Eliot's own motherless "weather-resistant" trenchcoat was drinking it up like a sponge.

The place they went to was a large, subdued nighttime eatery at the corner of Nineteenth Street. They all squeezed into a circular corner booth, and various spectacular sandwiches and ice cream dishes were ordered from the waitress. Wally Pound, this very pleasant but very quiet fellow, sat next to him and ordered a mere grilled cheese and tomato.

They did not talk about magic. The conversation was loaded with a myriad of themes, each of which indicated that these particular members shared more of their lives than the bi-weekly meetings. And there were references to other people, some of whom might have been members, but certainly not all. It seemed now that more than magic united them; it seemed that there were many purposes in their lives, many sections of reality Eliot had never seen firsthand: ballet, poetry, chamber music, philosophy. Not a single mention of girls. Not even a feminine name. Nothing about sports, little about movies, nothing about school. Eliot took quick bites of his triple-decker pastrami, turkey, and swiss cheese sandwich. No, there was really no doubt about it, he had fallen into something exceptional.

TEMPLETON'S MAGIC SHOP

The following Saturday, Wally Pound telephoned and suggested they have lunch in town and then go together to Templeton's. They met at exactly noon at the corner of Broad and Chestnut and went to Bain's Cafeteria. The weather had finally broken; it was a sharp, sparkling December day.

Eliot saw that Wally was waiting for him to ask questions about the club. But at this point he really had none. What he did want was the chance to know a member well enough to risk showing one of his own tricks. But Wally was not an easy fellow to get to. He would say things which seemed to open up a line of conversation, only to drop it cold after Eliot's response. This happened quite often. Through the whole meal Eliot never had the feeling that he was making himself known.

Wally's face was clear and simple, his eyes blue, his skin fair, his jaw angular. He seemed frail, but his handshake had been powerful. He wore a dull corduroy jacket and a green plaid tie; he was exceptionally clean. He seemed joyless, even somber, as though shaped by greater responsibilities than the average person his age.

After the meal, Eliot brought a half-dollar out of his pocket. "I've been practicing the French Drop," he said.

Wally nodded in appreciation of this fact.

"I'd like you to watch how I do it," said Eliot. He had been practicing the sleight for hours every day since the meeting.

"Right," said Wally, "go ahead."

Eliot placed the coin between the tips of the left thumb and forefinger, brought his other hand over it, and then whisked the hand away while dropping the coin into his left palm.

Wally paused for a moment with his coffee cup at his lips. "That was very bad," he said, and then resumed drinking his coffee. Eliot sat motionless with the coin still palmed, waiting for further comment. But Wally said nothing.

Finally Eliot asked him, "What did I do wrong?"

"Look at your left hand."

Eliot regarded the hand which was concealing the coin. It seemed perfectly all right, but he'd be damned if he would ask Wally again.

Wally took a coin from his own pocket—a silver dollar—and did the sleight. It was beautiful. Eliot compared his own left hand to Wally's. Of course. His thumb was sticking out like a flag.

"That's called the fishhook. Dead giveaway that you're palming something."

Eliot made the move again, this time carefully allowing his thumb to stay relaxed. "How was that?"

Again, Wally simply did the sleight. But this time it was not at all effective. It was obvious that the coin was still in the left hand. Wally paused for a moment and then startled Eliot by showing him that he had actually taken the coin into his right hand, that he had not done the sleight at all.

"You get it?" said Wally.

Eliot slowly shook his head in puzzlement. He felt quite stupid.

"You were taken in by misdirection. Where my eyes go, your eyes go. If you want someone to think the coin's in your right hand, you have to keep looking at your right hand. The second time I kept looking at my left hand, even though I had actually taken the coin away. The first time, when I really did the sleight, I kept my eyes on my right hand. That's misdirection. It's the most important thing in magic."

*

Templeton's Magic Shop was in a smart office building near City Hall. Until now, the only magic stores Eliot had seen or been in were the tiny, disarranged, dirty-windowed novelty shops on Market Street, where magical apparatus took second place to cellophaned

13

sex manuals and such gag items as simulated spiders, turds, and vomit. The proprietors of these shops were invariably sleazy, with heavy-lidded narcotic stares that followed one all about the store and endowed every item they sold with the character of swindle.

But here he and Wally ascended in a humming, soothingly lit gray elevator which met its landings precisely, opened its doors responsively, and contained the circulating atmosphere of money's tender loving care. They alighted on the seventh floor and immediately faced the handsomely etched glass door, with the rabbit coming out of the hat and the very business-like "Templeton's Magic Supplies" printed beneath it. At the bottom of the door, in smaller letters: "Max Falkoner, Mgr."

Wally opened the door and Eliot followed him into a large, sunny, oblong room with a glass counter running its full length. The store was full of people, mostly teenage boys, animatedly talking to each other in clumps of twos and threes. Behind the counter, a short, swarthy man wearing a brown *cubavera* sport jacket was standing head to head with a customer and concentrating on a small black square cloth which lay on the counter between them. On the mirrored wall behind him was a riot of lacquered and chrome boxes, blocks, shining swords, cups, silks, flowers, chickens, skunks, rabbits, huge copper pans and electrical apparatus, tumblers, pitchers, tall glass tubes, gigantic playing cards, several smaller versions of what looked like the Wick-Bunche guillotine, alarm clocks, candlesticks, a top hat, and much else that was stunning but utterly unrecognizable to Eliot.

The opposite wall was covered with framed autographed publicity photos of magicians—some grinning behind fanned cards, some pulling rabbits out of hats, some answering the marvelous and strange functions of the apparatus in the store. One magician was lifting a live duck out of that same copper pan, another held lit candles between his fingers, one was standing on a stage that was covered by the artificial flowers, one plunged a sword through the neck of a pretty girl. Many wore turbans and exotic costumes and had girls floating or being sawed, boys climbing ropes, or spectators trussing them in chains. Some were dressed clownishly, some posed in pairs, and one was a woman holding eight linked metal rings before her. She struck Eliot as quite beautiful, with powerful smooth features, fair hair that seemed silver on the glossy, black and white print, a calm high forehead and strong, but seemingly colorless eyes. He had a feeling that this was the woman Blake had spoken of with such awe, the founder of the club. And, sure enough, the bold, perpendicular handwriting at the bottom corner of the photo said, "Love to Max Falkoner, Irene Angel."

Beneath the wall of photographs there were some soft chairs and a low table with magazines on it, professional journals: *Tops, Jinx, Genie.* Wally sat down while Eliot wandered up and down the length of the counter, which contained an amazing variety of smaller items: black and flesh-colored gadgets of all sorts, some built to contain cigarettes, some made to fit around the thumb or fingers. There were ropes, dozens of decks of cards oddly named (forcing deck, one-way deck, doubleback, Svengali, Stripper, Thunderbolt, Brain Wave, Deland), billiard balls and shells in various colors, clips, scissors, plastic eggs, razor blades, small silks, dice, and—at the end of the counter—some twenty magic wands. *He had forgotten about magic wands,* so much more the symbol of true magic than the rabbit in the hat. The ones in the showcase were all black with white or silver tips and much thicker and more powerful looking than he would have imagined them to be. He badly wanted one for his own.

Eliot turned and beckoned Wally, who was now smoking a pipe. He put down his magazine and came over to him, trailing white clouds of sweet, fruity smoke. Eliot pointed to the wands.

"Are they expensive?"

"Depends. Those two over there are cheap."

"Why? They look just like the others."

"Well, they're not all ordinary wands. That one over there's a breakaway wand, that one's a wand-to-table—I think it costs about fifteen dollars—that silver-tipped one is a squirter and the one next to it's a shooting wand." Wally pulled the pipe from his mouth and blew the smoke up into the air.

"I think I'll get one of the cheap ones," said Eliot.

"What for? You can make one with a piece of wood and some paint."

"Yeah, but I couldn't make one that looks that good."

"Look, if you're going to buy a wand, you might as well get a gimmicked one that you can do something with."

"No, I just want a plain, simple magic wand."

"That's crazy."

Eliot shrugged. "I just want a simple wand."

"Say, you know they expect you to do a trick at the club before long. If you haven't got too much money, maybe you'd better use it for that."

"But I thought . . . I mean, I told Blake I was a beginner. . . ."

"Don't worry. They won't expect much from you, but you have to do something before the voting."

"But . . . Christ, I don't know *anything*. I'll probably screw up completely! You saw the way I bungled that French Drop."

"Do you know the multiplying balls? That's a good starter."

Eliot shook his head no and was now quite alarmed. He felt that nothing of magic had as yet seeped into him and that it was unfair to expect him to perform yet. Wally trotted to the other end of the counter. "Max, could I borrow a set of multiplying golf balls for a minute?" The man behind the counter reached down and handed Wally a small cardboard box. Wally did something with his back to Eliot and then turned around to face him. The man behind the counter stepped back to watch, but the other customers in the store paid no attention.

Wally set his pipe on the counter and methodically took three paces to the center of the floor. He held out one empty hand and then showed the other to be empty also, though clearly there was already some funny business going on. But it looked pretty good. He gazed up, reached into the air and produced a golf ball. He made a surprised expression and placed the ball between his thumb and forefinger. Immediately, another ball appeared between his first and second fingers. He nodded his head, again apparently in surprise, shrugged his shoulders, pursed his lips— mimicking something that Eliot couldn't quite fathom—and placed the second ball between his second and third fingers. He was obviously pantomiming some kind of act—someone who keeps finding balls appearing or something—but it was really not clear, and Eliot wished he would talk a little bit so that he'd know what to be looking for. Another ball materialized again between his first and second fingers; there were now three. Eliot prided himself on observing that there were improvements to be made in this presentation—and Wally produced a fourth ball. Then he smiled in a rather complex way, as though to say "thank you" or "isn't this odd?" or something of the sort, and proceeded to reverse the effect. The balls disappeared one by one, the last one vanishing by the French Drop.

The man behind the counter applauded.

"Not bad, Pound Cake, not bad at all." Max Falkoner was short, heavy, round-faced, one eye squinting in the smoke of a dangling cigarette. To Eliot he looked like a cross between Winston Churchill and the king of clubs. His few strands of black hair were combed flat over his shiny head, and he had almost no eyebrows. He took off his *cubavera* and rolled up his right shirt-sleeve. He slowly showed his right hand to be empty, then closed the hand into a muscular fist. Out of that fist there popped a rather large red billiard ball. With the finger of his other hand, he daintily pushed the ball back, removed the cigarette from his mouth, and flicked some ashes into the fist. Now a yellow ball popped out. This he repeated twice, the ball changing from yellow to green to white, until finally out came a lemon which he then threw to Eliot. Eliot dropped it; it bounced on the floor hard, solid, and unquestionably a lemon from a lemon tree in some distant clime.

The man unrolled his sleeve and buttoned it. He pointed to Eliot. "A new sore-assed Apprentice?" he asked.

Wally nodded yes and made the introduction. The man reached his hand out to Eliot, and Eliot shook the hand with great gusto. A warm, strong hand, thick fingers, hard skin, squared off fingernails. Max stepped back and stood motionless behind the counter with his eyes riveted on Eliot. He had stuck another cigarette in his mouth. "Give my regards to Broadway, Remember me to Herald Square," went through Eliot's mind; dit-dit-dit, attention all the ships at sea, Walter Winchell, *Variety*, movies starring Dan Dailey and Mitzi Gaynor, the Empire State Building, sharp black-jacketed

New York cops vs. flabby Philadelphia park guards wearing pale gray opened-necked shirts.

"That was a great trick," said Eliot. "How much does it cost?"

Max Falkoner smiled and Eliot realized the question was inappropriate, but he didn't know why. Max continued sizing up Eliot until suddenly he took the unlit cigarette out of his mouth, pointed it at him and said, "I've got the trick for you. You do silks?"

"He's pretty green, Max," said Wally Pound.

"Relax, this one he'll do." He reached into the counter for a large envelope with the words "Flag Blendo" printed on it in headline-sized black letters. He turned his back for a moment and then showed three small silk handkerchiefs, red, white, and blue. In an instant they were transformed into a large American flag. The trick was nice, but it didn't really appeal to Eliot as much as the other one. But Falkoner was such a professional, and he had pointed that cigarette in a way that meant he knew what the right trick for Eliot was.

"How much?" asked Eliot.

"Ten bucks."

"*Ten?* Jesus, I don't know. Is it hard to do?"

"Completely mechanical."

"I don't know. I'd sort of like to learn some sleight of hand tricks."

Again, Max Falkoner silently regarded him, then carefully folded the flag and put it back into the envelope.

"Eliot Appleman, my friend, you want to do sleight of hand? You want to work surrounded? You want to make things disappear? You want to stick a lighted cigarette up your nose and pull it out of your ear? You want to be an ace with coins? You want to handle a deck of cards like you were the general of an army?"

Falkoner beckoned Eliot to step closer and pulled out a deck of cards which he then spread face down on the table. "Now," he said, "think of three cards." Eliot did so, selecting the queen of hearts, the six of diamonds and the eight of clubs. "You have three cards in your mind?" Eliot nodded yes. "Shuffle them," said Falkoner and Eliot laughed. "All right, concentrate on those cards, and now select three cards from these that are face down on the counter. Don't

18

look at them . . . fine . . . now sign your name on the backs of these cards . . . okay? . . . good. Seal them in this envelope. Right. Now, here's what I'm going to do . . . merely by sleight of hand. When I say the magic words, the cards in the envelope will be blank, and the ones you selected—which will be the same ones you merely thought of—will appear in the bottom of your right shoe, *between your sock and your foot!* And with your signature on the backs!"

Eliot turned to look at Wally, who was thoughtfully pondering Max Falkoner and puffing assiduously on his pipe. It was hard to tell by his expression if Wally knew the trick or not. But then, quite quickly, he returned his glance to Max Falkoner and glued his eyes to Falkoner's right hand. He had read the other day that if you want to know how a magician does a trick, you must keep your eyes on his right hand.

"Now, you understand what I'm going to do?"

Eliot nodded that he did.

"All right, here go the magic words:

> Ahn, tahn, tahn-ta-nass;
> Quviss, quvoss, kom-panass;
> Allo, dallo, socker-dallo;
> Kikki, rikki, ross!"

At this Eliot laughed. Max Falkoner gave out a collegial smile. "Showmanship," he said, and Eliot nodded understandingly, still watching Falkoner's right hand, which was poised motionless on the counter, the counter behind which he was still standing.

"All right," he said. "It's done."

Eliot did not move.

"So, open the envelope!"

Sure enough, Eliot tore it open and found three blank-faced cards, none of which bore his signature on the back. Falkoner continued to look at him as Eliot, stupefied, shook his head and moved through the crowd to one of the soft chairs. He sat down, looked at Wally, and then began untying the laces of his right shoe. He slowly began to remove his luminous red sock. When the sock was half off, he suddenly paused and froze his movements. He felt his ears burst into flame and sank his eyes under his lids. When he opened his eyes a moment after, he was gazing at half of a bare foot, his own.

He looked first to Wally Pound, who was puffing on his pipe and looking at him compassionately. Then, still clutching his sock, he turned to Max Falkoner. Falkoner was putting out his cigarette and with his other hand was reaching into his shirt pocket for another. His eyes, too, were still on Eliot. Another moment passed. Then Falkoner reached behind the counter and lobbed a metal shoehorn to Eliot. It hit his knee and struck the terrazzo floor with a deafening clang.

"Applefriend, buy Flag Blendo. For ten dollars you get a solid ten dollars' worth of magic."

*

The American flag was actually two flags sewn together at the edges, save for an opening at one corner where there was a one-inch metal ring. The smaller red, white and blue silks were attached together to a slender ribbon which was connected at the other end inside the flag. The trick consisted of showing the smaller silks while holding the flag bunched up behind them and pulling the ribbon so that the smaller silks were sucked into the flag. Eliot was disgusted with it. Over and again, practicing before the mirror in his parents' bedroom, he was stymied by the damned thing's snarling and knotting, the bunched-up flag sliding out of his hands before the critical moment, or simply by the fact that even when the trick worked it was all too obviously a faked flag with something lumpy hidden inside.

By and by, as he mastered the mechanics of the trick, what disturbed him most was the whole idea of it: three colored silks merging into an American flag. He wanted something mysterious or beautiful; this was ludicrous. And the patter that came along with the trick on a mimeographed sheet was also repulsive: some crap about Betsy Ross and George Washington.

On Wednesday he went directly from school downtown to Templeton's Magic Shop.

"Applefriend, what's this bellyaching? That's one good trick you bought."

"Look, I just don't like it. I don't like anything about it."

"Do it. Take it out of the envelope and do it."

"That's not the point, Max, I know how to do it, all right."

Falkoner scratched his ear.

"All right," he said. "You want to buy something else?"

"Well, I'd like to exchange it. I was looking through the catalogue. . . ."

"Ooop! Hold it right there. What'd you buy? A couple pieces of silk worth two bucks? A flag worth another buck? You bought a trick, a secret. I can't take it back now, kid. That's the policy. . . ."

"What secret? For Christ's sake, a lousy hole in a flag is no secret."

Falkoner made a wheezing sound with the cigarette held tightly between his lips. His nonexistent eyebrows raised, and his tiny dark eyes brightened. Eliot realized he was laughing.

"What's so funny?"

Falkoner paused. "Hey, Eliot Appleman . . . listen. The hole in the flag is a secret. On another trick a *lousy* piece of celluloid is a secret, and on another a lousy sliding drawer is a secret. That's what we sell; that's what you buy. All right? Now look, what exactly don't you like about the Blendo?"

Eliot sighed. Ten dollars shot.

"Well . . . for one thing, it's a kind of comedy trick and I didn't want to do comic stuff. . . ."

"So? Who says you gotta play it for laughs? The trick can be a big smash finale if you do it right. Junk the patter that comes with it, give a short lecture on the colors of the flag, do the move, and then have a backstage blast of the Star Spangled Banner and you got them standing in the aisles applauding. *Standing in the aisles!*"

The Linking Rings

Eliot Appleman, Myron, his father, and Helen, his mother, had for the past five years made their home in a suburb of the city known as Chestnut Hill. Their street, Pelham Lane, was a block of newly constructed, red-brick duplex apartments, an island of lower-middle-class Jewry surrounded by magnificent parks and hostile Gentiles. The neighborhood, therefore, held terrors as well as wonders for Eliot: terrors human in the form of young arm-bending, pride-destroying rednecks; wonders natural—the Wissahickon Creek, deep, quiet stretches of forest, rocks, endless trails, wildflowers, insects, birds of all kinds. There, in those parks, he knew his greatest joys, and there he had made the decision, so dear to his mother, to study medicine.

Myron Appleman was a man who had sold many things at many times in his life: flowers, insurance, gasoline, tile, lamps, women's shoes, and, now, men's clothing at Gimbel Brothers. He had nothing in the bank, but neither did he owe money to anyone. He was sinewy, reticent, strong-willed, incapable of cheating or lying. He was unaccustomed to touching people, although when he put his hands to wood, metal, or many years before, to the violin, he was a creator of beautiful things. His wife was his reciprocal: plump, soft-eyed, easily moved to laughter or tears. Her mission in the house was peace and affection. Eliot was born with his mother's brown eyes flecked with green, her smooth skin and rounded features; from his father he had received broad shoulders and strong limbs. For a son, she was the mother to be chosen and protected. But *he* was the father, distant and superb.

As a child, a very young child, Eliot knew the names of the planets and the stars. He was fascinated to learn about the sun, its size, its power and heat; but it was with hungry awe that he thought about the planets most distant from the sun: Uranus, Neptune and Pluto. Six years old, he imagined that he would grow up to be an astronomer whose special study was those three planets. "The stars," said his father, "are even farther away." But to Eliot the stars were part of God.

*

Eliot had chosen Wednesday night to go to Templeton's because that was the night the Sorcerer's Apprentices met. He had planned the day carefully. He had told his mother he would not be home for dinner, he had left his books at school, and had looked forward to eating in town alone and then walking around before going to the meeting at eight o'clock. But the encounter with Max Falkoner had depressed him and now, standing outside on Broad Street with the Flag Blendo still under his arm, the hours ahead weighed heavily. He wished it were later so that he might talk to Blake about the trick and get his advice.

It was five o'clock; the sun had already set, the sky was cold, and a half-moon glistened. People were hurrying past him in great clots into the subways and buses. They poured out of the buildings and were going home; they all seemed like his boring relatives—uncles, aunts, cousins—though amid them all there had been one, a second cousin named Elaine. They had been children together. He had fallen in love with her when he was five, and he had seen her only once since then. He had heard she was studying music in New York, far away.

Philadelphia itself seemed like a boring relative. To the right was City Hall, which smelled of urine and was covered with pigeon shit. To the left was South Broad Street, with a few luxurious hotels, office buildings, banks, the Academy of Music conducted by Eugene Ormandy, and then it suddenly stopped being downtown and became a big sour space in the Negro section. Behind him and before him, Market, Chestnut and Walnut Streets presented shops, stores, first-run movies—all shiny dots of meaninglessness. And there behind him, on the minus side of Broad Street where the city sold things cheaper, where hot dog buns were colder, there next to the big Main Post Office Annex, a gigantic beautiful stone building one block wide with mahogany and steel-barred windows devoted to the task of selling three-cent stamps, there next to it was Gimbel Brothers, on whose second floor Myron Appleman, father, sold forty-four dollar suits with Lincoln-like integrity.

Wednesday night the stores were open until nine. Good. Eliot moved from his post in front of the office building that housed Templeton's Magic Shop. He passed Wanamaker's, a store he hated. He hated the arched stone facade, the high, church-like dome of the main floor, the merchandise sealed behind glass, the stuffy sales people, the rock-like, solid, unchanging permanence of Wanamaker's. The sameness of it. Its self-sufficiency.

Gimbel's was different. There were always tables full of special items to touch, handle, examine—bargain-priced things, things that pleaded to be bought, a constant flux, a variety, dimensions. Philadelphia didn't have many places more interesting.

He entered on the Ninth Street side, wandered through the flower department, paused by the collection of rock-gardens, stuck his finger into the gravel beneath one of the miniature trees. Nearby was the garden supplies department. He squeezed a green plastic hose and reflected that the old orange rubber hoses were better; one could never squeeze them that easily.

Across the aisle was Gourmet Foods. Eliot stealthily opened a jar of Dijon mustard and put it to his nostrils. Damned good stuff. He quickly sealed the jar and placed it back upon the shelf. No one had seen him. He began to ponder, in a tentative way, what he should steal. A jar of imported mustard? He had never lifted anything from Gourmet Foods, but he decided that the mustard, no matter how exquisite, was not worth the risk. He picked up a container of macadamia nuts, unscrewed the top, and slid one into his mouth.

He drifted into the shoe department, browsed around a collection of loafers and noticed, with disgust, that a pair he especially liked cost about the same as the Flag Blendo. He was beginning to think it important for him to steal something particularly valuable. Shoes, of course, were out of the question. It occurred to him that skill at sleight of hand might prove very useful in his hobby of shoplifting, though how it would ever be possible to make off with the right pair of loafers he couldn't imagine.

He passed by a counter full of socks marked down to fifty-nine cents, fingered some without looking at them, and spent a moment at another counter heaped with long-sleeved sport shirts. Then he proceeded through an arcade into the book department. Here, two weeks ago, he had stolen a Modern Library Giant edition of *Moby Dick.* His method had been beautiful. The Modern Library section was off in a corner. He had removed the book, thumbed through it, and then started to move away with it. But then he thought he saw someone watching him, so he started walking, book in hand, toward the cashier, his eyes loaded with the sincere intent to buy it. He even locked glances with the salesgirl as he approached her head-on. It was his feet that effortlessly pulled him out of the book department. He had found himself standing in front of the stamp collection. He leaned over the counter and examined some Hungarian triangulars, placing the stolen book on the counter as he chatted with the salesman.

It had been a true discovery. No more stuffing things under coats or in pockets. The secret was to act exactly as though he wanted to buy the article and then at the last moment, float by the cashier as though it had already been purchased. Eliot vaguely sensed a connection between this and the concept of misdirection.

Once again, he browsed through the Modern Library section. But there was nothing there of any interest. Those damned Modern Library books were all alike anyway; they vanished as soon as they landed on a shelf. He could not remember ever finishing one of them. Besides, they were too cheap. He wanted something equal in value to the Flag Blendo.

He circled about the art books, but the prices frightened him: eighteen-fifty, twenty dollars, twenty-five dollars. They were beautiful books. He picked one up, and the old thrill of terror shot through his palms. He dropped the book back on the pile.

He looked around. He could have stolen it; no one was watching. And that was almost enough. He began to breathe freely.

He spied a large, handsome dictionary on the next counter. Now that was something he really wanted. His own was shabby and simpleminded; half the words he looked up were not in it. The price of this one was eight ninety-five. He picked it up, glanced through it, and then made his move.

Once again he was in the stamp department, with the book burning in his hand. It was the most expensive thing he had ever stolen. He nonchalantly made for the exit, stepped out on Eighth Street, and walked half a block. There he stuffed the book into the Blendo envelope and reentered the store.

He took the escalator to the second floor and walked around in the sporting goods department. His step was light and buoyant; the gloom had lifted. It was odd, but that business of acting as though he were going to purchase the book, and then leaving the store as though he *had* purchased it, almost made him believe he had bought it. He felt he truly owned the book and had paid something for it.

The sporting goods department was adjacent to the men's clothing department. Eliot leisurely meandered along the racks of fishing rods, football gear, boating equipment. When he came to the end of the corridor, he stole a glance to the left. There was his father standing underneath a mannequin, waiting for his turn to take a customer. He stood with his hands behind his back, his legs spread, his face set in that expression of waiting that Eliot knew only from the times his father would sit on the couch, being in one of his rare good moods, and benignly tap the upholstered arm with his fingers and whistle silently. Other salesmen were not standing that way; they were in groups of twos or threes, chatting, laughing. They were all paunchy; some had sneaky, wire-thin mustaches. There was not a customer in the place. Eliot was always afraid that one of these days he would come upon his father waiting on a customer. It would break his heart to see that.

He suddenly felt he did not want to be seen by his father. He hurried past the entrance to Men's Clothing and found himself in the bedding department. He ran his hand along the various rows of sheets, pillow-cases, towels, mattress pads. Then he crossed over to Housewares, turned lamps on and off, lifted ashtrays and blown glass knickknacks, stared into the light through some large globes of colored glass. The image of his father standing under the mannequin stayed before him. He made six percent on all sales; that meant that an ordinary suit netted him about three dollars.

Eliot exited by the escalator in the back of the housewares department. He tightly clutched in his hand the envelope with the Flag Blendo and the stolen dictionary.

*

Blake plunged his hands deep into the side pockets of his suit and disdained even to touch the Flag Blendo. He had been nodding his head affirmatively and understandingly all the while Eliot was telling him his problem. Finally, with a compatriotic smile and a swift penetrating squint, he interrupted:

"You're right, Eliot; it's not for you!" He was wearing a tan sharkskin suit with tiny black checks and a wide, musical sweep of lapel of a sort Eliot had never seen. It looked great on him, emphasizing his breadth and height and the flat, clean planes of his face. (That night Blake entered Eliot's dreams disguised as the G-clef sign, that gorgeous volute he could never draw, and the checks on Blake's suit became quarter and eighth notes.)

"It's just a cute gimmick; it has nothing to do with magic. Red, white, and blue silks merge into an American flag. That's trash. An American flag is a *manufactured item*. You bring in a manufactured item like that and you'd be amazed at what the audience can imagine: anything from mirrors to elephants could be built into it. Don't laugh; it's true, Eliot. And by the way, Max knows it better than anyone. Next time you see him, ask him what Irene would have thought of the Flag Blendo."

"Did he know her, too?"

"He knew her very well."

"I saw a picture on the wall there. *Beautiful* woman."

"That's with the linking rings, isn't it? Now, *she* knew magic: mysteries compounded of simple clay—you follow? Suspension of fundamental laws, transformations of nature, *things* of nature moving right before the audience in impossible ways."

"But what about those big production boxes? Aren't they manufactured with all kinds of devious things built in?"

"Of course," said Blake, now sitting down. "But then you've got to look to what's produced. The classic symbol of magic is a rabbit,

27

you see, something real and alive, out of nature, not a manufactured item. Doves, flowers, bowls of water, even bowls of fire, Eliot, fire! *That's* what makes a production effect.

"Ask yourself: what's the ideal trick? The boy climbs a rope, vanishes, his limbs fall to the ground, the magician throws them in a casket, and then out jumps the boy alive and kicking. The magician manipulates death, gravity, the structure of the human body. Eliot, every trick you do—if your act is serious— must have you controlling laws that others must submit to. That's why you have to work with simple, fundamental objects. Elaborate apparatus is only good when fantastic things happen with it, things that are so impossible they could never happen no matter what apparatus one has. The apparatus then serves a definite purpose: it makes the audience believe you have access to powerful *objects.* That's why good apparatus has to either look weird and outlandish, from another world, or it has to be simple and familiar. So, there are two kinds of magic: one where *you* have the power directly, like the fakir, or the other where you possess objects that have the power. Irene's favorite was the linking rings: simple, perfect circles of steel. The audience examines them . . . let me show you."

Blake glided across the room and spoke for a moment with one of the members. He was handed a bunch of large metal rings and returned to Eliot with the rings jingling on his arm. Some of the other Sorcerers gathered about as Blake paused about two feet from Eliot.

Eliot counted eight rings that looked separate, while Blake peeled off two of the rings and held one in each hand. Then he gave them to Eliot. They were just what Blake said: simple circles of steel about ten inches across. Blake took them back in one hand. From his other arm another metal ring slid down to his fingers. He held this ring up and struck it against the two which Eliot had just examined. There was a resounding clang, and suddenly the rings, now linked, were dangling from Blake's fingers. There then followed a dazzling series of maneuvers in which rings were linked and unlinked at Blake's will. He handed Eliot two linked rings which then unlinked in his own hands. Eliot examined them also, and they were without a flaw. It was most pleasing to watch and hear:

the pretty, shiny rings rotating, glimmering, clanging musically, passing each through the other until quite soon it seemed perfectly natural that, for a moment, the law of solids had been overcome. Eliot was willing to believe it, this he noticed in himself. It was like surrendering to beautiful music, surrendering to the effect of these intriguing rings moving in and out of each other in Blake's long, beautiful hands.

Watching Blake work, he was aware of the same feeling he had had when Wick had used the guillotine on Gordon Bunche: that some *subtle device* enabled one solid to pass through another. Now, however, this feeling seemed appropriate, involved as it was with these airy, sonorous circles that could just as well have been geometrical images in the mind. The only thought that troubled him at all was that a piece of steel, be it ever so slender, is still a piece of steel.

Blake concluded by showing *all* eight rings linked, and then swept them together into one hand. Only then did a childhood memory dislodge itself in Eliot's mind: a Christmas present of a magic set. A pair of magnets had been the main fascination; the rest of the tricks had been tossed aside—incomprehensible and disappointing to a child of five. Among the discarded tricks had been a set of red plastic rings three inches across, some linked, some unlinked and one "broken" to allow the solid rings to pass through it. Not realizing that this "break" was the key to the whole trick, Eliot had twisted apart the split ring for the wretched, momentary pleasure of it. He had played handcuffs with some of the other rings, and the rest had disappeared into a box of dead toys.

This must be the same trick that Blake had done, and now he would discover what had been left out of the child's set. He asked to see all the rings and Blake obliged. To his amazement and strangely wrought delight, Eliot discovered the same split ring, the same sets of three and two linked rings, and two *bona fide* separate rings.

"You know the trick, of course," said Blake.

Eliot, aware that he was smiling in what must have seemed an inappropriate way, shook his head no. Blake quickly explained the principle of the key ring (the ring with the gap in the rim, the *broken* plastic ring, the one first destroyed), and showed how that ring was the one that passed through the others, showed how he substituted the ones already linked for those that were genuinely separated, and showed how he concluded the trick by placing the key ring between the set of two and three linked rings, and grasped each of the single rings in either hand along with those already linked to make it appear that there were eight linked rings.

Eliot was overjoyed. There was not that flat, ugly sense of swindle that had gone with the Flag Blendo—perhaps because he had already learned to expect some foolishly simple secret. But more likely because that simple little crack in the key ring didn't really solve a damned thing. There were the switches, the misdirection, the flourishes, the actual *vision* of rings passing through each other, the sleight of hand, the constant clanging of the rings—all of which took a skill and mastery of movements which could have made an amazement out of genuine, solid, actually separate rings. No, the "secret," the crack in the key ring, was purely a challenge, a call to arms: *Make this BE a secret! Learn to use it to create magic!* Again: one didn't need a ring with a crack in it to run into this challenge; *anything* could become magical with the skills of Blake.

"It's one of the truly great conceptions in magic," said Blake. "It's an infinite trick, when magic can really be an art. A magician-artist confounds other magicians who know the secret of the trick he's doing!"

After the meeting, and after the hour of food and conversation at Hamburger Heaven, Eliot actually looked forward to the subway and the bus. The evening, which had threatened to go sour because of Max Falkoner, had ended on an upbeat. Blake had rekindled all of Eliot's enthusiasm about magic and had even arranged for him to borrow Don Papermaster's set of linking rings.

So now Eliot walked through the dark plaza of City Hall carrying the Flag Blendo, the stolen dictionary, and the linking rings in a separate paper bag. He slid a dime into the turnstile and descended into the acrid gloom of the subway. Apparently, he had just missed a train; he was the only one on the platform. And this late at night, it might be a half hour before another one came.

Since no one else was there, he set down the Flag Blendo and the dictionary and removed the linking rings from the paper bag. The sounds of them banging together echoed eerily in the huge dank spaces of the station. He took hold of the key ring and passed the tip of his finger through the break in the rim. Then he repeatedly smashed the key ring against another of the rings, trying to effect "penetration" of one ring though another. At one point, however, the key ring dropped from his hands. He stood frozen in terror as he watched it rolling to the edge of the platform. Luckily, it stopped and spun to a rest just short of the edge, even as Eliot conjured up in his mind images of leaping down after it in the face of tales his father had told of the power of the third rail, comic book villains in orange suits being killed with one jagged zzzap. The third rail: "You mean even if I just *touched* it I would die?" And even now, just standing at the striped edge of the platform could give Eliot the same thrill of horror that he had had as a child, even though he now knew that they coated the thing with some nonconductive material and even though he often saw workmen walking upon it and commercing with it as though it had no death in it.

Eliot picked up the key ring, and the shrieking subway exploded into the station. It was dimly lit and dirty, one of the older trains with peeling straw-backed seats and hand supports darkened by perspiration. The windows rattled as the car moved, and in the outer blackness lights shot by like comets. But Eliot happily contemplated the events of the evening and played in his mind various routines for the linking rings. Of course, the most spectacular part of the trick as Blake presented it was the finale where all eight rings were shown to be linked. Perhaps he could go one step further; perhaps he could end by having them linked *in a circle,* one great ring composed of lesser rings. He could call it The Triumph of the Circle.

IN THE SCHOOL OF SAINT JOHN THE BAPTIST

In the middle of December, Edgar Wick announced that he was putting together a full two-hour act for midnight bookings in the local movie houses. He and his partner, Gordon Bunche, needed a third person as an assistant and occasional stooge. Eliot volunteered for the job.

He felt bound to. The previous week, his debut with the linking rings had been a fiasco. Halfway through, they went berserk in his hands. His face turned red, his legs wobbled, and he felt like someone trying to break out of an enormous, jangling set of handcuffs. The rings began linking and unlinking on their own power and did a fair job of fooling *him* more than anyone else. The Sorcerers sharply criticized him for trying something so hard his first time around, and some of them even said he should have worked a purely mechanical trick like the Flag Blendo. But Blake stood up for him and praised his ideals, adding that of course he had a long way to go before he could handle the rings.

So he volunteered to work with Wick and Bunche. Wick took him aside and assured him that he would pick up valuable experience, but this Eliot doubted. The past six weeks had merely confirmed his first impression of the two of them: creeps, peculiar growths. Each week the grave, cadaverous Edgar Wick wore the same black gabardine suit and dark blue bow tie. Eliot speculated that under that suit was another black suit, and under that yet another, and so on down to the bones. At least Bunche, slob though he was, varied his attire with an amazing array of hokey, motheaten sweaters, none of which reached all the way down to his belt, and some jacket-trouser combinations capable of causing real pain.

Rehearsals were to be held in the auditorium of a Catholic high school at Fifty-third and Spruce, deep, deep in West Philadelphia— bus, subway, bus, and trolley car, a distance covering the entire *Philadelphia Inquirer,* including the women's section, and *Time* magazine front to back. The Saturday afternoon of the first rehearsal was a Philadelphia winter classic: cold, heavy clouds tight as metal, sleet falling in all directions, buses stalled, traffic clogged. Eliot, ears wet and nose running, was a half-hour late even as he was making his last connection. And that particular trolley carried him into regions of the city he had never seen. It must have been what Columbus felt, the world really is round, there's always more of the same over the horizon—always more and more of Philadelphia, row houses, nubbly little lawns, meaningless tamed trees, brick walls, Fords, Chevies.

When he alighted from the trolley, it was in a Catholic neighborhood. Their concentrated presence here was unredeemed by parks and fields like those near his own house. Concrete sidewalks and street after street ruled by Catholics: crosses, statues of the Virgin in windows, settled as thick as the Jews in Strawberry Mansion, *goyim* without flowers and brooks. The street was a mosaic of cold strangers worshipping something unfathomably alien to the God of trees and rivers.

Inside the School of Saint John the Baptist, Eliot was afraid of encountering a priest, though in fact he was not at all sure that priests had anything to do with Catholic schools. He knew that nuns did, and he would not have been alarmed if one suddenly passed next to him in the hall. It would not have been difficult to address her as "sister," as he had seen it done in movies. But would it be proper for a Jew to call a priest "father"? And even if proper, he doubted that he could bring himself to do it. How could one say "father" without, at the same time, meaning oneself as son?

The auditorium was on the first floor at the end of the main corridor. As he approached it, he heard the tinkling sounds of a piano, a frenetic jumble of notes on the upper keys. He entered from the side and saw Gordon Bunche bent over the instrument with his nose nearly touching his fingers. His head rolled back and forth with great excitement, though his eyes seemed fixed on those few keys he was pounding. Gordon immediately looked up at Eliot, retracted his hands from the piano, and held them perched at his chest like the claws of a tiny rodent. Behind him, the stage was loaded with apparatus. In addition to the orange guillotine, there were three magicians' tables, a large swath of black cloth draped across a six-foot high frame, a skull on one of the tables, a bugle on another, a sizeable wooden chest, and a good deal else that Eliot could not make out. The echoes of the twittering piano slowly died away, and from the other side of the auditorium, Edgar Wick rose in a cloud of cigarette smoke.

"You're over an hour late."

"I'm sorry, Edgar. The buses were running slow."

Wick moved toward him with the cigarette pointed into the air like a torch; the great spaces about him amplified every footstep. Eliot removed his wet coat and threw it over a chair.

Wick silently moved past and beckoned him to follow. The three proceeded to the stage and Wick began explaining the act. Being a midnight show, the gimmick was spook and spirit magic, and the opener would be some black art routines that Wick had devised "over a period of years." For some reason, this phrase had the effect of making Wick seem younger, rather than older. Perhaps it was the peculiar puppet-like way he stood—heels touching at right angles, elbows to the side, very little movement of the hands. When he then spoke of having worked on something "over a period of years," Eliot saw a little boy wonder discoursing to a group of delighted relatives, a child groaning under the weight of his own head and yearning, really, for the sandbox. Only with Wick, it was not spheres of the intellect that he had prematurely entered, but, alas and ever again, the "Kingdom of the Dead": ghosts, mummies, demons, skeletons, zombies, the nasty little puppies of the Wolf of Death.

Wick handed Eliot three pieces of black cloth, which were apparently some kind of costume, and then explained that with the proper lighting, this material would make Eliot invisible against the black backdrop. Eliot's job would be to move various white objects around while Wick pattered about ghosts and poltergeists.

The costume, made of flimsy, stiff cheesecloth, consisted of a pair of pants, a pullover top, and a hood with eyeholes scissored out. Backstage, Eliot began putting the costume on over his clothes. While he was not exactly fat, he was not exactly thin either. The buttons and buttonholes of the pants did not even kiss. The shirt was too tight and the sleeves too short. Obviously, he would have to remove his own clothes first.

But that morning Eliot had unfortunately selected a pair of undershorts patterned with large red windmills, and these windmills were clearly visible through the thin black cloth. He proceeded to remove his shorts and try the costume over his naked body. That was all right; nothing of him showed through the costume now, but the pants were still so tight that he felt his stomach churn in confusion the moment he buttoned them. The hood was a problem, but not an insoluble one. The eyeholes were too close together, so after a few attempts to adjust them, he settled for vision out of one eye.

He folded his clothes and placed them on a narrow table that was cluttered with dozens of silver crucifixes of various sizes. Some of them had the figure of Christ sculpted on them. He hefted one of these in his hand and was suddenly seized with the old urge to steal. Without pondering the matter further, he stuffed it into the pile of clothes. After all, he had not yet stolen it; but if he later decided he wanted it, it was there safely hidden in the folds of his underwear.

He removed the hood and made his way back to the stage—where, in his present state of dress, it was quite chilly—and was met by the gurgling cackle of Gordon Bunche's laughter. Was it because Eliot was wearing gold socks? Well, no one told him about this costume business. Or was it because portions of his midriff peeked out? It turned out to be neither. In fact, it turned out that Gordon was not even laughing. He was coughing. Violently. He was doubled up at the edge of the stage, his arms flopping at his sides, his face purple. The sounds were those of laughter, the posture that of a man weeping, but the heaving of his chest and his bulging eyes were clearly due to some sudden seizure alarming to behold.

At least it was so for Eliot. Wick seemed not at all perturbed. He stood to the side waiting patiently for the coughing to subside. But before it did, Gordon actually fell down to his knees and clutched his throat. Then he rolled over on his side, his eyes popping out of his head, the strange staccato laughter issuing from his throat.

"Call a doctor!" said Eliot.

"No need. It'll be over in a minute."

And, sure enough, the fit abruptly ended, and Gordon slowly picked himself up off the floor. His face and eyes were totally red, his lips slack and moronic. He walked about in a daze and Wick guided him to a glass of water. He greedily slurped it down, and for some reason, Eliot's heart went out to him. Gordon had obviously suffered a few minutes of agony there. But it was all treated so matter-of-factly as if to suggest that it was, in a way, his natural state. His chewed-down fingernails, his scrofulous skin, his bulbous nose, and now this crushing, but apparently commonplace, coughing fit all seemed to interlock.

"Well?" said Wick.

"Okay," said Gordon. "I'm fine. I'm sorry, I really am." He turned to Eliot. "That was my asthma."

"Very nice," said Eliot.

"All right," said Wick in his most authoritative twang. "Let's get the show on the road."

Wick explained that during the actual performance, the entire stage would have a black felt backdrop and that there would be a variety of white objects covered with pieces of the same material. A strong, glaring light from the front would make everything invisible. Eliot, dressed in black, would on cue remove these black coverings one by one, and the white objects would "appear" to the audience.

Wick went to the large wooden chest and began removing several white things from it: a white bird cage, a white candelabra, a white chair, a pair of white shoes, a white picture frame containing, of all things, a negative, white-on-black photograph of Gordon Bunche, and, finally a white violin and bow. These objects he arranged in front of the backdrop and then covered them with pieces of black cloth. Eliot stepped in front of them and reported to Wick that in his whole life he had never seen anything less invisible. Angered by this remark, Wick's resemblance to Peter Lorre increased for a moment and then slowly faded like a sunset.

"When the blinker lights around the proscenium are on, it will dazzle the audience and render the objects invisible."

"Right, Edgar!" said Eliot.

"Put on your hood."

Eliot obeyed and adjusted it again so that he got full vision out of his right eye. He found it was easier if he kept his left eye shut. Gazing through the right eyehole at Eliot's eye, Wick briefly explained his patter. He would tell the audience that he was going to materialize a dead person on the stage, a relative or friend of someone in the audience. Gordon, planted in the third row, would be the chosen "volunteer." Several attempts fail and then the magician reminds the audience that the spirits of the dead often take residence in the furniture of the room in which they die. But, says Gordon from the audience, his brother had a stroke while playing the violin and the house burned down around him. All the better, says the magician, since the objects died along with the man. The spirit of the man was sealed within the objects, and death is the other side of life, all of which, as Eliot dimly understood it, was somehow to account for the whiteness of everything.

"Now," said Wick, "as Gordon names each object, you pull the cloth away."

From out in the auditorium, Bunche's voice cried out: "A chair!"

Eliot unveiled the chair.

"Hold it," said Wick. He meditated for a moment. "The chair is the first object. Take the cloth from the top slowly, very slowly."

"A candle holder!" said Bunche, his voice echoing in the empty spaces.

"That one comes off quickly," said Wick. "Alternate, quick and slow, quick and slow."

"Right," Eliot answered, and peeled the cloth from the candelabra.

"A bird cage!"

Voilà, bird cage.

"A photograph of me!"

"Now," said Wick, "do this *very* slow. That picture is a real punch effect, a negative print."

At this, Eliot balked.

"For Christ's sake, Edgar, who's going to believe that? Everyone will figure out Gordon is a plant." He felt stupid talking from behind that black hood. He tried to put an expression of friendly concern in his one revealed eye. How could he have known that this one single item was dearest to Edgar Wick's heart? That, in all truth, it was the only original addition Wick had made to a black art routine which, unknown to Gordon or anyone else, he had not himself devised, but had purchased by mail.

Wick slid his hands into his pockets, straightened his back, and took four steps in different directions, which brought him back to his original place. Already beyond Peter Lorre, his face was approaching that of a kamikaze pilot. Slowly, Wick turned his head to the side in the general direction of Gordon Bunche.

"Who does he think he is?"

Bunche answered, hesitantly, "Well, Edgar . . ."

But Wick interrupted. "What does he know?"

Eliot opened his left eye and started to explain, but was forced instead to listen to the following interchange.

"He has to learn his place!" said Wick.

"But, I really really think he may have a point. . . ."

"You have a point, right on the top of your ugly head!"

"Oh, Edgar!"

"Gordon, why don't you sit down and shut up!"

"I will not! If I have something to say, I'll say it!"

"Baa! Baa! Baa! You jackass!"

"You can't bully me!"

"You can't bully me!" Wick answered, in a singsong mimic.

"You never let me have an opinion!"

"You never let me have an opinion!"

"*Stop* that!"

"*Stop* that!"

"You . . . you . . . you. . . ."

"Go flush yourself down the toilet with the rest of the shit." With that, Wick, calm and pale once more, languidly turned to Eliot, who at this point was glad he had the hood on to conceal his grin. Bunche, a brilliant purple, began to cough again. The empty spaces echoed with the sounds, but Wick raised his voice and spoke over it.

"Perhaps you simply don't understand," he said to Eliot. "Death is life's shadow. Death is black. These things are merely white. They are undead. The realm of the undead is therefore like an undeveloped photograph of life. That's why the photograph is so important." Wick paused and his rigid posture slackened for a moment. He took his hands out of his pockets and brought his fist down upon his palm. "*Now* do you understand? The photograph is the real clincher!"

Eliot had no intention of pointing out that this explanation had nothing whatever to do with his objection. That might make Wick even angrier and then who could tell what he would do to poor Gordon Bunche, who even now was coughing his guts out in the front row. Eliot could not see Bunche. Hooded as he was, it would involve a ninety-degree turn of the head, and even that might evoke more of Wick's ridiculous fury. Besides, that cough, which before had sounded alarming, now seemed merely craven.

Whatever: it was clear that these two *schlemiels* would never get anything off the ground, least of all a two-hour stage presentation that any theatre would buy. Well, he had known in advance that there was nothing to be learned from them. He had volunteered simply as a gesture to counterbalance his failure with the linking rings. But this was all such bad magic that he began to worry about being contaminated by it. He wished fervently for this all to be done with so that he could leave this sheer, empty auditorium. He felt cold beneath the crappy black costume he was wearing.

He pulled off his hood. "Okay, Edgar, let's finish this."

Bunche stopped coughing—abruptly. But Wick did not choose to make anything of the hood. Eliot had expected at least a peremptory glance. Instead, Wick went to the pitcher of water, refilled the glass there and then walked to the edge of the stage and handed it to

Bunche. There was something incomprehensibly pitiful about this. Suddenly Eliot felt stronger and more solid than either of them.

"Come on, Edgar," said Eliot. "What's next—the violin?"

"Yes," said Wick, still at the edge of the stage.

Eliot lifted the last black cloth and unveiled the white violin.

"Eliot," Wick said, and took one step forward, "my idea was that you pick up the violin and draw the bow back and forth just above the strings. It will look as though the ghost were playing. And then offstage a record will be put on. How does that strike you?"

Eliot grasped the instrument and lifted up the bow. "I have a better idea," he said. He placed the violin on his shoulder and slid it under his chin. He gripped the bow like a dagger and then tore it heavily over the strings, and back, and over again. The coarse sounds lacerated the air and stunned Edgar Wick and Gordon Bunche.

Eliot put the violin and bow down upon the chair. His face was flushed and he was smiling gleefully.

"Don't you think that's more effective, Edgar? I mean . . . you should see yourself; it even scared *you*."

Edgar Wick could only nod in agreement.

The rehearsal went on. They quickly ran through the working of the Talking Skull, the Floating Light Bulb, the Blooming Rose Bush, and the Spirit Bell. And while Wick still gave directions, it was now with a tone of voice that waited upon Eliot's approval. As for Eliot, he was simply glad that things were going along quickly and that he now seemed always to be doing the right thing. He was extremely bored.

With Eliot now in the act, Wick had added to the guillotine trick. At one point, as he lectured about Dr. Guillotin, the curtain behind him would part and again reveal the darkened stage with the black backdrop still in place. Eliot was to be standing there with his hood off and appear to the audience as a disembodied head floating in the air. The head was to be that of Dr. Guillotin himself, magically summoned by Wick to report about the painlessness of decapitation.

It was this part of the routine that Wick wanted to run through first. He and Bunche took seats in the third row and Eliot took his place toward the back of the stage.

"Are you ready, Eliot?"

Eliot nodded that he was.

"Fine. Now, imagine that the curtain has just parted. Wait for a moment, and then start speaking in a ghostly voice. Then move slowly toward the guillotine. Try to keep from bouncing up and down when you walk; it has to look like the head is floating."

Wick had not given him a prepared script. His job was simply to say something that would dovetail with Wick's patter about the imperfections and sorrows of earthly life and the peace that waited in the grave after a merciful death.

They were sitting in the third row waiting for him to start talking, and Eliot was trying to put together in his mind what he was going to say. He made two false starts, and each time Wick and Bunche leaned forward in their seats, their faces ablaze with expectation. But at the moment when he began for the third time, there came from behind him, obviously from out in the street, the loud sounds of a dog barking. Eliot could not resist the impulse to mouth the sounds as though it were he who was making them. Wick and Bunche, in tandem, again leaned forward and opened wide their eyes. The barking of the dog became more vigorous and finally ferocious; it must have been straining after a cat or something. Eliot continued mouthing the barks and quickly realized that Wick and Bunche thought the sounds were really coming from his throat. He expected that at least they would smile at his little joke, but they remained solemnly attentive. So, he bared his teeth and drew his face into a snarl, shook his head back and forth, reared up his hands as though they were the paws of an attacking wolf, and finally, he got down on all fours and slinked menacingly toward the guillotine. When the dog stopped, he stopped, stood up and bowed.

And they actually applauded.

*

On the trolley, Eliot's foot began to hurt rather badly. He had completely forgotten about the silver crucifix hidden in his underwear, and when he went to put on his clothes, it fell out of the folds and struck his right instep. He yelped in pain and kicked it under the table.

But it was only now as he stood in the crowded trolley that the foot really began to ache. And, it being close to five o'clock, there wasn't a chance of getting a seat here, nor would there be on the subway or the E bus. He tried standing on one leg, but each time that he was thrown off balance, he landed hard on his tormented foot. When he got off the trolley at Broad and Walnut, he nearly doubled over trying to walk. An hour of standing on a crowded subway and bus was out of the question.

Templeton's was only two blocks away, and on Saturday Max Falkoner usually kept the store open until after six. There Eliot could sit and wait until the crowds thinned out.

The shop was empty and Falkoner was standing by the window talking into the telephone. Eliot hobbled in and dropped himself into a chair. He sighed and groaned. Then he unbuttoned his overcoat and wriggled his arms out of the sleeves. He crossed his right foot over his knee and loosened his shoelaces.

Falkoner hung up the phone and strolled, with his hands in his pockets, down the length of the counter until he was standing across from Eliot. He took out a pack of cigarettes and lit one.

"Nu, Applefriend? What's with the ugly face?"

"I'm in terrible pain."

Falkoner dropped his matchbook on the counter and blew out a cloud of smoke.

"Something fell on my foot. It feels like it's broken."

"What do you mean, something fell on your foot?" Falkoner walked around the counter and came over to where Eliot was sitting.

"A heavy rock," said Eliot.

"A rock?"

Eliot grunted and winced. "A paperweight. *You* know, a big rock used as a paperweight."

"One of those onyx paperweights?"

"That's right."

"You mean, it just fell out of a window? And landed right on your shoe?"

"I was in my stocking feet," said Eliot, and then paused. Max was squinting at him through another cloud of smoke.

"Let's see what it looks like."

Eliot gingerly removed his shoe and his gold sock. The foot was truly enormous, smooth, purple. The swelling seemed to engulf everything but the big toe. Eliot gasped. "My God!" Falkoner kneeled down and gently poked his finger at the puffy flesh. Then he felt around the ankle and the sole.

"Do you think it's broken?" asked Eliot.

"Wiggle it."

Eliot did so. "It hurts when I do that."

Falkoner stood up and flipped his cigarette into the standing ashtray. "It feels all right to me."

"What do you mean? It hurts like hell . . . and look at the way it's all swollen up!"

Falkoner went behind the counter and disappeared into the back room. Eliot heard him knocking ice cubes out of a tray. As he was waiting there, it occurred to Eliot that this was the second time he had bared his foot in Templeton's Magic Shop. The last time he was searching for three playing cards inside his sock.

Max returned with the ice cubes neatly wrapped in a length of towel. He propped Eliot's foot on another chair and wrapped the towel around it. Then he dropped a magazine in Eliot's lap and went back to his desk behind the counter, where he began typing out some invoices.

Eliot was soon feeling ecstatic. Surrounded by glorious magical equipment, he realized that events had unexpectedly brought him into intimate contact with the Pro himself, Max Falkoner, the purveyor and complete master of the craft. As his foot grew numb, he began to feel warmed by the fact that Max Falkoner's very hands had applied the icy towel. Now he was alone in the store; no customers came in, and he was not there to buy. Outside, the sky had darkened and the windows reflected the brightly lit room.

Eliot wanted to start a conversation, but he couldn't think of what to say. There were only two things that he knew about Max Falkoner's personal life: that he had been a close friend of the mysterious Irene Angel, and the rumor that he had once found an envelope containing eighteen thousand dollars and had returned it to the owner, who had wept and given him a gold watch. At that point, Eliot's imagination now took over. Max Falkoner, he imagined, was about forty years old; his life had contained much bitterness and a few moments of great joy which flowed too easily through his generous hands. He had mastered his craft at the gambling tables of the world, where he had also learned contempt for the ups and downs of chance. Perhaps he was divorced, or his wife was an invalid. He probably had no children, and he probably lived in a downtown hotel.

"Max, . . . are you from Philadelphia?"

Falkoner paused for a moment, but did not look up from his typewriter. "Cleveland," he said. Ah. Eliot had thought New York.

"Well, what part of town do you live in?"

"Not far from here." He put another blank invoice into the carriage and concentrated on a pad of paper next to the typewriter.

"Are you married? Do you have any kids?"

Falkoner laughed. Eliot did not know why.

"Are you? I was wondering."

"Applefriend, you ask a lot of questions."

"I guess I do."

Falkoner stood up and came over to Eliot.

"How's the foot?"

"I don't feel a thing. Are you getting ready to close up?"

"Relax," said Max. He undid the towel; the foot looked much better. Then he went for more ice and again wrapped the towel around Eliot's foot.

As he was doing so, Eliot asked him about Irene.

"Blake says you knew her very well. What kind of a person was she? She must have been terrific . . . the way Blake talks about her."

Falkoner seemed to be studying Eliot for a moment. Eliot thought he knew why. Adults often looked at him that way when they were trying to gauge how mature he was.

"How old was she when she died?" asked Eliot.

Max silenced Eliot with a look and then disappeared into the office on the other side of the mirrored wall.

DOCTOR BETELGEUSE

Christmastime came and went on Pelham Lane. Snow fell. The Wissahickon Creek froze over; the woods were simplified. At night, the cold points of the stars were close and brilliant.

On the first Wednesday in January, Eliot was unanimously accepted into The Sorcerer's Apprentices. During the voting, he waited by a hissing radiator in the corridor and peered through a frosty window that looked down on people trudging through the deep snow. He thought to himself that no matter how the voting went, he would pursue his study of magic. He would master the linking rings as well as the other tricks he had acquired. In fact, in those few moments of waiting he even decided upon a professional name and motto: *Doctor Betelgeuse, Designs in Deception.*

When he was told the good news, he was also asked to remain outside while the room was prepared for the initiation ceremony. He returned to the window, enormously pleased. While he waited, he took out a half dollar and practiced some moves from The Miser's Dream, in which coins are plucked out of thin air. Reflected in the window, it looked good, *very* good. Doctor Betelgeuse.

In a few minutes, Kimberly Vogel, the sergeant-at-arms, opened the door and beckoned Eliot to follow right behind him. The room was darkened and the shades were drawn, and at the far end of the room a candle burned. In the dim, flickering light, three figures stood waiting behind a table. One of them, if only by his height, was Blake. As Eliot walked up the aisle between the other members of the club, he distinguished the president, Stillman Clipper, on Blake's right and Wally Pound on the left. He later learned that

Pound was there according to club tradition that required the presence of the most recently initiated member. Eliot attempted to smile as his eyes met those of Blake, but Blake remained solemn and concentrated. He stood with his hands behind him, his back stiff, his legs spread. In the candlelight, the flesh on his face seemed wondrously thin and pale.

Eliot was led to the table upon which, besides the candle, was a skull (it may have been made of rubber) encircled by a metal ring that held several big keys. There was also a large book that seemed bound in copper.

"Eliot Appleman," said Blake in airy, clear tones of address. He repeated the name with precisely the same inflection, "Eliot Appleman," and then he paused and nodded to the sergeant-at-arms standing behind Eliot. There was the sound of an electronic humming and the scratching of a phonograph record. The voice was a woman's. Eliot immediately surmised that it was Irene Angel. It seemed to begin in the middle of a sentence:

". . . I greet and welcome you. You are being admitted into a circle of young men seeking to perfect themselves in magic. You must understand that you have not yet overcome a single obstacle and that you have not yet made the slightest achievement that will bring you closer to this goal. The pleasure you feel now is the pleasure of being accepted as one of us, and the warmth we feel is in welcoming you as a raw beginner. Beyond that, *nothing* has been done. . . ."

The voice went on. "In the months to come, your motives for wanting to do magic will become clearer to you, and you will begin to learn the true secret of magic, the secret of secrets and the meaning of secrets. Even secrets are not what they seem; even that which is hidden . . . conceals."

The record stopped with a slight scratch and Blake said, "Fix the blindfold." This Eliot expected; he had been certain there would be a blindfold. After it was tied, Eliot was instructed to hold out his hands palms up. Said Blake:

"The man of magic does not see as other men see, yet he must see more clearly. Above all, he must trust his vision. I am going to place, one at a time, various objects into your hand. You may do anything you like with them—smell them, taste them if you like. However, since the object may as well be a dead fly as a raisin, your vision must be sure. Here is the first object."

Eliot felt something soft, cold, and light drop onto his palm. It was something to be crushed and when he did so, it seemed to exude liquid, yet his hand did not actually become damp. Suddenly, he sensed that he was killing something, and at the same moment it sprang before his mind as a flower.

The next object was a kind of chain with something in the middle. He immediately realized that he would know this one, and his hands took over for him. Without actually being aware of what the object was, he allowed his hands to piece the ends of the chain together and quickly locate a tiny knob. The right hand wound it.

"A watch," said Eliot, delighted.

It was amazing what the hands knew and what they could see. They were eager to show more of their powers. They were like creatures freed from an oppressive master, the eyes.

Next, something very slender and weighing next to nothing was placed in his hands. A long, thin rod. Flexible. His hands and fingers raced up and down the object until: it broke. He heard a piece fall on the floor. It made a faint, wooden sound. What was left in his hands was a rod about three inches long that was now highly brittle. Sharp at the ends. He was completely in the dark. His hands broke it again. It seemed to want to be broken, though he feared that the more he broke it, the harder it would be to identify. Its brittleness was essential. The flexibility had been a deception; this seemed to be what his hands knew. Again and again, his hands broke the pieces he was holding, until finally he was left cupping a dozen tiny fragments that now seemed bone hard and cutting. He should have waited before breaking it like this, he should have restrained his hands. It had been foolish to trust them so far.

But then Eliot had a revelation, the kind which always seemed to come to him when he needed it, but which always seemed to be coming for the last time. Eyes were blind, hands had overreached themselves, ears had collaborated with hands in deceiving him, smell—as usual—could give no knowledge. It was left for the sense of taste, and if that failed, then the mystery of this object had passed him by.

Even as he was thinking this, his hand was bringing the pieces of the object to his lips; in fact, it was perhaps the hands that had given him the revelation in the first place. Perhaps he had been wrong to blame them. And the very moment the little rod touched his lips, the mystery dissolved: it was a piece of spaghetti! He did not actually have to taste it to be sure of this, just its sharp touch upon his lips was enough; and so it was still the sense of touch showing its powers. First hands, now lips, and Eliot felt there was some kind of lesson in this, maybe even a lesson that the initiation was supposed to drive home, namely some great realization that to touch was the meaning and goal of *all* the senses.

But as though the Sorcerers were reading his mind and wanted quickly to disabuse him of this notion, the next object was so hot that he instantly pulled his hand away. Well, it was not an object at all, because nothing fell. But yes, before pulling away he had felt something crawling around his palm. Forgetting for a moment the solemnity of the occasion, he smiled and almost actually said "two hot moths." Very funny. That could have been the end of him, and maybe that was just what they wanted to test: whether or not he'd get so cocky that he'd sink to wisecracks.

The thing, whatever it was, had landed on his hand, had moved around for a second and then burned him. But maybe it hadn't burned at all, maybe it had bitten him, or maybe it was cold, so cold it felt hot. But it was definitely alive; it moved. Now what the hell: what is alive, small, hot and flies? Some strange incandescent beetle?

What is hot and flies?

Be scientific.

What is hot?

Fire.

But fire is not alive. Or is it?

What the hell *is* fire anyway? A hot nothing that moves. So all things that move aren't necessarily alive. Just things that move themselves. But doesn't fire move itself? Isn't fire a primal, primitive power, a source of worlds? In fact, fire is not even hot; things are hot to the degree that they have fire, and so. . . .

Blake's voice interrupted. "Your time is almost up."

"Fire," said Eliot, slightly disgusted with himself.

"Taste the palm of your hand," said Blake.

Eliot did so and sighed. Of course: a cigar ash.

Cool dry hands removed the blindfold. The candle had burned lower and Blake's handsome face was crawling with shadows. Again the record played.

"Here you will learn that there is never truth without illusion, nor reality without semblance. . . ." The woman's voice was now sepulchral, surrounded by echo as though she were speaking in an auditorium. "You will learn that truth is the last layer of illusion. For the secret within all secrets, the hardest truth to endure, is that everything is *on the surface,* that the senses do not deceive. . . ."

Then Blake broke in. "In accordance with these words by our founder, Irene Angel, you, Eliot Appleman, will now rise to take the oath of initiation." Eliot stood up. "But before proceeding with this oath which binds you to us in the fellowship of magic, will you submit to our questions?"

"I will," said Eliot, solemnly.

Everyone except Blake then gathered behind him. He was told that he must look straight ahead and keep his eyes fixed on Blake. At first, Eliot found that impossible, but Blake, his face still expressionless, said, "I am your audience; you must look at me without being moved by me; even though I am everything to you, you must not flinch from me."

Eliot's eyes settled into those of Blake. He felt himself relaxing a bit. There was a shuffling of feet and irritated murmuring behind him, together with sounds of papers. Eliot tried to concentrate on the undulating caverns of Blake's eyes.

The questions from the Sorcerers behind him came slowly at first.

"Who was the greatest man that ever lived?"

"Albert Einstein," said Eliot.

"What is the opposite of salt?"

"Envy," he quickly answered. He loved questions like this. Only Blake's dark, eerie eyes kept it from seeming a game.

"What is the largest number you can know?"

"Three."

"What is magic?"

Eliot paused, stared into the caverns, and said, "The ability to make people see what they're not seeing."

The questions then began to come faster.

"Who were you in your previous life?" That was Edgar Wick's voice.

"A Siberian wolf."

"What is the softest thing in the world?"

"Memory."

"What supernormal power would you like to have?"

"Telepathy."

"What is magic?"

Again, Eliot paused. Blake seemed to be smiling.

"The ability to keep people from seeing what they're seeing." He felt pleased with that answer.

The questions came still faster.

"What is the purpose of pain?"

"To remind us that we're going to die."

"What would you like your name to be?"

"Betelgeuse."

"Who would you like to be?"

"You."

"What is magic?"

"Power over nature."

Blake had not been smiling at all; his mouth had fallen open in what seemed to be a kind of trance. It was a little frightening. He looked like the mask of tragedy. But Eliot had no time to take his eyes off Blake's eyes, or rather, his lack of eyes.

The questions then came very fast, too fast to allow him to think before answering. He stopped trying to identify the voices.

"How would you kill the devil?"

"By shutting my eyes."

"What song would the strangest woman in the world sing?"

"A lullaby."

"How would you want to die?"

"I don't want to die."

"What is magic?"

"Power over others."

"What do you want to know about us?"

"What you don't want me to know."

"What supernatural power do you have?"

"Life."

"In what part of the body does shame reside?"

"The mind."

"What is magic?"

"Power over oneself."

"When does a boy become a man?"

"When he knows the truth."

"What do you want to learn from us?"

"Invisibility."

"What happens after death?"

"Death."

"What is magic?"

"Power over death."

"Who are you?"

"An only child."

"What is magic?"

"Power."

"What is magic?"

"Music."

"What is magic?"

"Truth."

"What is magic?"

"I am."

"What is magic?"

"*I!*"

At that moment Blake brought the flat of his hand crashing down upon the table. Eliot nearly leaped out of his skin.

"Sealed!" Blake shouted. "The answer is sealed!" He waited a moment and then said quietly, "Eliot, step forward to the table."

Eliot did so. "Put forth your left hand." Eliot did so, and Blake took hold of him with his own left hand. "You will now listen to the oath as it is recited, and afterwards you will repeat it after me."

Once again, the record.

"I swear on my honor that I will keep the promises that bind me as a member of The Sorcerer's Apprentices.

"I will never reveal a secret to anyone who is not a magician.

"I will regard all other magicians as brothers in spirit and will never undermine their work in public or private.

"I will never ask for another magician's secrets, but should he reveal them to me I will consider them my own.

"If I deduce another magician's secret, I will consider it my own, but I will tell him of it.

"I will never trust anyone's eyes but my own.

"I will not use what I learn for immoral purposes.

"I will obey the constitution and by-laws of The Sorcerer's Apprentices."

The lights went on, Blake extinguished the candle, and everyone shook Eliot's hand. He heard someone mutter "good answers" and his spirits soared.

*

After the meeting, Eliot took a roundabout way home so that for part of the ride he could have the company of Wally Pound. The bus was completely empty. Eliot and Wally proceeded, with one desire, to the back of the bus and sat together in the last row of seats.

"That was the first initiation using the records," said Wally. "It went pretty well." He puffed on his unlit pipe. His eyeglasses reflected the glare of the lights in the empty bus.

"I didn't realize that," said Eliot. "You mean you had Irene at your initiation?"

Wally nodded yes. The bus farted and whistled and pulled out of the station.

Eliot felt a painful surge of envy. "When was that?"

"Last March."

"No shit! I thought she died years ago."

"She died six months ago. In June."

"No shit. So, . . . I just missed knowing her?"

Wally nodded.

"You knew her pretty well?"

Wally shrugged his shoulders and peered out the window into the cold black nothing. "I sort of knew her."

"But she was really beautiful, wasn't she?"

Wally turned his head around, pulled his pipe out of his mouth, twisted it apart at the middle, picked out some shiny moist clumps of tobacco and flicked them three rows of seats away. "An excellent magician. Excellent."

Eliot sat back and sighed. Suddenly he heard his mouth saying, "And she killed herself. Jesus!"

"What are you talking about?"

"What are *you* talking about! She killed herself." Eliot drew his forefinger across his throat. "With a razor."

"Who says so?"

"Max," Eliot lied.

"He told you that?"

"Yep."

Wally looked extremely upset.

Eliot pondered for a moment. "What does Blake say?"

"I never asked; he never talked about it."

"Why not? Wasn't he in love with her?"

The bus hit a bump. Wally looked shocked—probably by the fact that Eliot said such a thing so matter-of-factly. His Clark Kent face seemed old, burdened, and alarmed. And he started giving out that sour odor: old tobacco mixed with sweat.

"How should I know?" said Wally.

"Well, I mean, maybe Max was in a position to know more than Blake, I mean . . . that's what I mean."

"Huh?"

"I mean, Max was having a love affair with her, right?"

Wally's eyes nearly jumped out of his head.

"Didn't you know that either?"

Wally shook his head. "Are you sure?" he croaked.

Was he sure?

"Sure."

Maybe Wally Pound was older than he, maybe he carried greater burdens. Maybe he was a far better magician. But clearly Eliot understood certain things that Wally could never know. Wally was gazing at him. Hungrily.

Eliot simply could not help himself. It was like the shoplifting.

"Blake worshipped her. I mean, *really* worshipped her. You know? Not a fleshly love. But a tremendously spiritual love." Eliot leaned forward and saw his own face in the black window. "In fact, they were distant cousins. Oh sure, she was much older than he, but he had known her all his life. He saw more and more of her as he grew up. And . . . as he grew up she was attracted to him; she saw his great magical talent." Eliot tore his eyes from his reflection in the window. There was not a trace of skepticism in Wally's face. He was completely taken in; fooled.

Eliot continued. "As Blake got older, his love became deeper. He spent all his time with her. Because he loved her so much, he learned all her magic, things she discovered for herself. She taught him everything. Then, finally, she took him to Templeton's and he met Max Falkoner. He immediately sensed what was going on between Irene and Max. How she was getting her money and her jobs. It disgusted him, nearly drove him crazy. . . ."

Eliot began to wish Wally would say something instead of sitting there with his mouth gaping. Even to interrupt him with a skeptical snort. It was almost unbearable that Wally was believing every word. Deliciously unbearable. Though . . . possibly . . . some of what he was saying was not completely false. The bus hummed on; it was still empty. Nobody else was getting on, and the driver was catching all the green lights.

Eliot continued. "But Blake held his tongue. He couldn't stand to think of Max's power over her. He wondered if it wasn't a hypnotic spell. Max told me how Blake used to come to him and try to fathom the secret of his power. After all . . ." Eliot gesticulated with upturned palms, ". . . wasn't Irene the greatest magician of them all? How could Max have that power? You know? I mean, just compare Max and Blake: Max is short and fat, Blake is tall and great looking, right?"

Wally moved his head in a small vague circle, applying yes to Eliot's yes and no to his no.

"Max talks through his nose, but Blake's voice is deep and beautiful.

"And . . . let's face it . . . Max is really a con man. I mean, he knows the business inside out and he's a great performer, and—in a way—a nice guy, but compared to Blake, I mean, it's like comparing Blendo with the linking rings. I mean, Blake is *more* than just a performer.

"Well. Apparently . . . apparently, Irene, being the fantastic person she was, saw exactly what was happening. Above all, she wanted to prevent a test of strength between Max and Blake. Because she loved each of them. Though with a different love. . . ."

By now Eliot was no longer even looking in Wally's general direction. His eyes were pointed at the back of the bus driver's head as though he were talking—or even just thinking—to himself. Surely somewhere, where it counted, all of this story, this absurd fabrication, was being stricken from the records even as it was being told.

"A test of strength. Imagine. Blake pitted against Max Falkoner. She shuddered at the thought. To prevent it from happening, she decided to give to Blake what she had given to Max. She seduced Blake. She initiated him into sex. But the result was just the opposite of what she had hoped for. It only increased Blake's passion. He now thought he could take Max's place completely.

"Meanwhile, Max found out what Irene had done with Blake and he began to lose his patience with that whole relationship. He called Blake in and dealt him the whole truth, no punches pulled. But Blake, though staggered, would not admit defeat. Max couldn't bear what was happening to poor Blake, or to himself for that matter (he's human). As a result, he went beyond the truth, he lied to Blake, he invented unimaginable perversities and physical degradations that he attributed to himself and Irene. Incredible things no madman in his wildest, filthiest fantasies would possibly even begin to imagine. Things involving the magic act, various tricks and gimmicks such as production boxes, levitation effects, the skull-vanish box, and so on. . . .

"Blake believed everything. Everything."

At that, Wally stood up in his place and crashed his head against a light fixture. The motion of the bus forced him right back down again, dazed, muttering that he had missed his stop.

Eliot reached up to pull the cord for Wally, but Wally held his arm.

"What did Blake do?'

Eliot, with his arm crooked in mid-air, gazed into the clean blue of Wally's fuddled eyes, eyes that would believe anything he said, cool, goyish eyes.

"He set Max on fire."

After a brief breathless second, Eliot roared, dropped his arm and gripped his ribs in laughter, fell off the seat and rolled in the aisles of the still empty bus as it barreled through the night.

PART 2

THE GIFT

THE EVENT

Eliot's first act as a *bona fide*, full-fledged member of the Sorcerer's Apprentices was to have business cards printed. DOCTOR BETELGEUSE, and under that, in elegant italics, *Designs in Deception.* He carried fifty of the cards stuffed in his wallet and liberally handed them out at the next meeting of the club. When one of the Sorcerers pointed out that he had left off his telephone number, Eliot grandly dismissed the objection with a wave of the hand. But that night he lettered in his phone number on the lower left-hand side of the cards. Only twenty of the two hundred cards came out neat enough to be usable.

But it didn't matter because he was already thinking of a new stage name after what he saw at that meeting. Of all the Sorcerers, Ronnie Pitkin was the only one who specialized in mind reading tricks. Was it only because he was now an authentic member of the club that he was able to appreciate Ronnie Pitkin? Appreciate was hardly the word. Eliot was thunderstruck by Ronnie Pitkin's hypnosis and mind reading routine, even though he had seen pieces of it many times before.

Until now, Ronnie Pitkin had simply made Eliot feel uneasy. Perhaps it was his discouraging good looks—he was tall, slender, athletically built, with silky blond hair and not a pimple on his face. He looked like a movie star. He had the same hawklike profile as Rory Calhoun. His drooping eyelids—exactly like those of Robert Mitchum—gave him a languid grace, as did his slow, flowing movements. His large, sunken eyes were deep blue and luminous.

Was it all envy? It was known that Ronnie Pitkin was a star athlete—a swimmer, not a team man. It was also known that girls swarmed around him. This even happened when the Sorcerers went out for hamburgers after the meetings. Waitresses, fully grown women, gave him a certain kind of look or bent over close to him when they could. Women at other tables would stare at him. But it never flustered Ronnie in the least. He stayed cool, with an apparent strength and self-possession that was amazing.

But for Eliot, the most troubling thing about Ronnie Pitkin had been his reticence. He spoke very little and never obtruded himself. You never knew what he was thinking, yet you were always aware of him. And when he did speak, even if what he said was of the utmost stupidity, he commanded silent attention from all the other members—except Blake, of course, who out-trumped everyone.

"I want a good mental effect, Max, a really good one." It was the following Saturday at Templeton's. Eliot tried to get there early enough to beat the crowds, but there were mobs of people already ahead of him. Max had little time for him and eventually Eliot found himself hustled into buying, for six dollars, a trick called "The Telematic Deck." When he examined it at home, he was as disgusted as he had been with the Flag Blendo. It was only a chintzy variation of the Svengali Deck, in which every second card is identical and cut slightly shorter than the others. This one was specially constructed to be wrapped with a rubber band and thrown out into the audience where someone would peek at a card and then throw the deck back up to the performer.

Bad, bad. But wait, maybe not. Eliot read the instructions carefully. One of the variations involved passing an ordinary deck with the same design on the back into the audience for examination and then secretly substituting the trick deck the next time it was passed out in order to do the actual "mind reading." That was good; that had possibilities. Luckily, he already had a regular Aviator deck that matched the trick deck.

It was Saturday evening and Eliot was eager to try the new trick on someone. What could be better than his father's pinochle crowd, who were just now gathering in the living room? He slid the Telematic deck into his back pocket and put the regular deck into his side pocket. He ambled out into the living room and casually started nibbling at the potato chips on the coffee table, being careful not to get his fingers greasy.

Noise and smoke already filled the room, although, fortunately, the game had not yet started. The whole group was there. Jack Pritzker, with his cannonball head and chewed-down cigar, was a foreman in an iron foundry and occasionally took Eliot to the Friday night professional wrestling matches at the Arena. Eliot hated the wrestling, but he liked Jack's loudmouthed vulgarity and warmth. There was Oscar Fitterman, the downstairs neighbor, with his pencil-line moustache and rodent-like eyes. There was cousin Julie, the racketeer of the Appleman clan—ex-nightclub comedian—who served a short jail term in Florida for real estate fraud, and did fantastic imitations of Jack Benny. There was Heshy Gitlin of the long nosehairs and the cockeyed bow tie; he owned a dry cleaning plant in South Philadelphia.

A princely group—presided over by his father, Myron Appleman, sitting silently at the head of the kitchen table and now staring quizzically at his son from behind thick spectacles that made his eyes seem twice their size.

"What is it, Eliot? What do you want?" said Eliot's father. Loud noisy greetings from everyone. Boisterous comments on Eliot's size, weight, sexual development, and IQ. Then, a moment of relative calm.

"I want to try out a new trick."

Uproar, amusement, condescension, the opening of beer bottles, Heshy getting up to grab a handful of potato chips, Myron Appleman smiling indulgently. The event begins, and what an event!

Confidently, deftly, Eliot set the stage, delivered the patter about thought transference, passed the regular deck out for examination, put it into his pocket while doing a bit of business with the notepad upon which he would write the selected card, grandly tossed out what he believed to be the trick deck (caught by Jack Pritzker), wrote down the card (nine of diamonds), asked for the deck back and then—calamity! It was the wrong deck! He had screwed up the secret switch and had actually thrown them the regular deck.

What to do? What the hell to do? The pinochle crowd sat there in silent anticipation, an old daguerreotype entitled, "Father and Card Players Anticipating Magic Trick." The expression on his father's face only intensified the horror of the situation—he had actually allowed himself to smile with a touch of pride in what his clever son was about to do! Cousin Julie nervously riffled the pinochle deck—but he, too, showed a little trace of embryonic familial warmth and pride. Heshy Gitlin snorted and munched his potato chips. Oscar the Rodent glared, his tiny eyes rapidly moving around to figure out the trick that was about to happen. And Cannonball Jack Pritzker—oh no! Good old Jack Pritzker, who peeked at God knows what card, had actually ground out his cigar and was looking at Eliot with something like wonderment.

Time passed—seconds, hours, years. Eliot closed his eyes and began measuredly pacing back and forth as though "picking up the thought waves." What to do? He could take a wild guess—there was, after all, one chance in fifty-two of getting it right, and then, if he were wrong, he could joke his way out of the room as fast as possible. Why not? What's one more humiliating experience in a life marked by pain and loneliness? Man's life on earth is brief, surrounded by death and meaninglessness. So what if four loudmouthed *nudnicks* have a laugh on him? In the cosmic scheme, would it matter?

But how could he face his father, for whom these clowns were peers and respected friends? And, speaking practically, it would spell the end of Eliot's magic career around the house.

But wait. All right, the situation was hopeless, but there was a way of softening it. Eliot suddenly remembered a piece of advice from Max Falkoner about what to do when a trick goes wrong. "When something goes wrong," he had said, "never apologize, never explain. When it goes wrong, make it *really* wrong." A powerful current suddenly surged through Eliot's body together with a wave of vertigo and a strange tickling at the back of his head. Feeling slightly mushy in the knees, and with his throat dry and his voice cracking, Eliot turned to Jack Pritzker and instructed him to take a dollar bill from his wallet and write down the serial number. As the number was being written down, the general level of chuckles, grunts, and snorts rose perceptibly around the table.

"Now," said Eliot, "pass the piece of paper to Mr. Gitlin." Jack Pritzker did so and then stuffed a fresh cigar into his mouth and folded his arms. "Mr. Gitlin," said Eliot, "would you please write your social security number underneath the number that Mr. Pritzker has written." Heshy Gitlin also complied, but with a dry snicker that was not more than thirty percent good-natured. "Please add the two numbers," said Eliot. Gitlin did so. Eliot then turned to Oscar the Rodent. "Mr. Fitterman, would you please take the last two digits of the year your mother was born and divide it into the number that is the sum of the two numbers on the paper."

Oscar Fitterman pulled a Parker 51 from inside his forest green plaid sport coat and obeyed, his thin black moustache twitching throughout the complicated operation.

Throughout all this, Eliot was pacing around the table, hoping to steal a glance at the paper while everyone was watching Oscar. A good idea, a real discovery, but it didn't work. He tried to see if he could determine the numbers by the movements of Oscar's hand. This didn't work either. And so now Eliot was at the end of his tether. What had been the point of Max Falkoner's advice? Failing to guess the card would have been bad, very bad. But was this any better? Why hadn't he thought of Blake in this situation, instead of the old con man, Max Falkoner? But maybe Blake's tricks never went wrong.

Eliot now stood there feeling naked and frightened. He took up the notepad and began writing down numbers. "Mr. Fitterman, please concentrate on the number in front of you."

At that moment, a strange thing happened. No, not strange, incredible. Eliot realized that he knew the number!

How could that be?

He looked around him at the faces burrowing into him from the kitchen table. An immense sensation of calm wafted through him, and his head felt like it was filled with the fumes of oil of wintergreen: cool, fresh, sweet.

Eliot wrote down the numbers on the large, yellow pad: 24391611. He tore the sheet off the pad, folded it in quarters, and then handed it to Jack Pritzker.

"Mr. Fitterman, please call out the number you have written down!" Eliot noticed that even his voice sounded different. He had never before felt such a sense of space. He wanted to laugh and sing. Oscar Fitterman called out the numbers—sure enough, 24391611. For a moment, Eliot almost felt that he was rising from the floor, leaving his body behind. At the same time, he sensed his eyes moistening and was afraid he would suddenly burst into tears.

"Mr. Pritzker, please read the number I have written down."

When Jack Pritzker opened the paper, he did not read out the number. Instead, he silently lowered it to his lap and slowly turned his head toward Eliot's father. He sucked on his cigar and blew a giant cloud of brown smoke out of the side of his mouth. "How the hell did he do that?"

Myron Appleman exploded in a voiceless laugh, his face bathed in sudden light and happiness. Everyone started laughing—Heshy Gitlin laughed so hard that a clump of half-chewed potato chips fell out of his mouth. Even Oscar the Rodent laughed—with a strange, rhythmic nodding of his head, his two big front teeth pushing forward with each nod. Cousin Julie said, "Wow!"

Finally, Eliot could stand it no longer. He threw his head back, grabbed his head with both hands and shouted out, at the top of his voice:

"Holy shit!"

With his hands remaining on the top of his head, Eliot paraded out of the kitchen and into his room. He shut the door behind him and, without turning on the light, sat down on the edge of his bed. His heart was pounding. Suddenly he jumped up—and just as suddenly down again. Who is ever going to believe this? What are the odds? One in a million? More—one in a hundred million! Incredible!

It was not until the following morning, when he was just opening his eyes, that Eliot remembered something about what had happened. There was that sense of *knowing* the number. What was *that* all about?

During Sunday breakfast—lox and eggs and onions—the great event hardly came up and Eliot was not eager to go into it. His father obviously considered it only a very good trick, and the excitement Eliot had felt had given way to a gnawing uncertainty about the whole thing. He wanted to think about it by himself before discussing it with anyone. Had it been only a card, a one in fifty-two shot, he could have lived with the idea of coincidence and taken undeserved credit for performing a good trick. But this went beyond coincidence—and there was that *knowing*.

He spent the afternoon downtown at the public library reading books dealing with telepathy and the new theories of J.B. Rhine about what was being called "extra-sensory perception." Finally, at about six o'clock, he telephoned Wally Pound, who immediately noticed something odd in Eliot's voice.

"Is something wrong, Eliot?"

"No, everything's fine. Wally, do me a favor. Think of a number, a big number."

Wally immediately went along with it. "Okay, I've got one."

Nothing.

Eliot was silent.

"Eliot?"

"Write it down," said Eliot.

"Just a minute, let me get a pencil."

Still nothing. What the hell.

Wally returned to the phone. "Okay, I've written it down."

"All right, concentrate on it."

Nothing, nothing, nothing. And then—Jesus Christ! Not a number or anything like that, but a complete, technicolor picture of Wally Pound sitting by the phone, wearing a purple sweater and gray corduroy pants, with a Band-Aid on the bridge of his nose. In the background was Wally's mother, a tall, beautiful woman with dark brown hair, wearing a long, brown silky robe.

Eliot shuddered. "Wally, tell me something. Do you have a Band-Aid on your nose?"

"As a matter of fact, I do. I bumped into the kitchen door this morning . . . Hey, Eliot . . . that's terrific!"

"And is your mother standing behind you wearing a brown robe?"

There was a pause on the other end of the line.

"Eliot? That's right! Hey, what's going on?"

"Wally, I've got to see you. I'm at the library now. They're just closing. I think I'm telepathic!"

"You're kidding! No shit?"

"Can you come down here?"

"Why don't you come here?"

Then suddenly, the number appeared. "Wally, Jesus Christ Almighty, I think I've got the number."

"What is it?"

"56340923380."

"I'll be there as soon as I can," said Wally.

When Eliot hung up the phone, tears were pouring down his face.

*

It was bitter cold in front of the public library. And dark. He hadn't thought of that when he asked Wally to come down, but then he hadn't been able to think of anything except what was happening. What *was* happening?

Eliot began pacing back and forth, weaving around the Corinthian columns of the library. His feet were getting numb from the cold, and every time he thought of what was happening, tears started again and froze on his cheeks. From time to time a pleasant image of what it would mean to have "powers" started to form in his mind, but it was immediately crushed by the overwhelming sensation of reality—big, big reality—which is never exactly either pleasant or unpleasant. By the time Wally arrived, Eliot was shivering from head to foot, both from the cold and from the facts.

The two boys walked hastily down Arch Street to an all-night Horn and Hardart self-service cafeteria, neither saying a word. In the frigid air, the fruity smoke of Wally Pound's pipe was somehow comforting.

But inside the restaurant, Eliot saw the Band-Aid on Wally's nose. When Wally took off his coat, Eliot saw that his purple sweater and gray corduroy pants were exactly as he had seen them in his mind a half hour before, and he started shivering again.

The cavernous restaurant, lit by dim, flickering fluorescent lights, was empty except for two or three bums slouched over their coffee with their hats and coats still on. Wally went to get the nickels from the change booth and compassionately gave some to Eliot. Eliot bought a hot chocolate and a dish of tapioca pudding; Wally had a cup of coffee and a turkey sandwich.

Eliot sipped at his chocolate and told Wally what had happened the previous night with the pinochle crowd, even though it was hard for him to speak. His chest kept quivering. But the warmth of the drink and the cup in his hands helped him. He felt immensely grateful that Wally simply listened quietly and trustingly, especially considering what a fool Eliot had made of him the last time they were together with that cockamamy story he had invented about Irene, Max, and Blake.

When Eliot had finished talking, Wally took out his pipe and his plaid tobacco pouch. He filled his pipe, lit it, and put on his hexagonal, rimless glasses.

"You want to try it again?" said Wally.

"Okay," Eliot said, reluctantly. He didn't know whether he wanted to succeed or fail. His heart started pounding again and he was suddenly feeling tremendously weary in his body, but also very relaxed and loose. Wally put the paper napkin on his lap under the table and took out his Scripto pencil. "I'll write down another number," he said.

Eliot closed his eyes and felt that tickling in the back of his head, but again got nothing. Wally waited patiently with an odd, vaguely self-satisfied look on his face. Finally, after a few minutes, Eliot gave up. "It's not working," he said, feeling like a fool himself. "All I keep thinking of is that stupid Russian magician we saw at the Mastbaum three weeks ago."

Wally sucked on his pipe and excitedly opened the napkin in front of Eliot. On it were written the words, "The Great Lobachevsky."

The two boys sat quietly for a long time. Eliot pushed aside his tapioca and Wally offered him half of his turkey sandwich. Eliot ate it slowly. He hadn't realized what a good friend Wally Pound was.

If their positions had been reversed, would he have reacted with as much kindness as Wally? He doubted it. He would have been consumed by envy. Probably. On the other hand, what was there to envy?

After he finished the sandwich, Eliot stood up and took off his coat. He was feeling a little better now, a little more himself.

"Can I ask you something?" said Wally. "Do you know what I've been thinking? I mean, have you been sort of reading my mind while I've been sitting here? Does it work like that?"

The answer, of course, was no, not in the slightest. But Wally's question produced an extraordinary picture in Eliot's mind. Without lifting a finger, he could make Wally Pound into his "slave," simply by letting him believe the answer was yes. Strangely enough, however, that prospect held absolutely no attraction for Eliot. And that fact interested him almost as much as everything else that was happening. He had never imagined himself as being an especially moral or truthful person. But, somehow, clearly seeing that impulse to "enslave" Wally made it powerless, as though such impulses could do harm only when they weren't fully seen.

Equally surprising to Eliot was his sudden reluctance to talk about the power. This, too, was unlike him. Very. But the more reticent Eliot became, answering Wally in brief minimal phrases, the more talkative Wally became. It was a strange sensation for Eliot. He had always been the talker; now he was the listener. How interesting. This was something new.

Wally quickly gathered momentum. He started by picturing the amazement of everyone in the club when they learned about Eliot's powers. "How do you plan to let them know, Eliot? Will you do some spectacular effect for them at the next meeting? Do you plan to tell everyone? Imagine how pleased Blake will be! I'm sure he'll want to feature you in the Annual Show—and, you know, rehearsals start next month. Maybe that would be the best way—to wait until we all have to present our acts to Blake for the show. And what about poor Ronnie? He's always been the mind reader of the club, but they've just been tricks. He may have to do something else."

Although Eliot was feeling very sleepy, the mention of Ronnie Pitkin perked him up for a moment. He savored to himself what it would be like to outdo the glamorous and magnetic Ronnie Pitkin. However, the image quickly passed and he became sleepy again. His eyelids began to droop.

But Wally went on talking, his imagination roaming far beyond the confines of the Sorcerer's Apprentices. "Just think what it will be like in a poker game, Eliot. You could make a fortune! Or in school, taking exams!"

Wally was no longer even looking at Eliot. He was gazing up to the ceiling, sucking loudly on his pipe, his eyeballs darting back and forth like two guppies in a fishbowl. Through the drowsiness, Eliot heard chunks of what Wally was portraying about the use of Eliot's powers in relationships with girls. Somewhere in the middle of that scenario, Eliot dropped off to sleep, though not before noting to himself how strangely uninteresting it all was when compared to the fact itself of this power inside him. Impressing Blake and the Sorcerers, impressing girls, winning money, getting A's—so what? At the same time, Eliot felt vaguely nostalgic about those things. What would life be like, what would he be like, if they stopped meaning so much to him?

He awoke with a start to prevent himself from falling off the chair. Wally had stopped talking and was now serenely gazing at the ceiling, his pipe unlit and a beatific smile on his face. He was in some sort of reverie. When he saw that Eliot was awake, he solicitously asked him if he would like another cup of hot chocolate. But Eliot wanted only to go home to a warm bed.

SIDE EFFECTS

It was the first meeting of the Sorcerer's Apprentices since Eliot's discovery that he was able to read minds. During the past two weeks he had kept more or less to himself and spoken about the power to no one except Wally. He had tested it several times. On each occasion it manifested itself in an unexpected way. There seemed to be certain limitations that were not yet well defined. For one, it did not work at all with his parents and, in a way, this was a considerable relief for Eliot.

But the greatest limitation was his own emotional reaction, or whatever it was, whenever he exercised his power. No matter what mood he was in when he tried it, its activation would cause tears to stream from his eyes and would be accompanied by a feeling that changed the complexion of everything he was doing. For example, there was a Freddie Chubb who lived at the other end of Pelham Lane. Freddie was one of the few neighborhood teenagers, all of them rednecks of one species or another, who did not actively hate Eliot. Not that Freddie was any less anti-Semitic than the other neighborhood boys. It was just that his own personality was so unpleasant that, as far as the others were concerned, he might as well have been Jewish. Freddie's father was a sergeant on the Philadelphia police force. To Eliot, this fact seemed to explain his insufferable arrogance. It certainly explained why, unlike Eliot, Freddie was never pushed around by Dick Fenton (six foot two, 190 pounds) or Tom Gurley (built like an ox), the neighborhood's two chief candidates for lifetime careers in Leavenworth.

One snowy afternoon Eliot had run into Freddie at Peterson's grocery. Freddie was big and fat, like his father, though without his father's bull neck and massive shoulders. He was more or less a blob. Trudging through the snow back to Pelham Lane, Eliot was carrying two heavy bags of groceries while all Freddie had was the *Evening Bulletin* and a small bag of onions. When Eliot asked him to lend a hand with the packages, Freddie's reply was a straight-forward "up your ass with a broken glass," followed by his renowned crowing laugh.

By the time they turned the corner at Pelham Lane, a bet had been made. Eliot had maneuvered Freddie into a contest involving the only subject that Freddie knew well: baseball. Eliot was no slouch at this, but Freddie really had a passion for it and easily fell into the trap when Eliot said, "A buck says you can't stump me."

Freddie stopped in his tracks and gave Eliot a look of utter disdain.

"A buck! Chickenshit! Make it ten. Make it twenty! In fact," said Freddie, his eyes growing narrower and narrower, the white snowflakes melting into his hot red jowls, "I'll bet you fifty goddamn chickenshit dollars I stump you with one chickenshit question, you asshole!"

Eliot shrugged and pretended defiance. "Okay, fat man, you're on!"

They began walking again. "You sure you got fifty dollars? I won't take payment in kosher pickles!"

Eliot said nothing to that, but continued walking in the absolute silence of the snow. For several minutes the only sound was the crunch of the boys' galoshes beneath them. Eliot marveled at the beauty all around as the snow suddenly thickened into a nearly opaque curtain of giant, wet flakes. It was a transfiguration of the world. The answer to Freddie's question appeared even before he asked it—249, the lifetime batting average of Pete Suder, the undistinguished second baseman of the last place Philadelphia Athletics. And then the tears and the shuddering started. At the same time, he saw that it was Freddie who did not have fifty dollars. In fact, Freddie Chubb's total savings amounted to exactly three dollars and eighty cents. And with that information came a vivid picture of Freddie being slapped in the face that very morning at breakfast by his father for spending a dollar thirty on a general admission ticket to the Warriors' basketball game.

The tears poured out of Eliot's eyes and it was all he could do to hold back the sobbing that was starting in his chest. And then there was this excruciating feeling of pity for fat Freddie Chubb.

"Look Freddie," Eliot managed to croak out before Freddie actually put his question, "I'm having some kind of allergic reaction to something. I'd better get right home." With that, Eliot bolted away as fast as he could through the deepening snow, being careful not to drop any of the groceries that now weighed so heavily in his arms. "Chickenshit! Chickenshit!" Freddie screamed after him, but the words were blanketed in snow.

Yes, that was a distinct limitation of his power, but thinking about it on the way to the meeting, Eliot felt sure that he could learn to control it. With time, he reasoned, his gift would become more matter-of-fact to him; he would adjust to it, as people adjust to permanent injuries that seem so unsettling at first. Of course, this power was more or less the opposite of an injury. But the same psychological laws surely applied. Comforted by these thoughts, Eliot allowed himself to drift into dreams of money, renown, and success with women.

*

Eliot arrived quite late—after the regular business meeting—and slipped quietly into the last row. Blake was addressing the club about the forthcoming Annual Show and acknowledged Eliot's entrance with an elegant arching of one eyebrow. Watching Blake speak, Eliot was struck anew by his commanding demeanor and his dramatic looks: the glossy, ivory skin of his face, the jet-black eyes and upturned eyebrows, the full, startlingly clefted lips, the patrician nose with its delicate flaring nostrils, the great smooth forehead and the long black hair combed handsomely back without a part. And his clothes: dark blazer with the new wide lapels; a solid red silk tie held with a sculptured silver bar; a white, richly textured shirt, the cuffs showing two inches and clasped by those tremendous silver heads of comedy and tragedy. And above all, Eliot was entranced by his warmth and his energy.

As to what Blake was saying, Eliot paid scant attention. Something about the need for a more balanced show with a wider variety of acts. Blake concluded by inviting everyone to speak briefly about their present act as they saw it: what they planned to use, any problems they might envision, when they'd like to try it out in front of the club. The chairs were then arranged in a large circle and Eliot waited impatiently while everyone spoke in turn. Wally Pound was sitting directly across from him, looking at him with great intensity and something like awe. Wally was the first to speak and, his glance coming back again and again to Eliot, described his silent routine: the multiplying golf balls, the Chinese sticks, the sympathetic silks, and the square circle production number. Joe Ferrante and Kimberly Vogel (the "Monte Carlo Boys") spoke next about their comedy act featuring the funnel and lota routine, the Mutilated Parasol and the combination Wand Through Balloon and Card in Balloon. Edgar Wick and Gordon Bunche, interrupting and contradicting each other, gave out a garbled version of the black art guillotine act that Eliot had rehearsed with them on that idiotic December afternoon in the School of St. John the Baptist. As Eliot had suspected, no theatre ever bought it.

Finally, it was Eliot's turn to speak. He was glad his turn came before Ronnie Pitkin, who was sitting to his left, giving off his usual smoldering emanations through his half-closed, crystal-blue eyes, his enigmatic smile and his loose, catlike posture. Ronnie, of course, would be speaking about his own mind reading act, and Eliot did not want to step too hard on a senior member's toes. Going before Ronnie would make it easier all around, Eliot reasoned. When everyone learned that Eliot could actually read minds, there would no doubt be general agreement then and there that his act should be the centerpiece of the show and Ronnie would be spared a certain amount of embarrassment. In any case, Blake could always be counted on to smooth things out.

Eliot had not given much thought to how he was going to break the news. He simply stood up and walked into the center of the circle (everyone else had stayed in their chairs). As he spoke, he slowly turned round on his spot, his gaze passing over all the faces of the Sorcerer's Apprentices. His voice boomed out; his heart pounded with joyous anticipation.

"I can read minds," he said. "I can actually read minds!" Elbows at his waist, his hands all by themselves lifted up at his sides toward his shoulders.

Silence. Eliot kept turning. Suddenly, he launched into a torrent of words, beginning with a detailed description of the great event at the pinochle game, followed by an even more detailed account of the Freddie Chubb episode, though without the conclusion. Sensing something strange coming from Wally Pound, he omitted any mention of what had taken place between them the day after the pinochle game.

More silence. Eliot started turning in the other direction. He was feeling a little dizzy, without knowing why. "And so," he went on, not really knowing what words were going to come out of his mouth, "I want you to advise me what to do. You all know much more than I do about stage business. How should I use this power for the best effect?"

Eliot was amazed at himself; he had no idea he would be standing up there putting the whole thing in that way, so diplomatically. He was beginning to feel a wonderful warmth and closeness toward everyone.

At first, he was simply puzzled by the burst of applause that followed. He only understood its meaning when someone shouted out (it was Sandy Hyman, the escape artist of the group), "Great line of patter, Eliot!"

They didn't believe him! Of course, why should they? Eliot saw that he was turning in a circle and stopped. He saw his hands up at his shoulders and let them drop down to his sides. He turned to look at Blake, who was only smiling benignly with a quizzical expression. He looked at Wally Pound, who instantly evaded his eyes.

"It's not a line of patter. It's a fact," said Eliot.

Eliot now started turning intentionally, looking at each face. Edgar Wick was shaking his head in disgust. To hell with him. Bunche started coughing, though softly. To hell with him, too. Wally Pound's eyes were still lowered. What's the matter, Wally? Blake simply continued to smile, but now with a sort of knowingness. Thank God, thought Eliot, Blake knows and understands. Or does he?

Finally, Ronnie Pitkin spoke. "Come off it, Appleman," he said in a deep, purring voice and without shifting a muscle of his lanky, sleepy posture. Eliot stared into Ronnie Pitkin's luminous blue eyes. Their coldness made him quaver.

"Ronnie," said Eliot almost in a whisper, "I'm not joking."

"Prove it to them." It was Wally Pound, speaking through clenched teeth.

With that, Sandy Hyman, the escape artist, clapped his hands and shouted out again. "Boy! This is either the nuttiest or the greatest build-up to a trick I've ever seen! He must have gotten it from Max!"

The mention of Max Falkoner's name calmed Eliot down considerably. He remembered something else Max had once said to him when he was selling him a particularly expensive and simple-minded coin trick. "It's not what you *do* on the stage that counts," he said. "It's what you *are* on the stage. Give me a *mensch* doing a pocket trick a *schmuck* doing a miracle every time."

Okay, Eliot thought to himself, I'll do it, and with self-control, too. The feeling of warmth toward the Sorcerers began to return. He hadn't planned to demonstrate his gift tonight, but what the hell, why not. It was naive to have thought they would simply believe him. In their shoes, he would have reacted the same way—although, maybe not. He remembered his own reactions at the show and at the first meeting he attended. He believed in magic, real magic.

Now, what to do? He turned to Ronnie Pitkin and, as always, was jarred by looking at him. What was it about Ronnie that was so unsettling and, at the same time, so fascinating? The hostility that Ronnie had just now manifested had nothing to do with it. It was really quite understandable. No one likes to be upstaged in his own special area.

But what better way to demonstrate his powers than by reading the mind of the mental magician Ronnie Pitkin himself?

"Ronnie," said Eliot, "you tell me what I should do."

Ronnie languidly uncrossed his legs and stared at Eliot's eyes. Eliot turned his own eyes away and, as he did so, he felt the sensation at the back of his head and was then almost thrown to the ground by the picture that appeared. It was the image of a dead body! It was a dead girl lying on a couch!

"All right, Appleman, I'm thinking of a six-digit number."

It was a lie. He was not thinking of a number at all! He was thinking of a dead girl! Suddenly Eliot was overcome by fear, fear such as he had never before felt. And now there were the tears coming, goddamn it!

Instinctively, Wally Pound called out, "I've got a better idea. Let's send Eliot out of the room and decide among ourselves something really tough."

Before any objection could be raised, Eliot quickly said, "Good idea," and hastened toward the door. As he left, he caught a passing glimpse of Blake watching him. Blake's smile was gone.

Out in the corridor, Eliot began pacing up and down the length of the passageway. He did not know and he did not want to know the meaning of that picture he saw in Ronnie Pitkin's mind. He did not even want to think about it. But why did Eliot feel such fear? He had never known an emotion like that. Never. Not when he was once almost hit by a truck, not when his father used to shout at him or punish him, not when he was caught shoplifting in elementary school, not when he was gashed in the head by a piece of broken glass and saw his own arterial blood spurting from his temple, and not even when he was trapped by the neighborhood rednecks, held down and pummeled, certain that he was going to be mutilated by them—terrified and enraged beyond endurance. But this suffocating fear that was still passing through him, what in God's name was it? And how could anyone ever bear it for more than an instant without killing himself?

Suddenly, Eliot stopped in his tracks. "Oh, Jesus," he said to himself, "Oh, Jesus Christ." He stared down toward the floor, his head bowed. He understood. He was not only able to read other people's thoughts; he could feel their emotions! That fear belonged to Ronnie!

But how could that be? Eliot's head swarmed with questions. Cool, contained, mysterious, handsome Ronnie Pitkin—how could that be? Eliot's knees practically buckled at the thoughts that started coming into his mind. Was that fear always there? Or only just now? *Where* was it? Where in the mind? Could human beings actually live their whole lives with something so painful in them? And how could it be so invisible if even just a taste of it nearly caused Eliot to faint? He had to understand this. Was it this fear that made Ronnie so silent, so detached, that made him seem so strong and . . . attractive, even magnetic?

At that moment, rotund Sandy Hyman bounced out into the corridor, his eyeglasses resting at the tip of his nose and his head, as always, tilted backwards at a forty-five degree angle. This escape artist had trouble going through an open door.

"Okay, Eliot, you're on!"

"Sandy," said Eliot quietly, "come down here."

Sandy Hyman waddled down the length of the corridor to the stairwell where Eliot was standing. Eliot intently watched him coming toward him and, by the time Sandy reached him, Eliot was able to say to him in a soft voice:

"Sandy, I don't have to go in there. They've selected the year 1930, the date is August 21, and the time, 8:42 in the morning. That's the birthday of Clipper's older sister. And it was selected because no one else in the room could possibly have known that before tonight. But just to make sure, tell everyone that Clipper really isn't sure about the time because he had two numbers in his mind. The other was 8:32 in the morning. Also, the baby was delivered by the same doctor who delivered him and whose name is Dr. Martin Lot, and Clipper's mother has always made a big fuss about that."

Eliot was ready to go on with more details about what had just taken place in the room down the corridor, but Sandy Hyman was already running toward the meeting room, his head tilted so far back it looked like it was about to fall off.

After Sandy Hyman left, Eliot slowly walked back as his composure returned. He paused for a moment in front of the meeting room door and then, brushing his hair back with his hand, walked in.

He found an extremely subdued group of young magicians waiting for him, all still seated in a circle, but in different chairs. Eliot tried to avoid looking at Ronnie Pitkin, but even a passing glance at him felt like a dagger in the chest. What struck Eliot most was how differently many of the Sorcerers now appeared to him. What was plus had become minus, and vice versa. The cadaverous Edgar Wick now looked merely quiet and serious; the absurd Gordon Bunche now had a certain sweetness and dignity about him. On the other hand, the "Monte Carlo Boys," Joe Ferrante and Kimberly Vogel, always the good-natured jokesters, now seemed tense and ill at ease.

But the biggest transformation was in the face of Stephen Blake. He was leaning gracefully against the table that had been pushed outside the circle of chairs. His arms were loosely crossed in front of him, hands gripping his elbows, the huge silver cuff links glittering. His "musical" smile was gone, and to Eliot he resembled nothing more than the silver mask of tragedy shining on his left wrist. The sharply clefted lips now seemed sullen, even ominous.

Some of the Sorcerers slowly began to mill around Eliot, but he could not take his eyes off Blake, who remained in his place. Eliot desperately wanted to hear something from Blake, something that would indicate Blake understood what had happened to Eliot and that he would help Eliot understand it, too. But Blake said nothing.

First to come up to Eliot and speak to him was Edgar Wick.

"That was wonderful, Eliot," he said, quite simply and sincerely. The two boys spontaneously shook hands. Wick was immediately joined by Gordon Bunche, who also shook Eliot's hand and touched his shoulder. Several other of the boys followed suit, congratulating Eliot in a few words and then stepping aside. Eliot was struck by how—the word was hard to find—normal these boys now seemed, as though the actual witnessing of something like a miracle took away all their idiosyncrasies, at least for the moment. They had suddenly become less "interesting," and more real.

More than half the Sorcerers kept their distance. Stillman Clipper was still visibly shaken, but finally he could restrain himself no longer and called out, "Aren't you going to tell us how you did it?"

The room was suddenly silent.

Clipper had broken the cardinal rule. No one ever asked a member how he did a trick. If you were good enough to fool the club, custom was to savor the achievement and only then voluntarily explain it later.

The silence grew painful and Eliot felt paralyzed. No one came to his aid. His "allies," standing near him, seemed as shocked as he was. As for the other Sorcerers, their eyes shifted for a brief moment to Clipper and then drifted into a general glare of outright hostility toward Eliot. Only Blake could save the situation, and he did nothing.

Finally, Wally Pound stepped forward and spoke for Eliot. His voice was cracking. He was taking a big step.

"I know it's hard to believe," said Wally, walking across the room toward the "enemy" side, "but the fact of the matter is that Eliot really is telepathic. I've seen proof." Relieved that he had taken his stand, Wally reached into his pocket for his pipe and struck a professorial posture.

"He doesn't know how it works. We've both been reading up on it, and we can't find any precedents in the literature . . ."

"Cut the shit," said Ronnie Pitkin in a voice louder than anyone had ever heard him use. "You're his goddamn confederate!" With that, Ronnie stood up and went to the closet for his coat. Several of the "allies" looked questioningly at Wally Pound, but stood their ground—with shifting feet.

Eliot tried to speak, but there was nothing he could say. He still couldn't bring himself to look directly at Ronnie, and so he stood there with his mouth open and his eyes down, his arms hanging limply. The "enemies" gathered closer together.

Blake did nothing, said nothing. What was he waiting for?

"Just tell us the secret," said Clipper, "and let's get on with the meeting."

"Yeah," said Sandy Hyman, wiping his glasses with an Eyesaver tissue. "Are you one of us or aren't you?"

At that, Blake stepped forward from the far table that he was leaning against, but still said nothing. His arms remained crossed in front of him, his face dark and impassive.

Eliot finally started to speak. "I . . . I . . ." His breathing came heavily. And then he plunged back into silence.

Ronnie Pitkin remained by the door, his coat hanging like a cape over one shoulder. He tapped out a cigarette and inserted it into the corner of his mouth without lighting it. "Stephen," he drawled, his voice quiet and husky again, "isn't he violating the rule of collegiality?"

Eliot heard that voice from behind him, but tried not to listen to it. The fear he had experienced when reading Ronnie's mind was still the uppermost emotion in him, stronger by far even than the outrage that he felt at the reaction of the Sorcerers to his demonstration.

"Yeah," said Hyman again, "let's vote on it!"

In the middle of all this drama, Eliot could not help blurting out, with a surprisingly steady voice, "Sandy, did anyone ever tell you that you are a *putz?*" And, having delivered that, Eliot found himself turning firmly on his heels to leave.

"Fuck you all," he said, "or most of you!"

But at just that moment, Blake, apparently satisfied that Eliot's demonstration had not been rigged, suddenly burst into loud applause. Eliot spun around again to see that the sunlight had returned to Blake's face.

And to Eliot's amazement all the enemies were also soon applauding him, even, finally, Stillman Clipper.

"Bravo, Eliot, bravo!" said Blake, approaching and drilling him with a look of tremendous intensity. Standing close to Eliot, he whispered to him, "Come to my house for dinner a week from Tuesday. And now, go home. Everything is all right."

Wally Pound overheard Blake's words and hurriedly brought Eliot his coat. They left together to the sound of continuing applause. But as they left, Eliot passed close by Ronnie Pitkin, who was still standing by the door with his coat draped over his shoulder. Feeling momentarily happy, Eliot looked smilingly into

Ronnie's face. Ronnie was not applauding. Eliot shivered with terror again. He quickly left with Wally Pound.

*

Even before the antediluvian elevator arrived, clanking and banging, Wally started talking about the events that had just taken place. He continued talking down to the street and out into the dismal cold rain.

But Eliot had only one thing on his mind—Ronnie Pitkin. Seated comfortably in Hamburger Heaven three blocks away on Chestnut Street, after having polished off a large chopped liver sandwich, Eliot finally interrupted Wally Pound's nonstop flow of words and told him about his experience reading the mind of Ronnie Pitkin. Wally was intrigued by the image of the dead girl on the couch— who was she? Was it a real person or only a fantasy?

"I don't know," said Eliot, "and I don't care." He very much wanted Wally to understand what was troubling him so much.

"The fear I felt in him, Wally, you can't imagine how strong it is. How can that be? He looks so cool and controlled. How can a person live with that inside of him? I can't understand."

Wally put down his knife and fork and looked at Eliot silently.

Eliot went on. "Do other people have that inside of them, too?"

"I don't know," said Wally.

"What could possibly cause such a thing?"

"I don't know."

"Wally, what the hell *is* the mind?"

"I don't know."

BLAKE

Stephen Blake lived in a section of downtown Philadelphia that was often written up in the Sunday papers as "historic" and "charming." But it held no charm for Eliot. The old colonial structures jammed together in narrow cobblestone alleys were oppressive to him, even on a clear, sparkling night like tonight. And Eliot's heart sank when he reached Blake's address, a dingy brick building squatting between a darkened Christian Science reading room and a run-down grocery store with a green neon sign flickering in the window. How could Blake, being what he was, live in a depressing place like this? Two weeks of high anticipation looking forward to this evening—and now, would all the hope he had placed in Blake come crashing down?

Eliot rang the bell, and when the door opened, his forebodings of the ordinary instantly dissolved. Blake stood before him in a handsome, cream-colored lounging jacket and a loosely knotted striped silk ascot. His smile radiated light. No sooner did Eliot step in than he was greeted with a barrage of completely unfamiliar sights and smells—some strange combination of herbs and something with a heavy floral essence that made his head swim. He clumsily took off his thick overcoat and his unnecessary galoshes (there had been a forecast of snow) and followed Blake down a darkened hallway covered with odd-sized paintings of flowers, birds, mountains and faces. Ponderous, creaking French doors opened into the living room.

And what a living room! What struck Eliot first was the dazzling color: textured crimson wallpaper, high windows covered by shimmering gold brocade drapes, overstuffed couches and chairs upholstered in soft shades of ochre and amber yellow, dozens of threadbare Oriental carpets piled together three deep in places. Everything was old and worn, but altogether it somehow gave the impression of opulence.

But what made Eliot gasp with excitement was the array of magical apparatus everywhere in the room, on every shelf and table, standing next to every chair, collected four and five deep inside a massive glass-enclosed china closet that reached nearly to the high ceiling, which was itself hung with a billowing gauzy material, like clouds. Eliot had never dreamed of anything like what he saw here! Some of the pieces he recognized, but most he had never seen or heard of or read about anywhere. Where did it all come from? What nations, what epochs, what worlds? There, on a nearby shelf, next to a standard wrist guillotine, was what seemed like a solid mahogany pentagon the size of a basketball, each surface carved with a graceful arabesque. Out of the top there projected a two-inch high mirrored blue glass pyramid, and in the point of this pyramid were inserted what looked like ten or twelve fine thread-like ivory sticks with burn marks at the top. What was it? What did it do?

On the shelf beneath it was an even stranger piece of apparatus, an intricately molded cast-iron dragonfly, nearly a foot long, with slender strips of colored glass for wings. Inside the hollow, grillwork eyes, Eliot saw white cubes like dice, only larger. The mouth of the dragonfly seemed to form some kind of lever.

Blake excused himself and left Eliot alone in the room. Entranced, Eliot walked toward the far end of the room where the larger pieces of apparatus were displayed. Next to a couch was a waist-high basket woven out of thick, coiled rope covered with a darkened, shell-like varnish. The top of the basket was shaped into the head of a cobra about the size of a man's head. "This must be from India," Eliot thought. He lifted the top of the basket and looked inside, where he saw seven, possibly eight spheres of different sizes. Seeing that Blake had not come back, he hesitated for a moment and then reached into the basket and took out one of the spheres, which was as heavy as a cannonball. Another was lighter and seemed to contain some kind of liquid. He hastily put them back and replaced the cover.

Moving to the far wall, his eyes passed over dozens of lacquered boxes with varying designs on them—Asiatic, Egyptian, African, some with faces of demons or wild animals, or simply staring eyes surrounded by stylized flames. Eliot gingerly lifted one of the boxes from the shelf. On each panel of the box was the representation of a monster composed of parts of animals, some grossly exaggerated. On one side the head of an owl was placed on the torso of a strange kind of fish. From the belly of the fish there protruded the huge sexual organs of a bull. On another side the body of a pig was surmounted by the head of a wolf. On another the head of a horse was joined to the body of a rodent, perhaps a rat.

Inside this strange box, which was about six inches square and about a foot high, Eliot saw numerous blocks of wood, each about three inches around, all fitted precisely into the entire volume of the box. He squatted down and emptied the blocks onto the crimson carpet. These blocks, too, were painted on all sides, but with different parts of the human anatomy and in precise scientific detail.

As he was squatting on the floor, trying to arrange the blocks into a figure of a human being—for it was clearly some kind of puzzle—Blake suddenly reappeared. "It's from Ethiopia," said Blake. "Here, let me show you." Startled by Blake, Eliot lost his balance and only Blake's gentle hand on his shoulder kept him from sprawling ignominiously on his backside.

Laughing noiselessly, Blake took the blocks and deftly arranged them in a horizontal row on top of the box that had contained them. To Eliot's delight, the figure of a man appeared—the pictures of monsters on the outside of the box now blending in with the drawings on the blocks to form the complete representation of a man. Blake turned the box on its next side and rearranged the blocks to form the figure of a beautifully clothed woman; and, again, the third side and a new arrangement of the blocks yielded the picture of an angel with his eyes closed in sleep; the fourth side together with the blocks yielded a man and woman in an embrace.

Eliot was enraptured with the puzzle, and with the magical way the figures of the monsters blended in with the lines of the human and angelic figures. "Charming, isn't it?" said Blake. "No one ever thinks of using the box itself to solve the puzzle."

It was more than "charming" to Eliot. He wanted very much to have the puzzle, at least for a while. It touched something in him, as though the puzzle were a kind of mystery. But Blake had something else on his mind and matter-of-factly scooped up the blocks. He dropped them unceremoniously into the box, which he then shoved out of the way on one of the shelves. Eliot's eyes kept wandering to the box—monsters on the outside, man on the inside, mysteriously requiring the parts of the animals for his completion.

Blake motioned to Eliot to sit in a huge, overstuffed chair next to the cobra basket, and Blake himself pulled over a wide-winged Morris chair in order to be close to him. Eliot sank into the chair as into a dream. It was incredibly comfortable and he let out a long happy sigh.

A strange-looking little woman came into the room, carrying a tray with a teapot, cups, and a plate of unidentifiable stuffed pastries. She looked like some gnarled old gnome with a long nose, tiny, glistening black eyes, and dull black hair carelessly pulled back into a bun from which strands of gray hair hung down. She was wearing a wrinkled and torn loose red dress under a threadbare cardigan sweater. Eliot laughed to himself that Blake would have a maid who looked like this. Blake summarily ordered the woman to place the tray atop a nearby padded footstool. "Careful it don't tip," she croaked out in a strong Yiddish accent. Eliot was shocked not only by the accent, but by her disrespectful tone, which did not seem to faze Blake in the least. He ignored her as she energetically strode out of the room. Not until a later visit did Eliot learn that this was Blake's mother. But by then such perceptions were no longer troubling to him.

Eliot had come with two burning questions—one about his mind reading powers and the other about Irene Angel. But now, enveloped in the soft chair and sipping exotic, rose-flavored tea, he wanted only to know about the wondrous apparatus that filled the room. He did notice in passing how strange it was that he was so interested in these artificial tricks, when he actually had the kind of power that some of these tricks only simulated. But he was confident that tonight Blake would explain to him everything about the mind reading.

True to the code of the magician, Blake revealed little about how the tricks worked and Eliot faithfully resisted asking him. But Blake told him everything else—their origins, their romantic histories, stories of the magicians who had used them, the kind of effects they were intended to have on an audience. By the time they got up to go to the dinner table, Eliot's head was spinning with wonder and excitement. He had not known, no one had ever told him, how much magic there was in the history of man. Blake had told him about the role magic played in ancient medicine, in art and religion, in the sciences of vanished civilizations.

Eliot followed Blake through a beaded curtain into an adjoining long alcove in which a small, round table was set for dinner. The piles of food looked delicious, but what caught Eliot's eye was the uncorked bottle of French wine. This alarmed him. He had never drunk "real" wine before, only sweet wine served at Passover celebrations. He had tasted French wine once, which someone had described to him as "dry," whatever the hell that meant, and he had hated it.

Eliot unconsciously devoured his soup while mentally gearing himself for the wine test. As he heaped his plate with the meatballs, potatoes, and cauliflower (which the "maid" had apparently prepared in the unseen kitchen), he nervously watched Blake filling the glass in front of him. His mouth now stuffed with one and a half meatballs and half a piece of potato, he suddenly realized that Blake was simply sitting at his place, holding his own glass of wine in front of him waiting. Blake hadn't even touched the soup yet, far less put any meatballs on his plate. The truth was Eliot had never had a meal with anyone, except his Aunt Louise, who did not start eating immediately upon sitting at the table.

Slowly and gingerly, Eliot put down his fork, while secretly making rapid little bites of the food in his mouth in order to swallow it all as quickly as possible. Unfortunately, just as Blake extended his glass to propose a toast (Eliot had never actually had anything to do with "toasts"; he had only seen it in movies), he choked on the big wad of food that he was trying to swallow. In order to prevent a spray of half-chewed material from erupting all over the table, he instinctively reached for the glass of wine and downed it in two large gulps.

Blake elegantly gave no sign of noticing what had happened, but simply filled Eliot's glass again. As the wine that he had gulped down raced through his body, Eliot felt a sort of message coming up to his brain from somewhere down below his chest. "Good," it said, "very, very good!" Although his eyes were filled with tears from the choke reflex, and although he still hated the taste of wine, the sense of warmth and strength caused by the alcohol had already reached into his heart, and with a sure and steady hand he lifted his glass in exact imitation of Blake's gesture.

"To Irene!" he said, before Blake could speak, "the mysterious mistress of magic!" Not quite believing these words had actually come out of his own mouth, Eliot gulped down the second glass of wine.

Blake continued to take it all in stride, as though events were following some carefully thought-out plan. He sipped his own wine and then tactfully moved his untouched soup to the side in order to keep pace with Eliot's furious attack upon the meatballs and, soon thereafter, the wedge of chocolate-flecked Nesselrode pie.

As the last of the pie disappeared, Eliot poured himself another glass of wine and, feeling himself quite the equal of Blake, bluntly put to him *the* question:

"I want to know the real truth about Irene!"

At this, Blake's face assumed a grave expression which briefly penetrated Eliot's wine-soaked mind and sent a chill down his spine.

"Of course," said Blake. "That's half the reason I invited you here. Come with me."

Blake's room formed a stark contrast to the living room. The walls were plain white and decorated only with a group of geometric designs wrought in heavy, black iron. Among these metal geometric figures was the six-pointed star, which to Eliot represented only the dull religion of his grandparents and family—

everything that was the opposite of magic and mystery. He reached over and touched it. It was cold and he instantly drew his hand away.

The room was sparsely furnished with a daybed, covered by a brilliant Oriental carpet and dozens of black pillows. Two isinglass lamps hung from long chains over the bed, on either side of which were matching low-backed ebony armchairs of Chinese design. The lamps gave off a low, warm light.

At one end of the room the entire wall was covered with the largest collection of phonograph records Eliot had ever seen, and in front of them was an expensive-looking record player set next to an enormous speaker housed in a rich, mahogany cabinet.

Feeling unsteady on his feet, Eliot sat down on one of the hard, Chinese chairs and only then noticed what seemed to be a kind of altar at the other end of the room. Actually, it was a mantelpiece cluttered with small, Oriental statuettes and dozens of framed photographs of various sizes. A burning candle stood in the middle underneath a large black-and-white picture of the insignia of the Sorcerer's Apprentices. Realizing he had never really looked carefully at the insignia, Eliot pushed himself up from his chair and wobbled over to examine it. His eyes went in and out of focus as he stared at the ink drawing of the large metal ring, in the center of which was a human skull crossed diagonally from behind by a black, white-tipped magic wand. At the bottom, seven keys were drawn hanging from the ring, but they were not ordinary keys. They looked Egyptian, sort of.

Eliot sighed and then sighed again. It was all so extraordinary. He felt that everything, the whole of life, was simply extraordinary and that he must be the luckiest person in the world. Forgotten was the dull reality of Philadelphia.

He nearly jumped out of his skin as suddenly the voice of Irene Angel rang out loud and clear in his brain. My God!

His impulse was to wheel around to see if she was actually in the room, but the sober part of his brain was telling him just to stand still and do nothing. It was probably an hallucination, it was probably the alcohol—maybe triggering the manifestation of his power in some unexpected way. He shut his eyes, but this made him too dizzy and he had to reach out and clutch the mantelpiece in order to keep from falling. Opening his eyes again, he stared at the blurred insignia of the Sorcerers as he listened to the voice:

"The womb of magic conceives but once and then withers away," it said. "You must seek the seed and bend all your efforts to nourish it when it appears. Amid the artifices of the stage magician, amid the trappings and techniques, there will appear the reality beyond all artifice. Be quick to recognize it. It is in you. It is beyond you. Cultivate your professional style, your persona, and then, and only then, you may find your true self."

Still gripping the mantelpiece, and aware of a great deal of bubbling in his stomach, Eliot realized that he did not have the foggiest idea what the voice was talking about and so it could not be an hallucination. At that moment, during a pause, he heard a scratching sound. Of course! He spun around and saw Blake seated with great aplomb on one of the Chinese chairs which he had moved next to the record player. Irene's voice was coming from the record now spinning on the turntable. The voice continued:

"If you work with diligence along the lines handed down by the magicians of the past, sooner or later a real magician with real power will appear. He will be young and unformed; he will be shy. And he will retreat in front of every lie and deception. But you must give him all your attention so that what he brings can be shared among you. Here is how to recognize him . . ."

Blake lifted the needle and the voice stopped in mid-sentence. He sat in the chair with his legs elegantly crossed and his hands loosely clasped together. He said nothing, but only looked at Eliot with a solemn, penetrating gaze. After a long silence, he motioned Eliot to sit down on the other chair. The record continued to spin on the turntable and Eliot found himself looking back and forth from Blake's eyes to the hypnotically spinning phonograph record.

"Are you that person?" Blake asked, his voice even more musical and sonorous than Eliot remembered. At first, Eliot did not know what Blake meant. What person?

"Are you the magician that Irene prophesied?"

Eliot literally looked around to see who Blake was talking to. His main concern at the moment was a stomach that was beginning to send out distress signals. Apart from that, he was not aware that he had any mind at all. He was little more than a state of vertigo that had to go to the bathroom.

Blake became silent again. As Eliot's stomach temporarily settled down, his eyes fixed themselves on the spinning record. After a few moments, Blake's words began to penetrate into his awareness. He no longer sensed or felt his stomach, or any other part of his body. And, it seemed, just like that, with no transition at all, he understood what Blake meant. He, Eliot, was the real magician foretold by Irene.

Was it really so? A sensation of exquisite pleasure filled Eliot's chest and head and even spread down to his stomach and below, especially below. Gone was every trace of fear and uncertainty.

Eliot crossed his legs in exact imitation of Blake's posture and tilted his head back. That Blake had not answered his question about Irene completely escaped him. The question of who she really was and what had happened to her, which had been such a burning issue to him, was now forgotten. He had never known such happiness.

Blake stood up. "Are you that person?" he said again, as he glided past Eliot without looking at him. He went to the mantelpiece, where he picked up something and then closed his fist around it.

"I need to test your power, Eliot," he said. "I want to be sure of you."

Eliot smiled and nodded.

"I understand, Stephen," he said.

Standing at the mantelpiece directly under the ringed skull insignia, the warm, low illumination of the room creating deep hollowed shadows at his eyes and lending to his lips a sharply bowed tragic curve, Blake explained the nature of the test.

"You want to know about Irene," he said. "You want me to tell you things about her?"

Still grinning, Eliot nodded.

Blake continued. "I'm holding her ring in my hand. I am going to concentrate on her, and what I want you to do is to answer your question yourself by receiving my thoughts. Are you willing to try that?"

"Certainly," said Eliot, relishing the challenge, and even as he spoke the word, his body all by itself pulled him erect in his chair. Spine and head perfectly aligned, his eyes immediately closed and he sat in silence, waiting.

A few moments passed without anything happening. Gradually, his dizziness began to retreat and his breathing became soft and gentle. But still, nothing happened and he began to be a little bit concerned that his power would not appear. He opened his eyes for a second and saw Blake standing motionless, gazing intently at him, his fist clenched at his chest. Eliot immediately shut his eyes again and continued to wait.

Suddenly, he felt the familiar tickling sensation at the back of his head, but this time it grew much stronger than usual and darted down the length of his spine. A complete picture of Blake's thoughts opened like a flower before him.

There was a large, elegantly furnished apartment. Sunlight filled the room. It was summer; it was warm. Big French windows opened wide, letting in a soft breeze through billowing, gossamer curtains. The smell of water in the air, a river, city sounds, traffic, boats from far below.

Irene Angel was seated in a wide, low-backed chair with flowers embroidered on the thickly-upholstered arms. She was wearing a ruffled white blouse with numerous slender gold chains and a brilliant, opalescent pendant. Her eyes were lowered; her face was smooth and calm. Her white high forehead seemed to glow; long, pale yellow hair streamed down her back.

Across from her, separated by a low table, Blake was seated on the floor, his legs crossed in front of him. On the marble table was a gold death's head ring. Irene was speaking, but Eliot heard her words in the voice of Blake.

"Wear this ring," the voice was saying, "as a sign of your high initiation into the mysteries of our ancient society. The young men for whom you will be responsible must be trained as you have been trained until that one appears who, like you, is born to our great lineage in magic. Speak only to him of the secret behind the secrets, the skull within the circle, the Great Death.

"You, Stephen Blake, are my apprentice in eternity. You are called to teach and lead as I have been called. What others strive for and never attain, you have been given. Accept this gift and, with it, the duty placed on you from above to lead the worthy."

Fadeout. The voice stopped; the image quietly evaporated in Eliot's mind and he was just sitting there in the room with Blake, his half-closed eyes looking at Blake's glossy black shoes. "Is that all?" he wondered. He checked himself; the vertigo was completely gone, his body felt fine all over, his breathing was soft and steady. Was that all? No surprises? No picking up someone else's feelings? No shattering side-effects of the power? Eliot remained motionless, waiting, wary.

Was that really all? And wasn't it sort of, well, uninteresting? He had expected to learn something personal and intimate, if not exactly racy, about Irene, some facts about her that could really be savored. But all that he had seen was just more of the same thing— apart from the information about Blake's high station in this whole set-up, or whatever it was. His disappointment in the vision outweighed his sense of relief—though, God forbid he should ever again have to experience the sort of thing that happened when he had read Ronnie Pitkin's mind.

But just as he was about to look up at Blake, the tickling sensation at the back of the head appeared again. For a brief, fleeting second, Eliot felt himself in front of a strange kind of decision, unlike anything he had ever known before. He sensed that if he now opened his eyes all the way and looked up, everything would go in a certain way, but if he shut his eyes and allowed the power to manifest further, a completely different future would be offered him. Tonight, up to this point, the power had treated him gently, with none of the searing pain or shocks it had brought him before. But who could say what it would reveal to him if he now let it go on?

Eliot chose to shut his eyes. In fact, he closed his eyes very tightly, bracing himself, like someone waiting to be struck. Wasn't the Ronnie Pitkin experience, agonizing though it had been, worth it just to have discovered something so extraordinary about the mind?

The image of Irene and Blake reappeared, only now there were many more people in the room. They were all, including Blake, sitting on metal chairs loosely arranged in two curved rows. There were about fifteen people, men and women, and Blake was the youngest. This gave Eliot a start. In this company, Blake seemed so youthful, so insignificant.

As for Irene Angel, she was seated in front of the two rows, also on one of the metal chairs. But now she was not there alone. Someone was seated next to her. Who was it? Eliot couldn't make it out. He saw only an indistinct figure.

Already, Eliot's thoughts started working: Why was this image so different from the first one? Which was true? Or were they both true? But he had no time to think further as a sharp pain gripped him by the throat. Suddenly, his vision telescoped in on Blake's face, which rapidly transformed into something hideous, as though the face were made of melting wax. Long dark lines appeared under the eyes and a kind of liquid seemed to be dripping down. The fine curve of the lips was twisted and blurred.

As the face continued to melt, other images appeared in the eyes, images that Eliot saw in precise detail. In one of the images, Blake was opening a drawer and stealing things from it. Eliot felt Blake's emotions in the image and experienced his thoughts: "This is mine, this is mine! This is meant to be mine!"

Eliot saw Blake holding the gold death's head ring in his hand. He saw him close his fist around it. He followed him as Blake stealthily looked around and placed the ring in his pocket.

Eliot was shocked by what he saw. He understood what it was to steal things, but not something so valuable, so significant as the gold insignia ring that belonged to Irene! And he did not understand the melting face. His power had always shown him actual things, but this melting face was surely only a kind of dream-image. Faces do not melt except in horror movies. Maybe, he thought, it was the influence of the wine on him. What else could it be?

With his eyes still tightly shut, Eliot felt something stirring in his own body. As though moving by itself, his right hand slowly lifted from his thigh and inched toward the pocket of his sportcoat. As this was happening, the images continued to unfold. He saw Blake standing before the members of the Sorcerer's Apprentices at one of the Wednesday night meetings. Everyone was there—Clipper, Ronnie Pitkin, Sandy Hyman, Wick and Bunche, Wally Pound—everyone. Blake was speaking. He was telling them that Irene had died. And it was completely untrue.

Suddenly, Eliot was nearly thrown to the floor by a wave of fear. The sensation of pain in his throat spread throughout his body. It was the same fear he had known when he was reading the mind of Ronnie Pitkin, only it was even more powerful now. It was Blake's fear.

Blake? Afraid? Of what? Why? Why was he stealing and apparently lying? Why was he telling the Sorcerers that Irene had died and left him to lead the club? Eliot's body started trembling. There was too much happening now. The face of Blake continued to melt; Eliot's own hand continued ever so slowly to move by itself toward his pocket; the fear continued to intensify in him. He saw Blake in one image after another working with individual members of the club. He saw him helping them with their magic, encouraging them, speaking kind words to them. In each image, Blake was playing the role of teacher, leader, guide, always speaking to the members about Irene, encouraging them to believe that they were specially destined for greatness or something of that sort. Eliot felt the pleasure in the minds of each of the members, the sense of self-importance. Something of the nature of warm release flowed through him as he saw these images, and it existed side by side with the sense of fear and, now, disgust, shame, remorse. Were they his own sensations and emotions or were they Blake's remorse? Eliot did not know. He didn't care to know. He felt trapped. He wanted to cry and was afraid to open his eyes.

Blake's face continued to melt. Eliot's hand continued to move—now entering his pocket, where it encountered a wet, wadded up piece of Kleenex, a deck of cards (the Svengali deck that he now always carried around with him), the wrapping from a candy bar, and . . . something else. What was it? Eliot remembered his initiation, when his hands had grown "eyes." But just as he was about to identify this unknown "something," the image of Blake's melting face changed, as though the skin were finally peeling off.

And now Eliot saw the bones—gold in color—beneath the skin of Blake's face. A scream began to well up from deep inside him. At the same time, his hand grasped the thing in his pocket. He took his hand out, clenched into a fist around the object, and held it tightly in his lap.

"Open your eyes, Eliot, and look at what is in your hand," said Blake in deep, sonorous tones. Eliot did as he was told, lifting his eyelids ever so slightly, afraid of what he would see. There in his own hand was the gold death's head ring! Eliot threw up.

*

Blake calmly guided Eliot back to the living room and sat him down again next to the cobra basket. He disappeared for a moment into the kitchen where he passed a few words to the "serving-woman." Eliot heard the woman grumbling about cleaning up the mess, but he felt no embarrassment.

He felt sick. He sat in the living room—sick. The hundreds of objects that a short while ago were full of mystery and wonder now seemed only weird. His head ached. His stomach ached. He still felt nauseous. He looked with bewilderment at the ring that was still in his right hand. "How the hell did I ever get into this?" he thought.

But, to his amazement, when Blake reappeared with the tea, everything began to come back—both the wonder and the sense of horror at what he had just seen in his mind. He eagerly drank the tea, and as his stomach settled down, he found himself square in the middle between the old sense of awe before Blake and the agonized realization that he had seen through him. He had seen his lies and pretense; yet the man who now sat across from him was, incredibly, even more compelling than before, even more alluring and miraculous.

Perhaps what he had just seen was not the truth. Perhaps the first vision was the true one. But the power had never deceived him before. Which was to be trusted? The question began to torment him. And it seemed to him that Blake was waiting for him to speak, to reveal his vision, in order to know if Eliot had passed the test.

But did he now even want to "pass?" Eliot was not sure. What would he be getting into? And what did he want? Holding the cup in one hand and the ring in the other, Eliot pretended to feel sicker than he was in order to buy a little time. He slowly sipped what remained of the tea, pondering what to say, how much to reveal of what he saw. Perhaps he should admit the whole thing and tell Blake about both visions. No, that would be dangerous. He did not really trust Blake enough for that, not after what he had seen and felt in the second vision. How could this magical person, who exuded such masterful self-assurance, be haunted by such fear? Eliot shuddered as the image of the melting face flashed quickly again in his memory. No, he couldn't trust Blake—or could he?

Then the words of Blake came back to him. "Are you that person?" What person? Someone singled out for some high destiny? Was he? Is that what this power meant?

Eliot felt he had to say something. Blake was looking at him with special intensity, as though demanding that he speak or else forfeit the whole opportunity.

He opened his mouth without even knowing what was going to come out.

He began to describe the room he had seen, elaborating all the physical details—the furniture, the curtains, the summer heat, the sounds—hoping that as he spoke about these neutral things, he would be able to choose what to reveal about Blake. He then described the first image: Blake seated alone at Irene's feet.

Across from him, he saw Blake nodding in approval, and he realized then that he would say nothing about the second vision. His decision made him feel small in his own eyes, but he could not help himself. He was shocked suddenly to hear himself saying, "Have I passed the test?"

Then, as though to deny his eagerness for Blake's approval, he impulsively reached forward to return the ring. But something he said or did must have revealed more than he had wished. A kind of puzzled frown appeared on Blake's face and, instead of accepting the ring, Blake took Eliot's outstretched hand in his own large, slender hands and closed Eliot's fingers around the ring.

"The test isn't over yet," said Blake. "I want you to put the ring on. I want you to wear it day and night for a week and then come back. Then we'll know."

Eliot slowly sat back in his chair and put the empty teacup on the floor. His first impulse was to refuse, but it had no force. As though watching himself in a dream, he saw himself sliding the ring on the third finger of his right hand. It fit perfectly.

THE HANDS OF MAX FALKONER

More nausea and a sickening headache woke Eliot in the middle of the night. He staggered to the bathroom and then returned to his bed where he lay sleepless for hours, absently fingering the ring on his right hand. The events of the previous evening gave him no peace until the morning light appeared. He abruptly sat up in his bed and, without thinking much about it, removed the ring. He then sank back onto his pillow and was quickly engulfed in a sweet, dreamless sleep.

The cool touch of his mother's hand on his forehead awakened him. "Eliot, you'll be late for school."

Her voice made everything seem normal and safe. Eliot sprang out of bed and hurriedly washed and dressed. He picked up the ring from the floor, dropped it into the pocket of his brown cardigan sweater and, after gulping down a waiting bowl of hot Cream of Wheat, rushed out of the house still buttoning his heavy winter jacket.

The day was cold and bright. Eliot bowed his head into the freezing wind, adjusted the load of books under his arm and ran to the streetcar. He squeezed himself into the last remaining seat at the back and began looking through his lessons for the day. Soon the trolley was jammed with students raising the usual uproar. Once or twice, Eliot glanced up from his books feeling strangely glad to be part of the motley crowd.

But when the trolley approached Jefferson High and the noisy crowd began pushing toward the exits, he remained in his place. It was not any kind of decision. He just saw himself sitting there while the car emptied out and the doors closed. The school slowly floated past him as the trolley rumbled on its way. He had never cut school before and was rarely even late for classes. But now he calmly watched the houses and neighborhoods glide by him, people of all kinds coming in and out of the trolley, and he did not even think of school, not even when he heard a distant clock striking nine.

He knew he was on his way to Max Falkoner, but he did not yet allow his mind to think of anything. After transferring to the subway and then pushing through the early morning downtown crowds with their blank Philadelphia faces, he found himself at the corner of Sixteenth and Chestnut Streets and entered the building housing Templeton's Magic Shop.

The door was dark, but Eliot rapped on the glass just in case Max was already there. No answer; Templeton's did not open for business until ten. Eliot unbuttoned his coat and sat on the floor, propping himself against the door.

When ten o'clock came and passed, he began to realize how much he was aching to see Max. He took the ring out of his pocket and stared at it, as the events of the evening with Blake unreeled before him. He would start to put the ring on, but each time he hesitated until, finally, looking around to see if anyone was watching him, he slid the ring on his finger. But when he did so, he experienced such a sharp sensation of pleasure down his spine and between his legs that he instinctively removed it.

Suddenly, Eliot looked up to see Max Falkoner standing over him, as though he had materialized out of thin air. A burning cigarette dangled from the corner of Max's mouth, which was set in its usual expression of ironic disdain. The heavily lidded eyes squinted down at Eliot through the smoke; the short, squat body stood motionless as a tree stump. Startled and overjoyed to see the sallow face of Max Falkoner, Eliot jumped to his feet, scattering his school books and papers on the floor around him. He scrambled to collect his papers in a disorganized stack while Max moved past him and opened the door.

Inside the magic shop, Eliot dumped his books and papers on a chair and followed Max on the run across the room. But when he unthinkingly attempted to go with Max behind the counter, Max stopped him with a fierce look. It was an ironclad, unwritten rule of Templeton's Magic Shop that no customer cross to the other side of the counter. Eliot beat down a small wave of resentment—was he still only that, an ordinary "customer"?—and retreated to one of the chairs lined up against the wall under the framed photographs of professional magicians.

He sat down and waited impatiently. Sounds of Max preparing for the day's business came from behind the mirrored wall with its glass-enclosed cabinets that displayed the higher-priced pieces of stage apparatus. A toilet flushed and Eliot found himself in front of the image of Max Falkoner as just a mere human being, with ordinary bodily functions, standing over a toilet.

The fluorescent lights noiselessly blinked on and Max finally emerged from the office area. Still without speaking or even looking at Eliot, he went over to the cash register, rang it open, counted out some currency and put it in the register, noting the amount on a pad of paper. Eliot sprang up from his chair, forgiving Max everything, and was about to pour himself out when Max once again—without a word—disappeared behind the mirrored display cases.

Simply put, Eliot felt like shit. Why did he always feel this way with Max, no matter what was happening? And why did he keep coming back again and again to him? Why did he always look forward with such eagerness to seeing him?

He did not dwell on these thoughts. He knew he needed Max's common sense about the whole situation he was now in—the power, Blake, Irene, the ring, the prophecy, everything, the whole incredible tangle. He was willing to risk crossing the "customer line" any number of times if only Max could help him to know what to believe.

Max reappeared holding two cups of coffee. He put one of them down on the counter, over the wand display, and slowly sipped at the other, eyeing Eliot.

"To what do I owe the honor of this visit?" he said, motioning Eliot to take the coffee.

Somewhat becalmed, Eliot went to the counter and picked up the cup. The coffee was black and Eliot hated black coffee, but he drank it anyway, reluctant to ask Max to put milk and sugar in it.

Eliot started talking—slowly and clearly enough at the beginning, but soon lapsing into a spluttering torrent of words. Through it all, he watched Max's face, hunting for a sign of some kind from him. Max gave nothing, except an occasional nod of the head. Max's lack of reaction only made Eliot talk more and more, and he soon found himself talking about everything under the sun, not only his power of reading minds—which, incredibly, did not seem to interest Max in the slightest; not only the events with Blake, with Ronnie, with all of the Sorcerers; not only the stuff about Irene, the prophecy— which did evoke a barely perceptible shake of the head from Max; not only all of that, but much, much more. Eliot was astonished by his own uncontrolled mouth. He talked about school, he talked about astronomy, he talked about the Phillies baseball team; he talked about the movies, about girls, about his mother and father, clothes, food, music, including his fondness for Tchaikovsky and his inability to dance; he talked about money; he talked about how much he hated Philadelphia; he talked about his weight, about his dream of becoming a research biologist, until finally, with an astonishment that knew no bounds, he heard himself talking about his "hobby" of shoplifting, something he had never told anyone, anywhere. And with that, seeing that, he stopped.

Max stuck a cigarette into his mouth and lit it with a chrome Zippo lighter, which he then deftly dropped back into the pocket of his brown *cubavera*.

A very painful silence ensued as Max continued to smoke his cigarette and drink his coffee. Never in his life had Eliot felt like this—that he was being weighed and found wanting. He wanted to run out of the store and hide in some way, but the impulse to stay was equally strong. Yet how could he just stay—without doing something, without talking about something—and there was nothing more to talk about!

He had bared his soul to Max Falkoner. Now what would Max do with it? Eliot could not endure the silence; nor could he do anything to end it. He felt that at any moment he might start to cry. Seeing that, he slowly reached into his pocket and took hold of the ring that Blake had given him and clutched it in his fist.

Just then, Max put down his cup, lit another cigarette, and reached into the counter display case.

"I think I have the trick for you," said Max. Eliot could not believe his ears. A wave of anger began to rise up in him and he clutched his fist tightly around the ring in his pocket. His anger and hurt intensified beyond measure when he saw what Max brought out of the case: a set of Spirit Slates, one of the oldest, most gimmicky mind reading tricks in the business.

Eliot felt the blood draining from his face. He did not know whether he would scream or cry. How dare Max respond to him in this way! He who actually *could* read minds! Who actually could do *real* magic, not the faked imitations purveyed by Max Falkoner! He who was . . . yes, *that* person foretold by Irene herself!

Eliot's heart was pounding in his ears and behind his eyes. Never in his life had a wound gone so deep. Never had he opened himself so far only to be mocked. Why had he trusted Max so much?

Tightly gripping the death's head ring in his pocket, Eliot coldly watched Max setting up the Spirit Slates trick. With a fury the likes of which he had never experienced in his life, he turned on his power, directing it at Max. Since the experience with Freddie Chubb, he had never used the power in this way, without the consent of the other person. He had never used it surreptitiously, never in the service of wounded pride or any other emotion of that kind. Always, he had treated the power as something not really his own, something given him. He had begun to suspect that this power to see through another's mask was not something he could ever possibly manipulate; this power brought him feelings and a kind of knowing that were terrible and real and bigger than he was.

But now all that was forgotten. As he watched Max's hands aligning the slates, one on top of the other, he felt the familiar tickling sensation at the back of his head and waited impatiently for the vision he knew must come. When a few moments passed and nothing happened, he was not perturbed; it had been like that with Blake.

He waited. Time passed. Finally, Max looked up at him and began speaking the patter that went with the trick, but Eliot kept his eyes fixed on Max's hands. He did not want to look at him.

But after a few moments, as though coming from a great distance, he heard Max's voice saying, "Snap out of it, Applehead!"

Eliot's eyes darted upward to Max's relaxed, heavy-lidded eyes. The exotic and slightly Oriental slants and planes of his face were no longer so intriguing. The black strands of hair combed flat over the broad, balding dome of his head seemed now repellent. The bemused, ironic smile, which for Eliot had always been a mark of Max's self-control and containment, seemed now to taunt and mock him.

Suddenly, everything went black in front of Eliot. Then, out of the darkness, with unbearable clarity, there appeared the figure of a woman in a hospital gown weeping over the motionless body of a newborn baby. The woman cried and shuddered, turning her face back and forth from the baby to the figure of a young man in white standing next to her. The man pulled the woman away as she struggled and wailed, and another, older man, grasped the baby behind the head and inserted a tube in its mouth. Eliot felt his own throat filled with pain. The man pushed the tube in and out and pressed down gently on the baby's chest. Eliot felt that, too. But most of all, he felt the horror and grief of the woman. How she needed this baby to live! She would kill herself if it died; she would kill her husband; she would kill the world.

Eliot was fully aware that he was standing in front of Max choking with sobs. He searched the vision again and again for something else. Where was Max in this vision? He was nowhere to be seen. What was this terrible scenario? What was this strange, absolutely unknown feeling of desperate grief of the woman, a despair that filled his own body from head to toe, his throat, his back, his chest, his sex. Eliot was aware of everything in that moment—the room he was in, Max standing behind the counter, his face now suddenly grave and impassive, as though he, too, Max Falkoner, were in the presence of this same vision and energy swirling within Eliot's body. Eliot was aware of sounds in the room, the ticking clock, the street sounds muffled by the curtained windows. He was aware of where he was, in this office building, in downtown Philadelphia, in North America, the planet earth, the third planet from the Sun in the great solar system that was only a speck in the vastness of the Milky Way. He was aware of what was going on at Jefferson High, the morning assembly, the algebra class he was missing.

But Max was nowhere in the vision. Who was the baby? Who was the woman?

A profound sense of calm gradually settled in on Eliot. Something like a soft cool wind again seemed to penetrate every tissue of his body. He opened his eyes to see Max looking at him with tremendous intensity and compassion. Eliot closed his eyes again, with a sense of resignation. He knew who the woman was: it was his mother. He knew who the baby was: it was himself. Before his eyes the same scene now appeared—but quietly, gently—that he had seen in the second vision with Blake. Irene was sitting in front of a group of about fifteen men and women. Next to her was the figure of a man, blurred except for his hands. They were the hands of Max Falkoner! But why? What did it mean? Why were Max and Irene seated together like that? What kind of a group of people was it, with Blake as only one of them? And the youngest, least significant one at that?

Eliot let go of the ring he was clutching in his pocket. Slowly, he gathered up his books and walked toward the door.

Just as he grasped the knob, he heard Max calling to him. He turned around to see Max with his hat and overcoat on, locking the cash register and coming out from behind the counter.

"Let's have some breakfast," said Max, opening the door for Eliot. Eliot stepped into the corridor and Max locked the door behind him.

They walked toward the elevators. Eliot did not know why any of this was happening. Why was Max doing the unthinkable act of shutting the store during business hours to go out with him?

Eliot hastened to keep pace with Max while his school books kept slipping around under his arm. One of the books fell as they entered the elevator and Max held back the doors while Eliot picked it up.

Sixteenth Street was already bustling with shoppers. The cold wind blew apart Eliot's unbuttoned coat. With one hand he held the coat together while struggling with the other arm to hold his books. Max forged ahead, turning down Chestnut Street where a new blast of cold air rushed at them. But Eliot did not mind the cold. He felt something new, a new emotion that was also strangely familiar, like something out of the distant past, intensely quiet and vibrant.

The vision he had of his mother and himself had caused something else to recede from his mind. His wounded pride? Gone. The dreams of power and importance that Blake had led him to? Gone. The doubts and forebodings about Blake? Forgotten, unimportant. Even the question about Irene did not really bother him so much. In any case, he was not thinking about it as they entered Bain's Cafeteria.

As he pushed along both his load of books and the cafeteria tray—which he unconsciously piled with scrambled eggs and bacon, a large container of orange juice, a buttered Kaiser roll and a bowl with a small package of Rice Krispies in it, not to mention the coffee and a small cinnamon bun—he saw only the newborn baby and the anguished mother. And he felt with great intensity the physical presence of Max, who was moving along ahead of him in the line.

When he came to the end of the line and started to follow Max toward a table, he realized that there was no way he could carry both his books and the tray crammed with food. He stood helplessly by the cash register watching Max moving to a table far in the back and then decided to try the impossible. With his left hand he lifted the incredibly heavy tray, and with one big grab he wrapped his right arm around the books and began slowly wobbling toward the back of the cafeteria. The tray started tilting dangerously. Coffee sloshed out of the cup and the cup itself fell off the tray, splattering hot coffee onto his feet and even into his shoes. No matter; he plowed on. The cereal bowl was now sliding. It, too, fell off the tray. He bent his body to the side in order to level out the tray and to prevent the juice and eggs from going, when suddenly his whole load of books dropped to the floor.

Eliot straightened himself up and looked toward Max, who was now sitting at his table, unconcernedly salting his eggs. Eliot felt not the slightest embarrassment. Laughing softly to himself, he simply went straight to Max's table because the only thing that mattered was to be with him. Eliot did not recognize himself at all. Ordinarily, an event like this would have thrown him into a fit of apologies and jerky attempts to clean up the mess. Now, with his body immensely relaxed and his eyes filled with light, he casually took his seat and placed the considerably lightened tray on the table before him.

"Well done, Applefriend," said Max without looking up.

They both ate their food without speaking very much. With a part of his mind, Eliot knew that this was an exceptional opportunity—being alone with Max Falkoner, no magic shop, no other people, no established role of counter-salesman. He knew that he could have been asking Max all the questions he had wanted to ask about Blake and Irene and about his power. But these questions did not seem all that important now. Eliot did want to understand why his power failed to penetrate Max's mind, but in a way it did not really surprise him that much. In Max's presence, the power only showed him something about himself—in this case about his own birth and about the feelings of his mother, feelings that had probably shaped his whole life.

But above and beyond all that, important though it was, Eliot felt there was something else to be spoken about, some other way of making use of this rare opportunity. Never before had the exercise of the power left him feeling so free and calm inside, even though what he had seen was as strong as any of the other visions. That fact did seem significant, but Eliot did not know what it meant or even what to ask about it.

Breakfast (Eliot's second) proceeded and ended with Eliot calmly accepting that he was not going to ask Max about any of the things that had seemed of such burning importance an hour ago.

For the first time in his life, Eliot felt absolutely content to sit in one place without doing anything at all, and without talking about anything, and without dreaming about anything. This did interest him. He was fascinated to see how pleasant it was to just observe the people around him. As he sat there in this state of mind, he suddenly observed something in himself that alerted him. He wasn't sure, but it seemed that for a fleeting instant the power started to act all by itself at the back of his brain, without his even wishing it! But it soon passed and he returned immediately to just sitting quietly, aware of himself and his surroundings.

But Max did not allow him to stay like that for long. Eliot's eyes widened as he saw Max removing a deck of Aviator cards from his jacket. He took the cards out of the box, broke the seal, and handed them to Eliot.

"Show me something," he said, as he began clearing the table by stacking the dishes and setting them on an adjoining table. Excitement mounting in him, Eliot took the cards.

Something really unprecedented was happening. He was about to have a lesson from the master himself. But why? Max never did this. He was always the businessman, always the professional, never showing or doing any magic that wasn't part of selling something. He was notorious among the Sorcerers for his tight-lipped refusal to treat them as anything but potential customers, as just another bunch of kids interested in magic tricks. No one drew the line between the professional and amateur as sharply as Max Falkoner.

Eliot's mind started racing as he took the cards. In recent weeks, he had been neglecting his work at sleight of hand. The mind reading had more and more seemed to him the important thing, and that power did not require much effort. Sleight of hand was quite a different matter and made quite a different demand. One had to practice constantly; one had to give it one's best attention. The hands had to be educated. One had to pay very serious attention to details. One couldn't dream. It couldn't be mastered passively, automatically. The mind reading, on the other hand, happened by itself; all he had to do was wish for it.

He slid the cards back and forth in his hands, savoring the feel of a brand new deck. The safest thing to show would be the Four Aces, where the aces are put into the middle of the deck and mysteriously rise to the top. It required relatively little dexterity and he was pretty good at it. As Eliot started separating the aces out, Max lit a cigarette and turned his face away with an expression of disdain.

Quite right, Eliot thought. He wouldn't learn much by showing him that trick. What the hell, why not try something really difficult. To hell with how he would look; the point was to learn something.

Eliot shuffled the cards and rapidly considered all the card tricks he knew. The one with the most astonishing effect was the card-in-the-pocket, where a card that a person peeks at instantly appears in the magician's pocket. It was damned hard to do. But he would try.

He squared up the deck and held it out to Max, positioning the little finger of his right hand at the appropriate place on the side of the deck. "Peek at a card," he said to Max. Max complied, as Eliot held tightly to the deck. After Max cracked the side of the deck in order to look at a card, Eliot slid his little finger in the crack in order to mark the place. Then he drew the deck back toward himself, while using the little finger to slide the selected card out of the deck into the palm of his left hand. The next step was to stand up, distracting the spectator, and secretly slip the palmed card into his pocket. Eliot stood up and made the move and then began his patter.

But Max was just sitting there shaking his head in disbelief and blowing smoke out of the corner of his mouth.

"Sit down, Appleman," he said, without giving Eliot a chance to finish the trick. "What do you think you're doing?"

"The card-in-the-pocket," said Eliot, innocently. His heart was beginning to pound.

"Is that what the sore-assed Apprentices are teaching you? You handle cards like they were cantaloupes. My dog could do it better." Max paused while Eliot absorbed that. "It's all right," he went on, "if all you want to do is impress your Aunt Josephine."

"I don't have an Aunt Josephine," said Eliot, feeling the absurdity of his words and feeling also the anger and hurt returning to him, but this time with a strange difference. Although Max was unsparing in his criticism, there was hardly a trace of condemnation in the sound of his words. This enabled Eliot to have strong reactions without being carried away by them, which kept his wish to learn alive.

"Just show me a basic move," said Max. "Do a bottom deal."

Eliot squared up the deck and grasped it loosely in his left hand. With his right hand he made as if to deal out the top card. With his left thumb he nudged the top card slightly forward, while with the fingers of his left hand he quickly slid out the bottom card and then pulled the top card back—the point being to give the illusion of the top card coming off the deck when, in fact, it was the bottom card that was removed.

"Lousy," said Max. "You blink your eyes at the crucial moment. Just when the card comes out."

Eliot tried again and saw that Max was right. Just at the moment when he should be paying most attention to the cards, he blinked his eyes and only imagined he was doing the move. He tried it again and the same thing happened.

"Do it again," said Max. "Keep your eyes open. Don't blink. Don't dream."

Eliot tried again, forcing himself to keep his eyes open throughout.

"Was that better?" he asked.

"No. It still stinks."

"But I kept my eyes open."

"That's what you think. Do it again."

Again Eliot tried; this time he was certain he didn't blink.

"Why do you look away from your hands!" Max shouted.

"Did I?" Eliot tried again and sure enough, instead of blinking, he looked to the side, again only picturing the move to himself.

"Do it again," said Max in a harsh voice. "Keep your stupid eyes on your hands."

Eliot tried it again and again, but each time just at the instant he pulled out the bottom card, his eyes rolled ever so slightly off to the side.

"This is incredible," said Eliot. "I can't do it!"

"Do it again," said Max. Eliot squared up the cards and prepared to try again. Just as he was about to make the move, however, he felt a sharp flash of pain in his knee. Max had kicked him under the table! Eliot let out a howl and looked at Max in disbelief. Max grabbed his wrist just as he was about to let go of the cards.

"Now do the goddamn move," said Max. "Watch the cards with your knee!"

Eliot was practically in shock. The pain in his knee was bad enough, but what the hell Max meant was completely incomprehensible. It was absurd. But the pain prevented him from thinking about it. He was completely confused. Meanwhile, Max was shouting, "Do it, you asshole, *now!* Watch the cards with your knee! Now!"

Eliot obeyed. It was flawless.

On the way back to the magic shop, Max turned aside all questions about what had happened in the cafeteria. The only word of explanation was something about the difference between amateurs and professionals, but Eliot could not quite grasp it. It had to do with blinking. Something like, amateurs always blink just when they most need to look. A half-second of dreaming separated amateurs from professionals. "There are very few real professionals," said Max.

When they reached the office building, Max made it very clear that he did not want Eliot to come up with him. As Max was about to leave, Eliot got up the nerve to ask him why he had kicked him. But a blast of cold wind blew the words away. Eliot remained standing in front of the glass door and, through his own half-reflected image, watched Max disappear into one of the waiting elevators.

When Max was gone, Eliot's eyes focused on his own reflection in the door. With a jolt, he suddenly remembered that he had left all his books in the cafeteria. He spun around and raced through the bitter wind down Chestnut Street, his nose dripping, his ears burning, freezing air cutting into his lungs. He felt filled with an inexplicable joy.

A Decision in the Dark

That same night was the night of the bi-weekly meeting of the Sorcerer's Apprentices. For the first time since he had joined the club, Eliot was tempted to stay away. After the experience with Max that morning, he did not want to face Blake so soon. He felt he needed time to sort things out.

But tonight's meeting was one of the most important of the year, when the planning for the next Annual Show would begin in earnest. Tonight, each of the Sorcerers had to propose the routine he would perform and then, over the next few weeks, Blake would make the final decisions, as well as set the sequence of the acts.

Eliot wanted very much to be in the show, but the last twenty-four hours—Blake last night, Max this morning—had thrown everything into question. Should he propose the Sympathetic Silks, the Milk Pitcher, the Card in Balloon and, perhaps, the Flag Blendo? All of them were fairly safe, mechanical stage effects requiring little or no sleight of hand. Or should he do a straight mind reading act, using a combination of mental effects and his real power? As for the routine he loved most—the linking rings—Eliot had long since abandoned the dream of doing that in the Annual Show. The linking rings required far more sleight of hand and stage experience than he could hope to master in the time remaining.

Even before the events of the past twenty-four hours, Eliot had worried about using his power in the Annual Show. In the first place, there was the resentment it had evoked in some of the Sorcerers, especially Ronnie Pitkin. But even more important, there were the inescapable side effects—or were they only just side effects?—of the power. Something else always came along with it, and God knows what would happen if he tried it on stage with hundreds of people in the audience! God knows what truths the power would serve up to him!

But now, added to all this, there were the opposing personal influences of Blake and Max Falkoner. Max, surely, would expect him to do a straightforward stage act using the tricks he had bought at Templeton's and had been practicing. But what would Blake expect of him? Blake, after all, was the actual leader of the club and had the right to make all the final decisions. At most, Max could only advise and suggest.

What would Blake expect, demand, of him? That question had gnawed at Eliot all day. After retrieving his books, he had wandered around downtown thinking about everything. Little by little, the joy he had felt after leaving Max ebbed away. Everything he had intended to ask him returned—about Irene and the "prophecy," about Blake and the ring, about the meaning of the power. . . .

Strange that all these questions which so preoccupied him had evaporated when he was with Max. What an opportunity he had squandered! Or, perhaps not. Perhaps he had been given something more precious. He didn't know. He didn't know anything!

He wandered through the department stores, through Gimbel's, Wanamaker's, Strawbridge's, through book departments, stationery departments, hardware departments, men's clothing. Strangely, the impulse to shoplift did not appear. Down countless aisles piled with beautiful wool sweaters, top-notch button-down shirts, the latest in flashlights and fishing lures, past towering stacks of expensive notebooks, past gleaming fountain pens, exotic office gadgets made of cork, chrome, and brass, through corridors of best selling nonfiction books with alluring dust jackets facing outward, not once did the impulse appear.

He needed to talk to Wally, but school wouldn't be out until three o'clock and it wasn't even noon yet. Eliot was already bored and his arms were aching from the weight of the school books. Perhaps a movie to kill the time. But none of the downtown theatres were open so early in the day except the News and the Roxie; the first showed nothing but newsreels and the other nothing but dirty movies which were never really dirty enough and, in any case, he would have to bluff about his age to get in, and why bother?

Eliot sat down inside a Nedick's hot dog stand mainly to get out of the cold and rest his arms. A steaming cup of chocolate and a jumbo hot dog blanketed with mustard and pickle relish lifted his spirits momentarily, but he soon found himself out in the cold again. Boredom had become depression. Slowly, he trudged down Market Street toward the Benjamin Franklin Parkway. Maybe the Franklin Institute was open. Eliot loved that place, with its science exhibits that one could work for oneself. He loved pressing buttons and watching the laws of the universe in action with levers, rods, lightbulbs, blocks of wood, and spheres of metal. He loved seeing the inner working of machines, the pendulums, the colored liquids, the amazing optical illusions that always made him feel that everything he saw in his whole life was some kind of illusion.

But above all, he loved the planetarium. The possibility of watching a show at the planetarium buoyed him up again and quickened his step as he aimed himself down Market Street past the pornography and the joke and trick shops.

The Institute was open. Eliot ran up the broad stone steps, paid his fifty cents and made straight for the planetarium. The sign outside the planetarium announced the program for that month—"Double Stars"—but the starting time was not until half past three o'clock. That meant two hours to kill. Eliot telephoned Wally's mother and asked her to have him come to the planetarium as soon as he returned from school.

Back at the entrance to the planetarium, Eliot looked around to see if anyone was watching, tried the door, and found it open. He quickly slipped inside and shut the door softly behind him.

He stood for several moments in the entrance. In the center of the great, dome-shaped space stood the instrument itself, poised like an immense, black, mechanical insect with its strange spherical bulbs, three feet across, joined at either end by hundreds of metal struts and slats forming an intricate pattern of open-work squares and triangles.

As always, however, it was the silence of this wondrous space that touched Eliot most, although he wasn't quite conscious of this. He told himself he liked the shows, the programs dealing with his beloved science of astronomy. In fact, the shows often bored him. But the silence of the room never failed to enter him.

Not a single sound penetrated from outside, yet it was not a dead silence; somehow it was not a "man-made" silence. Perhaps it was the shape of the hall; perhaps it was the low, diffused lighting emanating from around the dome's circumference, where the silhouette of the city skyline was painted; perhaps it was the feeling the room gave of standing alone under the sky, far away from the noise and furor of man. Whatever the reason, the silence always had the same effect on Eliot's state of mind—not soothing him exactly, but opening him to something vibrantly quiet within himself.

Eliot sat down in the last row of chairs arranged in a circle around the great central mechanism. He stayed near the door so that he would see Wally when he came in. He placed his books on the seat next to him, unbuttoned his heavy coat, and tilted his head back to gaze at the peach-colored, seemingly infinite space above him. Letting out a long sigh, he immediately dropped off into a deep, dreamless sleep.

When his eyes opened, the room was completely black and the space he was in was filled with stars. He didn't know where he was until he heard the voice of the lecturer and detected other people sitting in the chairs in front of him. He felt extraordinarily refreshed and relaxed. For a while he was content simply to sit there while the lecturer explained some theories about the origin of double stars and moved the pointer light around the sky. The quick, jerky movements of the pointer did not dispel his sense of being in the midst of infinite space.

Presently, the entrance door cracked open and Wally Pound poked his head in. Eliot gesticulated to him and called out his name in a loud whisper. Before the door eased shut, Wally hastily scurried over and sat down next to Eliot.

The two boys were now sitting together in absolute darkness and in a silence which seemed intensified by the droning voice of the lecturer. All that was visible were the thousands of points of light surrounding them. It was as though nothing existed.

After a few moments, Wally's voice whispered, very softly, "What's happening? What's the emergency?"

Eliot began to tell Wally everything, but somehow, hearing his own disembodied whisper in the dark cooled everything down. He was surprised to hear how objectively he spoke about the events of the past twenty-four hours.

But as for Wally, his reactions were anything but cool. Loud whispers of "Holy shit!" and "Jesus Christ!" echoed through the dark universe as Eliot calmly rolled out his experience with Blake. The darkness seemed to be having an opposite effect on the usually self-contained Wally Pound. His exclamations became louder and more frequent until, out of the inky void, as though from another dimension, a full-throated "Shut up!" brought the conversation to a halt. Eliot and Wally sat in silence again as the lecturer's voice droned on.

Eliot felt strangely safe—without a body and without a face—safe enough to reach into his pocket and, for the first time, take out the ring that Blake had given him. Sitting there, he knew he would go to the meeting that night; he felt no fear of Blake, and he felt, yes, under the protection of something else, something having to do with Max Falkoner. With a slight start, he realized that he had no intention of telling Wally or anyone about the experience with Max—and this fact interested him very much, and puzzled him.

In the darkness, and with practically no awareness that he had a body, Eliot slipped the ring onto the third finger of his right hand. He sensed nothing, and he left the ring on as the whispering conversation began again.

"So, what are you going to do?" Wally asked.

At that moment, his thoughts floating free, Eliot had no doubts. "Regular magic," said Eliot confidently, "Blendo, Sympathetic Silks, the Rice Bowls, maybe the Die Box or the Chinese Sticks or Zombie."

Wally's whisper grew louder again. "No mind reading at all?"

"No," said Eliot in a firm voice.

"But suppose Blake wants you to? What'll you say?"

Eliot smiled, but realizing that Wally could not see his face, he whispered back, "You'll see. I may just tell him my powers have dried up, or something. What can he do?"

Wally responded with a long, low whistle, which Eliot interpreted as an expression of admiration, but which actually was something else.

"This is going to be one hell of a meeting," said Wally in full voice.

"Shut up!" said the darkness.

PART 3

BETWEEN TWO MAGICIANS

BLAKE'S WAY

Eliot and Wally were among the first to arrive at the club that night. Only Clipper and the sweaty Sandy Hyman were there arranging chairs and setting up their magic apparatus. As the other Sorcerers trickled in, Eliot's sense of self-composure held firm, even when Ronnie Pitkin arrived, looking handsome as ever with an expensive suede overcoat draped around his shoulders and his silky blond hair falling rakishly over the side of his forehead. Not even the hatred emanating toward him from Ronnie's luminous blue eyes could shake Eliot. As the others came in—Gordon Bunche coughing into a giant, dirty handkerchief; Edgar Wick dressed in his customary shiny black suit; Joe Ferrante and Kim Vogel (the "Monte Carlo Boys") laughing and cutting up; Bennie Schulweis ("Benngali") with his loud plaid jacket and light-up bow tie; tall, painfully shy Terry Laken ("The Great Lakini") who never spoke; science whiz Don Papermaster ("Dr. Magic"); fat, stuttering Sonny Margolis ("The Wizard of West Philadelphia")—as they all came in and found their usual places, Eliot remembered the first time he had come to this room nearly six months before. He remembered standing outside the door watching the shadows of the Sorcerers, heavy with purpose, moving back and forth across the frosted glass. Now, he was one of those shadows.

Then Blake entered. Suddenly, the room became still. Blake seemed uncharacteristically grim as he cut through the center of the room and took his place at the front table next to the president, Stillman Clipper. When Blake passed by him, Eliot felt a wave of force and, in one instant, his self-composure began to weaken. He glanced down to make sure the skull ring was clearly visible on his right hand and found himself trembling. In vain, he tried to bring back his sense of security; he called forth images of his meeting that morning with Max Falkoner, but that only helped a little, not enough.

As the meeting began and the parliamentary matters were dealt with, Eliot struggled to reaffirm the decision to stay with ordinary magic for the Annual Show. He kept thinking of Max, but it had no effect on his emotions or on the trembling in his body. He began to worry that Blake knew he had not worn the ring as instructed. But Blake was a fraud, wasn't he? Eliot had seen that, hadn't he?

The time came for the main business of the meeting. Each of the more senior Sorcerers presented his proposal for the Annual Show. There were very few surprises, although there was considerable tension as Ronnie Pitkin outlined his new mind reading act. Still, Eliot felt a little reassured by that. At the same time, it began to seem odd that no mention was being made of the last meeting when Eliot had revealed his powers. But Eliot did not think much about this; he was too intent on holding to his decision, while each of the members completed his statement.

Finally, it was Wally's turn, which meant that he, Eliot, as the newest member and the last to speak, was next. As each of the Sorcerers outlined his act, the club secretary, Terry Laken, dutifully and soberly took notes. Blake kept silent throughout, apparently reserving his comments until the end.

While Wally was making his presentation, Eliot was rehearsing to himself what he was going to say. He would modestly begin by stating that his inexperience dictated that he perform relatively easy tricks. He would start off with the Sympathetic Silks (where the knots connecting one set of silk scarves are magically transferred to a separate set of unknotted scarves); he would follow this with the Chinese Rice Bowls (where, with the help of an ingenious little plastic disc, a quantity of rice is transformed into water); then he would do the Zombie (where a shiny aluminum ball floats mysteriously under a silk cloth) and conclude with none other than the Flag Blendo!

Wally finished and Eliot moved to get out of his chair. But just then Blake began speaking, glancing at Terry Laken's notes and offering his comments on each of the proposed acts. This caught Eliot by surprise, and he remained suspended for several minutes, neither in nor out of his chair, unable to figure out what was happening. Had Blake forgotten about him? That was impossible. Then why hadn't he been allowed to speak? Eliot slowly sank down into his chair. Something started burning in him.

He tried to catch Blake's eye, but that had no effect. Blake just looked through him. Eliot then looked around at the other Sorcerers. Surely, they realized he had been passed by and that an injustice was being perpetrated. But they seemed completely unaware of it; they were all listening with rapt attention to Blake— all except Wally Pound, whose eyes darted nervously back and forth between Blake and Eliot. As for Ronnie Pitkin, he slowly and methodically turned his head toward Eliot, coldly met his eyes, then just as slowly turned his head back.

Eliot was overwhelmed with outrage and confusion, and then, fear and hurt. In part of his mind, he simply couldn't take in what was happening. "There must be some mistake," said his thoughts over and over. He kept making helpless gestures to catch Blake's eye—little movements of the hand, especially the hand with the ring on it, little movements of his head. But beneath these thoughts, his chest was aching and he was fighting back tears, resisting the impulse to get up and leave the club forever. Granted, he was the newest member, and granted, he was still learning many basic things; still, he knew he was as good as or even better than some of the others. He surely had more composure in front of an audience than the silly Gordon Bunche and Edgar Wick; his sleight of hand was probably as good as that of the bumbling "escape artist" Sandy Hyman; he was more serious than the loud-mouthed Bennie Schulweis; he was more clever than . . . as good as . . . more deserving than . . . etcetera, etcetera.

And as for the mind reading—"My God," thought Eliot. "I could cream them all." That was it, he was sure; it was jealousy, envy. They couldn't bear that he alone had the gift of real magic powers. Hadn't Blake himself said that he was that special "person" prophesied by Irene? They were simply all afraid he would steal the show. Of course.

But then why was Blake the one who was ignoring him? Maybe he was only protecting the feelings of all the others.

These speculations, however, did little to comfort Eliot. As he sat there, he was wounded over and over again by Blake's indifference. He heard nothing of what was being said and, after a seeming eternity, the meeting drew toward an end with Eliot in a state of shock. As soon as the formal part of the meeting was over, he bolted out of the room without saying a word to anyone, not even to Wally Pound.

Outside, in the cold, dark night, halfway down the block, his hands under his arms, the wind freezing the tears on his face, he realized he had left without his coat and school books. He could not go home without them. He could not go back to get them. There was nowhere to go where he could get out of the cold and still watch the entrance of the club building to see when the meeting was over so that he could slip in and retrieve his belongings. Added to that, this part of the city, south of Market Street, was dangerous at this hour. The street was deserted—no people, no cars; the only sound was the electric crackling of the trolley car wires in the cold, dark air. Above, the stars were clear and brilliant.

Eliot paced up and down the length of the block feeling colder and more miserable with each passing moment, his nose running, his feet turning numb, his chest quivering. At the end of the block there was a phone booth, but that provided little relief as he could not move around inside it. But it was better than nothing. He jammed shut the broken door and an absurd overhead light went on, making everything outside appear even darker and more dangerous. There he stayed for a long time, watching the entrance to the club building, thinking no thoughts.

Finally, a figure emerged from the building. It was Wally! And he was carrying Eliot's books and coat.

*

Eliot left the ring on his hand for the rest of the week and was amazed and disgusted with himself for constantly thinking of Blake, counting the days until the appointed evening for the next meeting with him at his home. From time to time, he would take out a deck of cards and try to practice along the lines that Max had demonstrated, but to no avail. His mind would always be drawn to Blake and to the "test" that he was now afraid he would fail. He thought of going to see Max, but worried that Blake might find out about it.

Was the Annual Show so important to him, Eliot wondered, that he had become a slave to what Blake thought of him? As for the disembodied calm and confidence he had felt in the planetarium, that seemed now to have belonged to someone else, not to him. He could not bring it back; he could not even wish to bring it back.

On the appointed night, Eliot went to Blake's house with no plans, no thoughts, except a craving to be relieved of his hurt feelings. He had arrived hours ahead of time and walked round and round Blake's neighborhood while a mixture of cold rain and wet snow swirled about him, soaking his shoes (he had neglected to wear his galoshes) and his pants.

The meeting with Blake that night started out very much like the previous one. Blake was gracious; a dinner had been prepared; there was wine. But throughout the dinner Blake said nothing about the Annual Show or the club meeting. Eliot sensed that he was being manipulated in some way, but he didn't know why, nor did he have any power over his reactions. As the dinner drew to a close, and with his stomach already aching from the emotional tension, Eliot could contain himself no longer. He gulped down his second glass of wine and, to his horror, he heard himself say, in a quivering, pleading voice:

"Why didn't you call on me at the meeting?"

But instead of anger, which Eliot expected in response to this question, Blake only smiled and filled Eliot's glass with the last of the wine.

"What would you have said?" Blake asked, lightly.

At that question, Eliot froze. He knew that this moment was the culmination of the "test" that Blake had arranged for him. And he was astonished to see that, more than anything else, he wanted to pass this test, even though his power had already revealed Blake to be a fraud.

Eliot closed his eyes and tried again to evoke the image of Max Falkoner. He tried to remember the resolution he had come to sitting in the bodiless darkness of the planetarium. But again, it had no effect. He tried to remember what he had felt practicing the bottom deal with Max, even the kick in the shins. But it had no effect.

With his eyes closed, he began to feel dizzy from the wine, and when he opened them he found himself looking directly into Blake's face, which now assumed an expression of startling seriousness and gravity.

"Finish your wine," Blake commanded.

Eliot obeyed. He had to answer. But, as he was swallowing his wine, he realized that although he had to answer, he did not have to answer truthfully. His thoughts now started to move. He had discovered the way out of this situation. He would simply lie to Blake.

"Well, I was going to say that I would do whatever routines you recommended."

This seemed to please Blake, and Eliot breathed a little sigh of relief. Nevertheless, a new and even deeper unease began to settle on him. Maybe it wasn't a lie. Maybe he *would* obey Blake. He wanted to obey someone. And he wanted to be the "person" Irene had prophesied. He began to feel that he had only tricked himself, not Blake. Why else was he feeling so damned happy that Blake was pleased? His childish emotions had won out, as they always did.

What followed left Eliot troubled in a way he had never experienced in his whole life. Blake flatly ordered him to devote himself solely to developing the mind reading for the Annual Show, urging Eliot to use the power every day until he had fully mastered it. Blake gave Eliot to understand that only in this way would he be able to take his proper place as the "person." When Eliot, to his dismay, confided to Blake about the "side effects" of the power, Blake brushed it aside. "That will not be a problem," he said, "as long as you wear the ring and do exactly what I say."

The instructions Blake then gave him were quite simple. Whenever he exercised his powers, Eliot was to hold his hands together so that the fingers of his left hand were touching the golden skull. This, said Blake, would prevent the "side effects" of the power from bothering Eliot and, eventually, it would prevent them even from appearing. Blake ordered Eliot to practice this at least once a day and to meet with him, Blake, every week. In addition, he was to keep everything concealed from all other people, especially the Sorcerers.

The name of Max Falkoner was not mentioned at all.

Finally, as Eliot was leaving, Blake took both his hands in his own and, looking deeply into Eliot's eyes, said, "Remember, the ring belonged to Irene."

Then he closed the door, leaving Eliot staring at the ring in the darkness.

THE GOLDEN SKULL

At first, it was hard for Eliot to carry out Blake's instructions. He did not quite believe that the "side effects" of the power could be reduced so easily, especially as up until now their force had been increasing on each occasion. The first day, he did not try at all. But the next day, determined to make the attempt, he cast about for some innocuous situation or person to try it on. On the way home from school, he stopped at a White Tower and ordered a hamburger. The counter man was a complete stranger—a tall, fleshy man in his fifties with a scarred face and missing teeth. As he was serving the hamburger, Eliot put his hands together under the counter, making sure he was touching the ring, and turned on the power. What he saw in the man's mind was reassuringly boring: he was thinking simultaneously of a bet he had just placed on the Warriors' basketball game that night and of getting revenge on his boss, who had unfairly accused him of something. The "side effects" also appeared and, as they did so, Eliot tightly grasped the ring with his left hand. What came forth was painful enough—the man was systematically stealing from the cash register in order to buy whiskey and, of all things, comic books! Eliot breathed a sigh of relief and unhooked his hands. What he had seen was pitiful, but it didn't really bother him that much.

Only as he was leaving did the final image flash before him: a picture of the man in his flea-ridden hotel room, standing over a sink and wretching up blood. The image went through him like an electric shock. He grabbed hold of the ring again, but too late to soften the reaction, and he had to go into a drugstore and sit at the counter until he calmed down. He reasoned to himself that he had learned something from this experiment. In order to protect himself from what he was seeing, he had to hold onto the ring until he was sure the process was well over. He left the drugstore assuring himself that the exercise had been a small success.

On the following day he selected another stranger, a young Negro man working on a street repair team near school. Eliot stood for a few minutes in the doorway of a jewelry shop watching the man operating a pneumatic drill. Again, he clasped his hands together and opened himself to the power. This time what came forward nearly caused him to laugh out loud. The man was imagining himself doing it with a woman to the rhythm of the pneumatic drill. Eliot looked around in embarrassment and hastily walked away. But in his haste, he had again let go of the ring too soon and, before he was ten paces away, he was struck by the image of the man standing over his father, who was lying in the street with a wound in his chest. Instinctively, Eliot started running as fast as he could back toward school.

The third attempt had quite a different outcome. Once again, Eliot chose someone completely unknown to him, this time a young child, a little girl about seven years old sitting across from him on the bus and clutching a small violin case. She was a very pretty child with large eyes and long dark braids tied with white ribbons hanging down the front of a bright red coat. Her big eyes followed every passenger that walked by. Eliot clasped his hands together, waited for a few moments, and saw the little girl at her music lesson. Her teacher, an elderly man, was praising her, saying, "Very good, Sonia, very, very good!" She was running the scene over and over again in her mind. Eliot kept his hands together and, as the girl stood up to leave, he saw the elderly man saying to her, rather harshly, "You must pay more attention to your fingering!"

The child exited, but Eliot kept his hands clasped together and did not relax them until he reached his stop. As he walked home under the great oak trees lining Wissahickon Avenue, he congratulated himself at having this time escaped without anything dire happening. But the last words of the violin teacher kept coming back to him: "You must pay more attention to your fingering!" This made him think of Max Falkoner and the sleight of hand lesson at Bain's Cafeteria and everything connected with it. With a jolt, he realized that he had gone almost three days without thinking of Max at all. How could something that had meant so much to him be so completely erased from his mind?

Of course, Max would probably disapprove of what Eliot was now doing. Probably that was why he had put Max out of his mind. But how could what he had felt with Max be so easily set aside? Eliot went on reasoning to himself and by the time he walked through his front door he resolved to visit Max the next day, even though it was Saturday and Templeton's would be packed with customers.

*

When Eliot walked into Templeton's the following morning, he was not surprised to see two of the Sorcerers in the store—Terry Laken and Sandy Hyman. There was a noisy throng of other people as well, most of them young. The adult magicians, the professionals, did not generally come to Templeton's on Saturdays, although today seemed to be a major exception. Eliot recognized the famous nightclub magician, known simply as Lambert, talking to a group of admiring teenagers. And wasn't that none other than the renowned John Scarne, reputed to be the greatest card man in the world, standing at the counter discussing some moves with Max and surrounded by an even larger group of onlookers? In other parts of the store, small clusters of people gathered, talking, arguing, gesticulating amid the flashing of brilliantly colored silks, billiard balls, ropes, small boxes and the staccato bursts of cards being riffled.

No longer feeling any resentment toward his fellow Sorcerers, Eliot greeted them warmly as he snaked through the crowd toward the counter where Max and John Scarne were standing in head-to-head conversation. As soon as a tiny opening appeared at the counter, he slipped into the inner circle surrounding the two men and anchored himself within arm's reach of the great Scarne.

The heads of the two men were nearly touching as they looked down at a deck of cards spread face up on the small black velvet demonstration cloth. The smoke from Max's dangling cigarette floated into his eyes, but didn't seem to disturb his concentration as he slid a single card out from the spread, tipped it over with his left hand and then, with his right hand made a pass over it which changed the card's color and denomination when it was turned again. The crowd gasped. Scarne's jagged face at first tightened and then broke out in a relaxed smile of appreciation. As for Eliot, his amazement knew no bounds. He knew Max was good, but that even the great John Scarne came to learn things from him—that was incredible!

As Scarne took the deck in his hands, Max glanced up and looked directly at Eliot. In an instant, Eliot felt and sensed everything that had passed between them in the past. It was like waking from a dream. Suddenly, Blake and the task he had given Eliot receded.

Max casually reached down under the counter and shoved an envelope toward Eliot. As Eliot hesitantly picked it up, Max said only, "That's your routine for the Annual Show," and matter-of-factly turned back to Scarne.

Eliot immediately withdrew from the crowd to a corner of the store and ripped open the envelope. He could hardly believe what he saw. It was a routine, carefully diagrammed and handwritten by Max, for the most demanding and wonderful trick of all, the trick Eliot loved above all others: the linking rings!

*

Barely able to contain himself, Eliot raced out of the store with the bulky envelope stuffed in the pocket of his coat. He needed a place where he could study the whole thing in privacy. Outside, the first hints of spring warmed the air and then, suddenly, the wind would come up, bringing winter back in full force. With his unbuttoned coat flying out to the sides, Eliot ran from store to store looking for a place to sit and finally settled on the lobby of the pretentious Bellevue-Stratford Hotel.

Ignoring the suspicious looks of the elderly bellhops and desk clerks, he sat down in a mushy sofa and devoured the information in the papers that Max had given him. Although it was impossible to follow the details without having a set of the rings to work with, Eliot was able to see that Max was proposing far more than the basic linking rings sequence.

By the time Eliot had read through everything and re-read it, he saw something of the demand that lay ahead. As of now, he was not even capable of really working the simplest moves with the rings. Before him there stretched weeks and months of extremely hard work. The sleight of hand that the routine required was far more complex than merely palming a card or sliding a card out from the bottom of the deck, not to mention the stagemanship that would be needed. He saw himself having to practice every day, at every spare moment. He knew there would be many things he would have to give up and that he would have to arrange his time carefully, something he had never been able to do in the past, whether for school or even for tasks that deeply interested him. Always, his initial resolve faded at a certain point, and always he had settled merely for getting by in whatever he had undertaken. And this present task would be even more difficult because it was not just a mental task. He knew he could not bluff or charm his way through it. And there would constantly be Max passing judgment on his work. He would have to see Max often—after all, would Max have given him this task if he didn't plan to guide him? An awesome challenge. Far beyond his powers. Every chance of falling on his face. Many sacrifices ahead. Working constantly under the terrible eye of Max Falkoner.

Eliot was ecstatic.

*

But on his next visit to Blake, everything changed once again. Eliot had resolved to tell Blake about Max, to inform Blake calmly that he wished to do the linking rings in the Annual Show. Blake never gave him an opening and Eliot's fear of how Blake would react soon mounted to overwhelming proportions. Fear and . . . something else in himself that Eliot did not want to acknowledge, something having to do with what he was beginning to feel when exercising his power to read minds.

After visiting Templeton's and getting the extraordinary assignment from Max, Eliot devoted most, but not all, of his time to the linking rings. True, on the following day, Sunday, alone in his bedroom, he had worked hours with the rings, making sure he understood the outlines of the complex routine Max had worked out for him. And true, the more he practiced, the more he saw how much he would have to work on his sleight of hand and stage magicianship, a realization that made him, if anything, more eager than ever to devote himself unsparingly to this task. But the fact was he also continued with the "task" Blake had given him. In fact, it would have been hard for him not to.

It was already becoming pleasant.

Blake smiled approvingly at Eliot's report of his progress on the "task."

"A fine start," said Blake, "but now you must try it with people you know."

Eliot surprised himself by how willingly he accepted the new assignment.

THE FIRST TRIUMPH

The occasion came the very next day at school in Hayden G. Petrie's American History class. Mr. Petrie was a short, physically frail, but tremendously forceful man close to retirement age, whose chief characteristics were a piercing stare and a spinal injury that required him at all times to wear a metal neck brace. No one had ever seen him without it. Whether he was seated in the cafeteria, or at the morning assembly, or behind the wheel of his black Plymouth, or pacing methodically through the school corridors, his short, but rigidly upright form was unmistakable from great distances. Generations of Jefferson High School students had lived in fear of his authoritarian methods, his fierce surprise quizzes, and his terrifying, lightning-like class interrogations. Bolted straight up behind his big desk or standing like a ramrod in front of the class, and unable to move his head, his whole body would suddenly, and with blinding speed, turn in one piece to confront one or another of his hapless students. Few could withstand these confrontations. Even good students crumbled as Mr. Petrie, or Peachy, as he was called behind his back, pushed and probed until he found some weakness in his victims. Many considered it uncanny the way he could pick out the least prepared student, but in fact it was the shock of facing him that made even those who had done the reading forget everything they knew. After devouring his prey, he would sigh, tilting his stiff body backward and, in a raw, raspy voice, crow out, "Do a job, lads, do a job!"

Because he had a free period before Peachy's class, Eliot was always able to get there early enough to grab one of the desirable seats in the last row, though everyone knew there was no real place to hide from Mr. Petrie. And today, Eliot wanted very much to hide, not having read a word of the class assignment. As Peachy rolled on about the Constitutional Convention of 1787, Eliot stealthily reached a hand down into his lunchbag and unwrapped one of his hamburger sandwiches, releasing into the atmosphere a great invisible cloud of garlic and fried onion. Bending over behind the gigantic back of Harvey Mednick, he slipped part of the sandwich into his mouth and, of course, at just that moment heard Peachy call out his name in sharp tones.

"Mr. Appleman! Please cite the constitutional basis of the Federalist philosophy!"

Eliot immediately spit his mouthful back into his lunchbag and sat up straight. The custom in Peachy's class was that whoever was called on would try to stall until the person next to him could look up the answer and either whisper it out loud or write it on a scrap of paper and slip it into the victim's hands—a particularly dangerous procedure because it involved producing visible evidence. These methods, however, really worked only for questions whose answer involved a simple date or name. The present case, where a lengthy answer was required, had a very high failure rate.

"Would you please repeat the question, sir?" Eliot called out as Norm Steinberg, seated to Eliot's right, scrambled through the textbook.

Mr. Petrie rose vertically from his chair as though pulled up by a chain and slowly marched toward the class. A bad sign. Nor did he stop at the front row, but kept on advancing, an extremely bad sign, and did not stop his relentless march until he was standing directly in front of Eliot. And there he stood, his eyes riveted on Eliot from behind quarter-inch thick glasses and his quivering paper-thin nostrils situated directly above Eliot's smelly, half-open lunchbag. A look of disgust, bordering on nausea, passed over his face as his eyes lowered to the lunchbag.

Of course, by this time Eliot knew the situation was hopeless. Not having had a chance to help him out, Norm Steinberg was tilting so far over the other way that he nearly fell out of his chair.

"Huge Harvey" Mednick's wide back, so protective a moment ago, now seemed like a prison wall.

In such situations, Eliot's strategy—which had developed in his bones when he was a young child—was to use boyish charm or, failing that, through sweetly confessing whatever it looked like the other person wanted to hear, to throw himself humbly at the mercy of the conqueror. But Mr. Petrie's expression of physical disgust went right through the interstices of Eliot's acquired personality and was received in his solar plexus as outright hatred of him. This, in turn, provoked in Eliot's body such a reaction of organic fear that, to his own amazement, the impulse to fight and kill, hitherto unknown to him, rose up from within him. And, to his further surprise, this impulse made him feel strong, powerful, and full of a certain kind of energy. Finally, when Mr. Petrie, his crazily magnified eyes now directed back on Eliot, repeated his question in insultingly sarcastic tones, Eliot, without thinking twice about it, clasped his hands together, returned Mr. Petrie's challenging gaze and turned on his power. Immediately, as on a screen, there was displayed before his eyes nothing less than the full text of Article I, Section 8, of the United States Constitution with its famous "delegation of powers" by the States to the Congress, as well as the Tenth Amendment, all of which formed the legal basis of the Federalist philosophy so dear, as it happened, to the otherwise frozen heart of Mr. Hayden G. Petrie.

Focusing his gaze right between Peachy's eyes and clutching the skull ring, Eliot coolly "read" out the passages, word by word:

The Congress shall have Power to lay and collect Taxes, Duties, Imposts and Excises, to pay the Debts and provide for the common Defence and general Welfare of the United States; but all duties, Imposts and Excises shall be uniform throughout the United States;

To borrow Money on the Credit of the United States;

To regulate Commerce with foreign Nations, and among the several States, and with the Indian Tribes;

To establish an uniform Rule of Naturalization, and uniform Laws on the subject of Bankruptcies throughout the United States;

To coin Money, regulate the Value thereof, and of foreign Coin, and fix the Standard of Weights and Measures;

To provide for the Punishment of counterfeiting the Securities and current Coin of the United States;

To establish Post Offices and post Roads;

To promote the Progress of Science and useful Arts, by securing for limited Times to Authors and Inventors exclusive Right to their respective Writings and Discoveries;

To constitute Tribunals inferior to the Supreme Court;

To define and punish Piracies and Felonies committed on the high Seas, and Offences against the Law of Nations;

To declare War, grant Letters of Marque and Reprisal, and make rules concerning Captures on Land and Water;

To raise and support Armies, but no Appropriation of Money to that Use shall be for a longer Term than two Years;

To provide and maintain a Navy;

To make rules for the Government and Regulation of the land and naval Forces;

To provide for calling for the Militia to execute the Laws of the Union, suppress Insurrections and repel Invasions;

To provide for organizing, arming, and disciplining the Militia, and for governing such part of them as may be employed in the Service of the United States, reserving to the States respectively, the Appointment of the Officers, and the Authority of training the Militia according to the discipline prescribed by Congress;

To exercise exclusive Legislation in all Cases whatsoever, over such District (not exceeding ten Miles square), as may, by Cession of particular States, and the Acceptance of the United States, become the Seat of the Government of the United States, and to exercise like Authority over all Places purchased by the Consent of the Legislature of the State in which the Same shall be for the Erection of Forts, Magazines, Arsenals, dock Yards, and other needful Buildings;—And

To make all Laws which shall be necessary and proper for carrying into Execution the foregoing Powers, and all other Powers vested by this Constitution in the Government of the United States, or in any Department or Office thereof.

Having recited this, Eliot paused and then capped it with a triumphal, full-throated intonation of the Tenth Amendment:

The Powers not delegated to the United States by the Constitution nor prohibited by it to the States, are reserved to the States respectively, or to the people.

During the course of these recitations, not only did the jaw of Hayden Petrie slowly drop lower than anyone had ever seen it drop, but there actually appeared on his face something remarkably like a smile. Later, in the corridors and bathrooms, it was said that by the end of Eliot's performance tears of joy were glistening in Mr. Petrie's eyes. In any case, far from acting defeated, the terrifying Mr. Petrie sang out for all to hear, "Good job, lad, good job!"

Whatever Mr. Petrie felt, Eliot—still gripping the ring—experienced triumph and strength such as he had never known before. The "side effects" of the power appeared, but he simply paid no attention to them. It was something about Mr. Petrie's neck or the constant pain, or something. . . . It simply did not attract Eliot's attention away from the sense of personal power that was pulsing through the very tissues of his body, enhanced by the silent, admiring looks of his classmates.

THE WEDNESDAY GAME

The event in Mr. Petrie's class was Eliot's first taste of direct combat with a feared enemy resulting in a personal victory, and he found it very sweet. So much so that it became the first in a series of similar "triumphs" in all his classes, though none was so exquisitely pleasurable as that first one. Some two weeks later, however, an event outside school occurred which was its equal in bringing intensely pleasant sensations down into his body.

It involved a serious poker game. Every Friday night a *semi-serious* poker game had been taking place among a circle of Eliot's classmates who had in common, among other things, persistent bad luck in finding anything to do on weekends that involved girls. Being naturally at home with cards, Eliot usually came out ahead, sometimes by as much as eight or ten dollars.

Eliot loved the game. He loved the food—the license to eat unmeasured quantities of potato chips and pretzels; he loved the joking, the horsing around, the by-play. And he loved the money, the excitement of being in on a large pot and the rush that came when he won. One thing, however, always puzzled him, and that was the crushing sense of despair that he felt whenever he lost a big hand. He would tell himself it was only a few dollars, that it didn't mean so much, but to no avail. At such moments, it seemed to him that the whole universe was against him. He could never understand the equanimity shown by some of the others when they lost. Down deep, he felt much more kinship with the steady loser, Sidney Levinson, who was constantly whining and sweating as he counted his ever-diminishing supply of nickels, dimes, and quarters. If money meant so much to Sidney, why did he keep coming to a game where he always, but always, ended up losing? What dream about luck kept him coming? Or was it something else that brought him? Eliot didn't know. The whole, entire money thing was very confusing.

As for cheating, this was not a big deal. The way Levinson held his cards—parallel with the table—it was impossible not to see them. Occasionally, in a very large pot, Eliot would consider trying some sleight of hand, but a mixture of fear and ethics prevented him.

But there was another poker game that Eliot knew about in which the players were quite different and the stakes much higher. Stan "Zero" Zaretsky was a senior and the star of the basketball team. Every Wednesday afternoon this legendary poker game took place on the enclosed front porch of Zero Zaretsky's house, which happened to be on the same block as the house of Lenny Akers, a good-looking, affable classmate of Eliot's who that year had started playing—and losing—at the Friday night game, and whose most distinguishing feature was that he sometimes drove around in his father's Cadillac convertible. Lenny was the only member of the Friday night crowd who had any success with women and joined the game only on the Fridays when he did not have a date. From Lenny Akers, the Friday night group heard vivid tales about Zero Zaretsky's Wednesday afternoon game—as Lenny had started dating Zero Zaretsky's gorgeous sister Amy, a subject about which he also gave frequent instructive talks, and had become a regular visitor at the Zaretsky household.

What Eliot heard about the Wednesday afternoon game was as scary as it was alluring. The stakes: half-dollar ante and unlimited raising on every hand. And there were several kinds of games: in addition to the five-card draw and seven-card stud which were the staples of the Friday game, they played Baseball (seven-card stud with threes and nines wild) and a dangerous variant of seven-card stud called Anaconda, usually with a high-low split, which by Lenny's account produced killer pots sometimes exceeding fifty dollars. And there were the participants, starting with the great Zero Zaretsky himself. Zero was no doubt the heaviest person ever to be a varsity basketball player, not to mention a star player. His ruddy face was round as the full moon, and his large body was perfectly globular. Yet there was no deadlier eye in the league. To see Zero Zaretsky stolidly plant himself at half court, while the other players were whirring like locusts around the basket, and with incredible grace loft the ball in slow motion into a high, perfect arc ending with a rimless swish, was to witness an event which for many bordered on the sacred. Off the court, however, Zero fell distinctly short of sainthood. Although the stories that he regularly ran errands for a crime syndicate may have only been rumors, they lent glamor and depth to his other widely verified activities, which included pairings with exotic women of all ethnic types, frequent and well-publicized skirmishes with high school officials, and a record-breaking number of semesters flunking the senior year curriculum.

The other members of the Wednesday game were not less distinguished. There was natty, diminutive, knife-wielding José Vilavicencio, and the black wrestler Joe Minyard, before whom even inanimate objects seemed to cringe, and Bart Torg, who looked like an escaped convict and whose credentials included a recent hearing in juvenile court on auto theft charges.

Eliot never dreamed he would find himself in this game, but it happened one Wednesday afternoon when he was tooling around with Lenny Akers in the family Cadillac. Lenny pulled up in front of Zero's house and went in to fetch Amy, taking Eliot with him. To get into the house, they had to pass through the front porch where the Wednesday game was in progress. Hurrying past the players, Eliot felt the game's intense vibration and his eyes bulged as he caught sight of the pot, made up of an incredible number of large coins spread out over half the table, in the center of which was an even more incredible mound of crumpled dollar bills, including several fives and tens. It stopped him in his tracks and he stood there gawking as Lenny raced away from him into the house. He felt like a little child watching the big boys. Zero Zaretsky lifted his great head and stared at him with a sphinx-like expression. But Eliot could not tear his eyes away from the money. Mentally, he counted the pot at about seventy dollars.

The next thing he knew, he was sitting between big Joe Minyard and tiny, aromatic José Vilavicencio. As in a dream, he was taking out his wallet and putting all his money (except for two dollars) on the table in front of him. In vain, he looked around for potato chips. When someone placed a bottle of Schlitz in his hands, he asked for a glass, but his request was ignored.

He sat there watching as the seventy-dollar pot was raked in by Zero Zaretsky, and he counted his own money. He had thirty-three dollars and fifty cents, a huge sum that represented a week's allowance plus five dollars under the table from his mother, plus seven and a half dollars that he had won at the Friday night game, plus a ten dollar loan repayment made that morning at school by Lenny Akers. He figured that he would go into the game for ten, at most. Losing any more than ten dollars would be suicidally depressing. Even losing five would be a nightmare for Eliot, or for that matter, losing anything at all. But why even think like that?

The cards were passed to him. "Deal," said Zero. Eliot felt joyful that Zero actually spoke to him and experienced a surge of confidence. "Five-card draw, deuces wild," he said while he performed his most elaborate riffle shuffle. The other four players glanced at each other with strange smiles on their faces as Eliot shuffled again, adding several stagy flourishes this time.

"Man, what you doing with them cards?" said José the Knife. Eliot began to explain about different kinds of shuffling as he started to deal. But as he did so, the black monster hand of Joe Minyard grabbed his wrist.

"Cut," said Minyard in a terrifyingly deep voice. Eliot instantly put the cards on the table and split the deck.

"Terrific cut," said Bart Torg, but Eliot knew there was nothing special about how he had cut the cards. What was going on? Torg, the escaped convict, finished the cut.

Eliot dealt, while counting his own money again.

"What's the ante, man?" said José.

Eliot placed a finger on a dime in front of him but, seeing the reactions of disgust in the others, pushed in two quarters.

"Fifty cents," he said, bravely.

From that point on, Eliot knew he was in trouble. The stakes were just too high for him. He found himself folding on every hand before it had a chance to develop. With increasing sadness, he watched his money ebb away fifty cents and a dollar at a time. It was unbearable. Why was he so afraid? He knew the game. He knew cards as well as anyone. He handled cards like a pro. He was smart. Why was he so frightened when large sums of money were involved? The sense of mocking menace in the attitudes of Zero, Minyard, Vilavicencio, and Torg was a factor, of course, but cards were cards and although the others played boldly and quickly, they were no better than he was in their knowledge of the game—on the contrary. It was the money, pure and simple.

Eliot kept looking around for Lenny so that he could leave the game gracefully, but Lenny was God knows where inside the house—probably diddling around with the beauteous Amy Zaretsky.

"Your deal, man," said José, and the game went on. Each time Eliot tried to stay in the pot, he crashed against his fear of losing money and folded his hand. He was beginning to feel humiliated. But something strangely familiar was creeping into his awareness. This feeling—this sense of meeting something in himself that he did not want to see—had a definite taste to it. And suddenly, he remembered. It was the same "taste" of himself that he had had when he was with Max Falkoner! Very strange. Very interesting!

The thought of Max triggered thoughts of his work with the linking rings, and a strong desire arose in him to go home and practice. In fact, his work with the rings was not going well. He had reached some kind of plateau and he needed to see Max about it.

"I said *deal*, man!" The sharp command from José brought Eliot back to the present moment. He knew now what he must do. He must not let himself get carried away by his fear. He knew cards, he knew the game. He had only to bring his attention onto what he knew—to what was right in front of him, and he would be all right. Slowly, deliberately, he dealt the cards, trying to keep his attention on his hands, as Max had taught him.

One at a time, he looked at the cards he had dealt himself, and his heart leaped into his throat when he saw the first wild deuce and then the second and then two nines and a jack. My God, he was sitting with four of a kind even before the draw!

The first round of betting brought Eliot back to himself again. Torg opened for a dollar, followed by Vilavicencio and Minyard. But Zero saw the dollar and raised another dollar! Feigning calm, Eliot tossed in two dollar bills.

Torg and Vilavicencio drew three cards, Minyard took one, and Zero Zaretsky drew three! The son of a bitch! How could he have raised on openers and still draw three cards? It was pure gall. Of course, Zero could afford to fool around—he was already sitting with a pile of winnings. Eliot pondered his strategy; he could stand pat, leaving others to think he was holding a straight or a flush, or he could draw one card and try for an unbeatable five of a kind. His heart pounding, he drew one card, pretending that he was trying to fill a straight. He drew a queen, leaving him with the original four nines.

As the betting started, there was enough silence for Eliot to try to come back to sensing his hands, but each time that he saw dollar bills flying into the pot, he completely forgot his hands, Max Falkoner, and everything else.

There was now about thirty dollars in the pot. Torg started the second round of betting with two dollars, Minyard dropped out, Vilavicencio stayed in and Zero, after a slight pause, slowly pushed in two dollars' worth of coins. As Zero was methodically counting out the quarters and dimes, Eliot calculated that by taking this pot, he would be about even and could leave the game safe and sound. He was certain now that his four nines was the best hand. But just as he was about to add his two dollars and then make his escape, Zero nonchalantly tossed in a giant wad of bills.

"I raise your goddamn asses," said Zero, laughing.

"Motherfucker," said Torg, the convict, "you're full of shit."

"You're bluffing, man," said Vilavicencio.

Eliot kept quiet, his heart still pounding, his eyes counting the money Zero had tossed in.

"What's the raise?" said Eliot finally, his voice quavering.

"How should I know, schmuck. Count it and see," said Zero.

"It's twenty-two dollars," said Eliot immediately. "You've raised twenty-two dollars!"

"Hey," said Torg, "he can count!"

Eliot looked down at his own money. He only had eight dollars left.

"I can't cover that," said Eliot, almost tearfully.

"Tough ass," said Zero, reaching out his star basketball hand to rake in the pot.

"Hold it, Zero man," said José, folding his cards. "I think baby-face got you beat."

"Yeah," said Torg, "he's got you beat!"

"Tough ass," said Zero again. "He can't cover."

It was now dawning on Eliot that he had been set up in some way or other. These people were play-acting—they were out to get him. Eliot's mind raced. He hadn't noticed any cheating, but he hadn't been looking for it either. Zero could have stacked the deck; any one of them could have done it. Of course. What a pigeon he had been! Why had he assumed he was the only one who could handle cards?

The theatre continued.

"Look man," said José, "you gonna make him cry! You're a bad man, Zero man!"

"Yeah," said Torg, "shame on you!"

Anger and rage started boiling up in Eliot. His eyes darted to his hands and to the ring.

"Hey, look at that neat ring," said Vilavicencio. "That's worth some money, ain't it, Zero man?"

At that point, Joe Minyard's incredibly deep voice was heard. "Put in the ring, little boy!"

Eliot became cold as ice. His self-pity was gone. His anger was gone. With a thin smile on his lips, he took off the death's head ring and held it in both his hands. *The power came on all by itself.* He saw what Zero was holding—nothing at all, only a pair of sevens. He saw Zero's thoughts—that he had no intention of letting Eliot win the money, that none of them did. And he saw other things as well—such as the name Gino di Donato, and the address of Zero's "employer," and the nature of the errands Zero ran for him. He then saw something else about Zero—his sexual impotence and the shame he suffered because of it, and the need he had for the drugs that were supplied to him by his "employer." This took Eliot by surprise, but he experienced not the slightest compassion for Zero. On the contrary, it delighted him. For the first time, the deeper revelations of the power did not trouble him at all. In the excitement of the moment, however, this new development passed unnoticed except for the fleeting thought of how pleased Blake would be to hear of it.

Eliot looked directly into Zero Zaretsky's big round face. "This ring," he said, "is worth a lot more than what's in the pot. I'd better call up my friend Gino and buy some courage from him."

And with that, everything quickly changed. Zero's face turned gray and his eyes darted nervously around the table. Obviously, no one else knew Zero's secrets. The other players were puzzled by what then took place. Zero simply caved in. With a sudden sharp movement, he turned his cards face up on the table and tried to cover himself with a loud joking remark—"Oh, let the kid keep his toy!"

Eliot slowly placed the ring back on his finger, spread out his four nines and pulled in the pot. The huge pile of dollars was like a drug; it made his head swim. He had actually done it! He had won big money; he was in the real world and he had won! These players were not even his equals; they were older, they were hostile, they were out to get him, and yet he had won real money from them— money, real coins, real dollars! So this was what it was like to be strong! It wasn't that hard, after all. Why had he been so afraid? These tough guys—these representatives of the real world—why, they were as weak as he was! Eliot felt like dancing for joy.

To add to his elation, he looked up to see that Lenny Akers had returned to the porch accompanied by Zero Zaretsky's unbelievably beautiful sister Amy, and they had both witnessed the whole triumphant scene. Eliot stood up and stuffed the bills into his pocket without counting them. Without offering a word of explanation, he walked out of the house with Lenny and Amy. None of the players looked at him. "How easy it all is," thought Eliot. And how it made him tingle from head to foot!

FALKONER'S WAY

The weeks and months that followed, however, brought Eliot suffering of a kind he had never known. More and more, he was pulled forcibly in two sharply opposed directions, with Max on one side and Blake on the other. Until now, although he had been moving back and forth from one to the other, there had been no clear sense that he had to make a choice between them. Now, however, and with increasing intensity, he began to feel as though he were two entirely different people inside one body.

It began the day after the Wednesday game. Still glowing from that triumph, he went to Templeton's Magic Shop for help with the linking rings. Although he knew he needed guidance from Max, he was convinced he had made some real progress. And so, he was completely unprepared for what took place.

At first, Max did not even let him take all the rings out of his sack. Eliot had been sitting in the row of chairs against the wall waiting impatiently for the last customer to leave. Finally, as Max was locking the door from inside, Eliot jumped up and reached into his schoolbag for the rings.

"Just take out the key ring and one other single ring," said Max, as he turned around to face Eliot.

Eliot did so.

"Now close your eyes."

Eliot obeyed.

"Put down your bag."

Eliot did so.

"Now," said Max, almost in a whisper, and with a gentleness that Eliot had never heard in him, "hold the key ring in your right hand and the other ring in your left hand, and stretch your arms out to the sides pointing diagonally upwards." Eliot did as he was told.

"Keep them there and don't move them until I tell you," said Max, so softly that Eliot could barely hear him.

Minutes passed. Eliot's shoulders soon began to ache. He sensed the silence in the room, but inwardly his thoughts were in an uproar. His arms began to quiver.

"Try, Eliot, try," Max whispered. "Don't give up."

Eliot felt the pain spreading down his back and through his neck. The silence in the room became more and more pronounced as the agitation within increased. He could sense Max moving closer to him as, in an even softer voice, he said, "Try . . . try . . . try to wish to not give up . . ." and then Max stopped speaking. Eliot was in intense pain. His whole body was aching and his shoulders and arms felt as though knives were sticking in them.

After what seemed an eternity, Max's soft voice was heard again. "You have muscles inside you that have never been used. Don't give up. Try to find those muscles . . . try, Eliot, try . . . they exist in your body. If you don't use them, they'll waste away and you'll be a child for the rest of your life."

The pain continued, with short intervals of numbness. Eliot's arms became heavier and heavier. He could sense them slowly sinking down.

"Try, Eliot, search for those muscles. . . ."

Every tiny sound, every passing thought distracted Eliot and each time that he was distracted, his arms sank farther and farther down under the pain and the numb weight of his arms.

Finally, his arms were hanging limply down at his sides. He knew he had failed to find whatever it was he was supposed to find. He remained in place until his breathing returned to normal and until the pain and numbness subsided. When he opened his eyes, he saw Max standing in front of him with an expression on his face of intense concentration and compassion.

"Keep your eyes closed," said Max, firmly.

Eliot obeyed. He had no comprehension of what was happening or why, but he was suffused with a sense of failure that drove out every trace of the elation and the feeling of strength that he had come with. At the same time, he sensed a subtle vitality flowing down his spine.

Max spoke again. "Don't move yet. Stay very still."

Eliot obeyed.

"Now," Max continued, "allow the power to appear. Don't move a muscle."

"But who should I direct it toward?" said Eliot in a soft voice, full of puzzlement.

"Toward yourself," said Max.

No sooner did Max say those words—so incomprehensible—than there appeared before Eliot the image of his triumph at the Wednesday poker game. The pleasure he had then felt returned to him, but it did not engulf him. He sensed two currents within his body—one of pleasure and the other of this subtle vitality that had just been evoked by Max, the first in the front half of his body and the second mainly in the back. He felt divided in two.

The power continued. It showed him a visual image of his own face as it had looked when he was confronting Zero Zaretsky. It was like the face of a wolf. Instinctively, Eliot moved his hands toward each other so that he could grasp the skull ring and protect himself from the effects of the power.

"Don't move," said Max, in a whisper, but very sharply. "Go on searching for those special muscles."

But what did Max mean? Eliot's arms were already hanging limply down at his sides, the fingers of each hand loosely grasping one of the linking rings. What did Max mean by saying he should go on searching for those "muscles," whatever they were? All the muscles in his arms seemed to Eliot so exhausted he could scarcely move them.

The power continued to operate. There now appeared the event in Mr. Petrie's class. Once again Eliot saw his face as it had looked then, only now it resembled not a wolf, but some other kind of animal, some kind of bird with brilliant plumage—a peacock!

Moments passed.

"Open your eyes," said Max.

Eliot did so.

"Now show me your work on the rings," said Max, his voice at a normal pitch. Max sat down on one of the chairs by the wall, crossed his legs, and inserted a cigarette in his mouth.

Mutely, Eliot reached into his bag for the rest of the rings and began the routine as he had been practicing it. As though from somewhere behind himself, he watched in shock at how poorly he performed. At every crucial point, he helplessly witnessed his attention repeatedly being drawn away from his hands and the rings. But what startled him most was observing the part of himself that was completely satisfied with how he performed, like a separate personality that offered very favorable judgment on everything he did.

Max did not spare Eliot's feelings. Gone was the gentle whisper and the compassionate look. Puffing away on his cigarette, he barked out a stream of insults as Eliot bumbled through the sequence of moves. By the end of the routine, rings were sliding out of Eliot's hands and clanging on the floor, rolling under chairs. Max laughed, mockingly.

"Appleman, that was a real treat! Forget the whole thing. Go home! I'm not interested in watching you play with yourself! Go home! There's no hope for you!"

Nevertheless, Max did not stand up to go. He jammed out his cigarette and lit up another one.

Eliot was not about to go. There was his usual impulse to cry and the usual impulse to run away. But, for some reason, these impulses did not engulf him either. They seemed on the same side of himself as the personality that he had observed judging his poor work favorably. He simply stayed in his place taking in the new barrage of insults that now belched forth, with the clouds of cigarette smoke, from Max's lips.

As the tirade continued to wash over him, Eliot began picking the rings up from the floor and from under the chairs. Having done that, he again stood quietly in front of Max, waiting for him to stop shouting. He felt filled with light, for some reason he didn't understand.

When Max quieted down, Eliot began the routine again, but he was immediately interrupted by a piercing shout from Max:

"Take that fucking ring off your finger!"

Without thinking twice about it, Eliot obeyed. Then he started the routine again. The light he had sensed seemed to pour into his shoulders and arms and down into his fingers. It was true: there were different muscles—or something like that! It was amazing! He was making no mistakes! And yet *he* wasn't doing anything. Those muscles, or whatever they were, were doing the routine.

But no sooner did he have that thought, than he lost contact with the sense of light, and the routine started going sour again. At that point, Max spoke again, but now his voice had become calm once more—calm and even.

"Attention," said Max, "pay attention to the light."

Startled that Max knew about the sensation of light, Eliot obeyed, again and again withdrawing his attention from his thoughts and, under Max's guidance, placing it on the sensation of light. Each time he did so, his hands performed the moves with precision and exact timing. And each time that his attention was pulled away from the light, he made mistakes.

"Stop trying to *do* the trick," said Max. "Let your muscles do it. Just keep your attention on the light. The light needs your attention, it needs *you*. Nothing else will work!"

As Eliot continued the routine, Max went on side-coaching. Each time Eliot made a mistake, Max brought him back: "Choose, Eliot, choose! Pay with your attention!"

But Eliot—something in him—soon began to grow weary and heavy. Each time he willed his attention back toward the sensation of light, his hands performed the moves perfectly, but he was growing tired of willing.

"You want to dream," said Max. "Don't give way to it. Fight, Eliot! Be a man!"

Again and again, Eliot brought his attention back—back from the thoughts and images that were so alluring. Although the routine was only five minutes long, it seemed like hours were passing. The mistakes began to pile up one after the other, and Max intensified his side-coaching.

"Search, Eliot, search!"

Eliot began dropping the rings again.

"Let them go," said Max. "Work with what's left. Search!"

Eliot felt he could not go on. He felt he had nothing left and he watched with disgust as his hands fumbled and slipped around with the rings. He felt he had to stop, but Max, handing him the rings he had dropped, insisted he start the routine over again without a pause.

It wasn't that he was physically tired, quite the contrary. Nor was he particularly upset emotionally. It was just that he seemed to have no more will, no more wish to try, no more attention to give.

But Max pushed him on. "You're far from the light," said Max, "but the light is close to you. Turn to it, Eliot, choose, choose! If you stop now you're finished."

Sweat began pouring from Eliot's face. His throat became painfully dry as he went through the routine again and again. He saw that it was pitch black outside, and in the distance he heard the mournful City Hall bell sounding six o'clock. His glance surveyed the room as he pushed through the routine for the tenth time, the eleventh time—never getting it quite right all the way. His eyes wandered to the magic apparatus on the shelves and then to the photographs of the professional magicians hanging on the wall to his left. And suddenly, in the middle of one of the most difficult moves with rings—where the key ring passes through the triple chain and connects it to the double chain—his ever-weakening attention was caught by the photograph of Irene Angel, the one showing her holding all the eight rings linked together. Her long blond hair seemed to glow. Eliot wanted to sink into that photograph, into her mysterious pale eyes and her strange, indecipherable smile.

And just as suddenly, Max's voice, loud and harsh, invaded Eliot's brain.

"Search, you sonofabitch, search!"

But Eliot had absolutely nothing left. It seemed he had lost everything when he was caught by the photograph of Irene. He felt empty, dead, nonexistent. His arms and hands kept on moving—

but like little mechanical puppets. Then, gradually, they slowed and stopped like toys winding down.

Eliot just stood there with his eyes down. He was afraid to look at Max. A moment passed. Then, quietly again, Max spoke. "If you still have enough energy left to be afraid, you have to go on trying. I'm going out for a sandwich. You stay here and work."

And with that, Max put on his hat and coat and left Eliot alone in the shop.

THE MIRRORED WALL

No sooner did Max leave, than Eliot set the rings aside and sat down on one of the chairs by the wall of photographs. He rested a few minutes and then, his mind in a sort of becalmed stupor, got up to practice. He stood facing the mirrored wall which held the shelves of the club and stage apparatus and began the routine from the start. The first basic move with the rings was the "melting" of the key ring into a single ring. Eliot held the two rings at chest height and watched in the mirror as he slowly turned the rings against each other. The slot in the key ring automatically came against the single ring, and the rings slid satisfying together with no sound, giving the perfect illusion of two solid metal objects mysteriously interpenetrating. Seeing it in the mirror brought up the old love he had originally felt for magic and for this particular trick. Again he saw that even though he knew the gimmick, and even though he himself was doing the trick, something in him actually "believed" a magical penetration was taking place.

Feeling the old enthusiasm coming back, it was not until he was halfway through the routine that he realized the situation Max had left him in. There he was, alone in Templeton's magic shop with all the magic tricks in the world displayed in front of him—and with all their secrets sitting there for the taking.

Eliot's heart began pounding. He quietly stacked the rings on the glass counter and looked around. The silence in the room was absolute, except for the humming of the fluorescent lights and the soft ticking of a clock somewhere behind the mirrored wall.

Eliot stepped behind the counter and, as he did so, he was hit with a new surge of electricity through his body—far stronger than anything he had ever experienced when shoplifting. It was a heady sensation and it made him bolt back around to the front of the counter again.

Wouldn't this be a violation of trust? But even as he was thinking this, he walked over to the door and locked it from inside. Moving back to the counter, and then behind it, he surveyed the magic apparatus on the wall. Dozens of ornately designed production boxes filled the bottom shelf. Eliot nervously peeked inside a dove box and noted the black felt "load"—well, he knew that secret already, so he hadn't really copped anything. On the next shelf was a large card frame—two sheets of glass banded together and inserted cornerwise on a richly varnished wooden frame. In this trick the magician throws a deck of cards at the two pieces of glass and the card, "freely" selected beforehand by a spectator, magically appears between the pieces of glass. Probably a spring load in the base of the frame, thought Eliot. But why not make sure? With trembling hands, he removed the apparatus. As he was doing so, he grabbed the trick next to it as well, a Sword Through Neck set of wooden stocks. He carefully placed both pieces of apparatus on the counter.

He waited a moment for his shaking to subside, and continued surveying the apparatus before him. There was a set of Passe-Passe bottles. He took it down. And wasn't that a Squeezaway Block? He grabbed it. And there—a Val Evans "Penetrating Glass" in which an ordinary household tumbler slowly sinks down through a plate. Eliot removed that, too. And what was that on the top shelf—wasn't that Multum in Parvo?—one of the most beautiful magical effects, where all the milk in a large pitcher is poured, without leaving a drop, into smaller and smaller glasses, ending with a mere shot glass. Eliot craved to know how, exactly, it was done. He hastily got a chair to stand on and took down the Multum in Parvo pitcher, glasses and tray, setting them on the counter next to the other tricks.

He now turned his attention to the front counter, which held not only close-up magic trick decks and various small paraphernalia such as wands, thumb tips, and body clips, but all those alluring envelopes that contained nothing but a single piece of paper upon which was written a secret to one very special, newly created trick. Sliding open the back panel of the counter, Eliot anxiously checked his watch. Only fifteen minutes had passed since Max had left—still plenty of time. He reached under the counter and let his hand choose one of the envelopes—John Scarne's Triple Coincidence. Eliot placed the envelope on the counter.

Shaking again, he turned first to the Multum in Parvo. As he suspected, the trick was based on the classic Milk Pitcher principle, with a plastic shell lining the pitcher, and each of the glasses also had something like a shell, except for the smallest one. He set down the trick and turned to the others, quickly divining the secret of each. As for the envelope, it was very loosely sealed and easily opened. Eliot devoured the contents, placed the paper back and resealed it by licking the flap.

Working quickly, he returned everything to its place and went back to the linking rings. He was drenched in sweat and breathing hard. Picking up the rings again, a new thought occurred to him. Maybe there was something in the shop that could give him a clue to the mystery of Irene! What of Max's file cabinet in the back of the store?

Eliot saw his face wincing in the mirrors. Was he really prepared to sink so low? To look into Max's personal papers? Wasn't this despicable? He felt his heart hammering inside his chest. No, he thought, it was not like that. It was because he wanted the truth. He needed to know, to understand. And he would only look for one specific thing—some facts about Irene. He would not look at anything else. He would be honorable.

Armed with this thought, Eliot edged toward the end of the counter and peered around the mirrored wall into Max's office. And there it was—a green, four-drawer file cabinet. He checked his watch again, took a deep breath, wiped his moist palms on his pants, and tiptoed toward the filing cabinet.

What he saw, however, as he came round the mirrored wall stopped him dead in his tracks. There was the squat figure of Max Falkoner calmly sitting at a tiny desk in the front part of the office area nonchalantly having a sandwich and a cup of coffee and reading a newspaper! He had apparently gone out for the food and had come back through the private entrance.

"How's it going, Applefriend?" Max drawled without lifting his eyes from the newspaper. Eliot was gripped by terror and shame and could not get a word out of his mouth.

Then his thoughts started flowing. Maybe . . . maybe, Max suspected nothing. He certainly gave no sign that he knew what Eliot had been up to. Maybe . . . maybe . . . he had only just come back with the sandwich and hadn't wanted to disturb Eliot's practicing. Of course. No need to panic.

"How's it going?" Max repeated, looking up at Eliot. There wasn't a trace of suspicion or anything at all in Max's face, apart from a sort of pleasant weariness, the face of someone who'd had a hard day and was relaxing a little between demands. He seemed absolutely ordinary, his Winston Churchill jowls a little baggier than usual, his balding head, covered by the thin wisps of gray-black hair, a little shinier and more vulnerable than usual.

Eliot croaked out an answer. "It's going okay, Max . . ." he said, and then added, "I was just looking back here to get a glass of water."

Max absently waved his hand toward the water cooler.

"Help yourself, old buddy," he said, and returned to his sandwich and newspaper.

Max seemed ordinary! Like an old uncle or something. Suddenly everything was feeling so flat—the linking rings a childish distraction, the Annual Show no big deal, Blake a kind of weirdo, Max somebody's old uncle, Irene—well, maybe she was still something special, but Eliot didn't feel very much about her either. And as for the Sorcerers, they were just kids like himself.

This sense of flatness and ordinariness was two things to Eliot—it was both depressing and also a relief. He saw that at this moment he was free to walk away from the whole thing—not only the tight spot that he had just escaped from, but the whole meshugginah situation—Blake, Max, the Sorcerers, the rings, the power—everything. He could walk away and go back to being just Eliot Appleman, with his safe, ordinary, understandable little life.

It was the same kind of feeling he had had when he first exercised the power with Blake and experienced that strange moment of decision to go further with the power, no matter where it led. He wanted magic at any cost—real magic; he wanted the miraculous in his life no matter what. But this present decision, this second break in the momentum of events, was much harder than the one he had made that first time with Blake. Then all sorts of new things were pouring into him and the decision almost made itself; he had only to incline toward it. But now he knew that there was some kind of heavy price to be paid. It was lovely scoring against his teachers, triumphing over fearsome enemies, grabbing prestige, money, and who knows what else through the power. He wanted those things— but he felt in his bones that this was not the miraculous he had dreamt of; these things were not magical, not the kind of magic he wanted, the magic that had to do with the stars and the distant planets, with God and his mysteries.

He looked again at the back of Max's head as he went on eating and reading. Was the kind of work Max demanded really the key to the miraculous?

Twice before, Eliot had tried to turn the power onto Max and both times it had failed. But now Max looked so ordinary, so vulnerable, that he suspected it could work this time. And so he tried. The tingling sensation in the back of his head appeared, the power began to function, but instantly the light in his body appeared as well, the same light that he had experienced just before when he was suffering under Max's fierce demands. And now, suddenly, he decided. He saw. He could not stay with Max. He wasn't worthy of his care. Hadn't he stolen secrets from him, hadn't he planned to peer into his personal life? Hadn't he lied to this extraordinary ordinary man? The power was rushing through him, bringing him to a deep sense of sorrow about himself. He was just a sneaky kid, he was not worthy to be a pupil of this man who, as he now began to realize, was not ordinary at all! What an effect the power was having on him! It brought no visions of Max's or anyone else's mind, only this crushing of shame and remorse—and yet with it came a strong sense of dignity of a kind he had never known.

At that moment, Max spun around in his chair facing Eliot. His face was completely transformed! He was no "uncle," no ordinary man. His dark eyes burned with a deep, intense fire; his very skin seemed radiant with force and energy. Eliot paled, but stood his ground. His voice was choking with tears.

"I have to tell you something, Max, and then I'll leave, I'll go home. I'm a piece of shit. I've betrayed your confidence."

Max said nothing. His face was like a tiger's. He sat motionless, but immensely relaxed.

"When you were out, I didn't work at all. All I did was sneak looks at the club apparatus and the routines in the sealed envelopes."

Still, Max said and did nothing. Eliot swallowed hard. The next thing to say was the most difficult of all. He tilted his head down to avoid Max's eyes.

"And I lied to you. I wasn't looking for a glass of water. I was going to rifle the file cabinet to find out about Irene and about anything else that interested me I'm very sorry. That's what I am and now you know. Now, I'll leave. I'm sorry. Thank you. . . ." At the last words, Eliot began to sob out loud and started to move away. He went back into the shop, picked up his schoolbag and left his set of linking rings on the counter. His shoulders shaking with sobs, he turned the doorknob and was halfway out the door when he heard Max's voice, like a lion's roar, "Appleman, come back!"

Eliot immediately ran back into the store and raced behind the mirrored wall. Max still seated at the desk, still looking grave and full of irresistible power.

"Come here, Eliot!" he commanded with a forceful gesture of his hand. "Now look," he said, pointing toward the back of the mirrored wall that separated the store from the office area. Eliot gasped. He saw the whole store as though he were looking through glass—it was a one-way mirror!

"Yes," said Max, "I've been here the whole time. I saw every move you made. I know what you are. Now *you* know. That's what your power is for."

Eliot felt his whole body spinning inside. Waves of bittersweet joy poured through him from his head down to the soles of his feet.

Max handed him a half of a sandwich.

"Eat this," he said, rising from his chair, "and then we work."

BLAKE'S PLAN

Not once in the weeks and months that followed did Max suggest that Eliot stop visiting Blake. Whenever Eliot tried to talk to Max about these visits and everything resulting from them, Max gave it no special importance. This Eliot could not understand. More and more he felt that Max and Blake represented two contradictory influences warring inside him. More and more, he wished Max would order him to stop seeing Blake. But apart from requiring that Eliot remove the skull ring when practicing the linking rings with him, Max seemed strangely unconcerned. Nor did he suggest that Eliot stop using the power as Blake told him to—directed outward to others and to satisfy Eliot's egoistic emotions.

As for Blake, Eliot never even told him about his work with Max. He never had a chance to. No sooner did he relate the events with Mr. Petrie and the Wednesday poker game, which Blake listened to with great delight and approval, than he found himself drawn even deeper into Blake's orbit. With much ceremony, Blake privately declared to Eliot that he was indeed that "person" whom Irene had prophesied, and at the next meeting of the club when Blake laid out the program for the Annual Show, he stunned everyone by placing Eliot as the next to last act on the program, just before his own.

It was commonly understood in the club that the more important the act, the further along in the program it was placed. Blake's act, of course, was always the last and climactic part of the Annual Show, and so there was considerable pride of place attached to the slot preceding his. Never had a member as new as

Eliot performed anywhere in the second half of the program, far less next to Blake. But Blake put the whole weight of his authority behind Eliot by announcing not that he was "that person"—this was for now to remain a secret between him and Eliot—but that after careful study, he was certain Eliot possessed the authentic power of reading minds. Saying this, he called Eliot forward and solemnly placed his arm around his shoulders and, as it seemed to Eliot, willed the Sorcerers to applaud, softly at first and then with some loud cheers. Blake then told him to sit down at the front table and then, still standing continued to speak.

To Eliot, all this was so intensely pleasant that he felt all his dreams were coming true. However, he could not help but perceive with astonishment how quickly those Sorcerers who had been hostile to him were now suddenly his "great friends." The only exception to this was Ronnie Pitkin, who Eliot observed maintaining an icy silence throughout.

But the astonishments of the evening were only beginning. Having gathered nearly unanimous support for Eliot, Blake proceeded to describe in detail the whole program of the show, based on the proposals that each of the Sorcerers had submitted. Eliot listened carefully as Blake outlined each of the acts and their sequence, anxiously waiting to hear what would be assigned to Ronnie Pitkin now that Eliot had obviously eclipsed him as the club's chief mentalist. To Eliot's surprise, Blake did not change Ronnie's act at all. It was to be the same mind reading routines that Ronnie had proposed—a sequence of mental effects including the billet knife, the Ultra Blindfold, and the Spirit Bell. Not only that, but Ronnie's act was to come just before Eliot's! If anything would show Ronnie's work in an unfavorable light, it was this. What could Blake be thinking?

It soon became clear what Blake was thinking. This year, he said, the show would be divided into three parts instead to two. The first two segments would consists of the usual magic routines, starting with Wally Pound's silent act and proceeding through the Wick-Bunche guillotine, Bennie Schulweis' and the "Monte Carlo Boys'" comedy routines and so forth. But the third segment would have a predominantly mental and psychic theme starting with Ronnie, followed by Eliot, and concluding with Blake. Ronnie's act would set the stage for Eliot's! Still sitting at the front table, facing the members of the club, Eliot avoided Ronnie Pitkin's baleful eyes.

Blake then proceeded to outline Eliot's act, without giving any indication that it had not been discussed beforehand, that it was all Blake's own idea and that this was the first Eliot had heard of it. Eliot was stupefied when he learned what Blake was asking him to do.

"My studies have shown me," said Blake, "that Eliot's power to read minds, marvelous though it is, is only the tip of an iceberg. This power can be used not only to read minds, but also to influence minds, to make people think whatever one wants them to think and to make them see whatever one wants them to see, and ultimately . . ." Here Blake paused for a moment, looking down at Eliot and savoring the effect his words were having on everyone in the room. The Sorcerers were all sitting as though struck dumb, their jaws hanging open. He finished his sentence, ". . . and ultimately to make people *do* whatever one wants them to do."

Again Blake paused and benignly looked down at Eliot. For his part, Eliot did not know where to look or what to do with himself. Was this some kind of joke Blake was playing? Was this all a dream—and if so what kind? He had to turn his eyes away from the Sorcerers, who were staring at him as though he were from another planet. Even Wally Pound was looking at him with bulging eyes.

Blake went on speaking, his gracefully clefted lips now spread out in a sort of smile. "After Ronnie's act, Eliot will start by reading the mind of one volunteer from the audience. But then he will do something that has never been done on stage before. He will ask every single member of the audience to think of a number and write it down privately. He will then ask each person to stand and will, one by one, call out the numbers they have written. Believe me, Eliot can do this!"

The Sorcerers gasped and murmured.

Blake went on. "Now comes the next phase. Eliot will go beyond mind reading into mind forcing. He will ask every member of the audience to concentrate on an image of their own choosing and again to privately write it down, fold the paper, and hand it to the person next to them. And, without telling them in advance, Eliot will project a single image into their minds so that when the papers are opened and read they will all be the same!"

At this Eliot sprang up from his chair in shock—not knowing where he was going to go, but completely unable to stay where he was. Blake's firm hand fell on his shoulder, however, and kept him in his seat.

"And then," said Blake, his voice calm and strong, "Eliot will speak about summoning a great magician who holds the secrets of the temples of ancient Egypt. At this point, the audience will be prepared to believe in practically anything!

"There will be a flash from offstage, and then I will appear on stage made up in the costume of an ancient Egyptian priest. Eliot will remain there with me as I begin my act, and after my first trick—the Sands of the Desert—I will dismiss him and go on with the rest of my act."

So that was it, thought Eliot. The whole thing was being set up to highlight Blake. Fantastic! But this thought had nowhere to settle in Eliot's mind. Any feeling of resentment toward Blake—that he was exploiting Eliot just to make his own act more dramatic—was immediately crowded out by the phenomenal, indigestible idea of "mind forcing." Had Blake gone crazy? Eliot remained frozen in his chair, facing the members of the club whose eyes were still riveted on him. He thought of the moment at his father's pinochle game when he had first discovered the power. Had he grown so accustomed to being able to read minds that he no longer felt how extraordinary and even miraculous it was? And if that was possible, why not "mind forcing" as well? Was one any less unbelievable than the other?

But Blake was not finished yet. There was more to come, although what Blake then said had no effect on anyone but Eliot. As Blake outlined his own act, Eliot felt as though he had been struck by lightning. Everything went black in front of him as Blake calmly advised the club that after showing the Sands of the Desert—where different colors of sand are mixed together in a bowl of water and then magically separated out again when the magician reaches into the bowl—he would then do his own carefully worked out version of the linking rings!

His act would conclude, said Blake, with an elaborate fire bowl production, but Eliot heard nothing of that. In a storm of inner agitation, he was vowing to himself that he would never let Blake or anyone take away from him his work with the linking rings. At the same time, chains of images unfolded before him around the new possibilities of his power—what Blake called "mind forcing."

ELAINE

Blake did not pressure Eliot to experiment with the new dimensions of the power, perhaps because he knew it would happen all by itself. As for Eliot's other life, Blake's announcement that the linking rings would be part of his own act only caused Eliot to redouble his work with them and to take care that Blake never found out about it. By now, he knew he could keep secrets from Blake, just as he was sure he could hide nothing from Max.

Over the summer months he saw Max more and more often, hoping that Max would say or do something that would enable him to break away from Blake. But the more he went to Max, the more he went also to Blake. With Max, he worked and sweated at the linking rings. Each time he visited Max, he discovered new areas of the routine where he was careless and inattentive, and by exercising his power under Max's sometimes fierce and sometimes gentle guidance, he saw new things about himself that shocked and dismayed him.

With Max, he saw that the only real thing he had was the attention he could give to his work; everything else in him had the stench of childishness and automatism. With Blake, he was treated practically like a god, as a great magician, as an initiate in some mysterious inner circle and—at the same time—as the honored disciple of an even greater magician, Blake himself.

As the summer wore on, Blake showed Eliot the workings of all the magic apparatus in his house—all those pieces of apparatus that had so fascinated Eliot on the first night he had come to Blake. From Blake, Eliot learned the secrets of magic tricks from

India, China and Japan, from Arabia and the lands of Central Asia—
Tibet, Mongolia. Blake showed him reconstructions of alchemical
apparatus of the kind used, so Blake informed him, by the followers
of Paracelsus four hundred years before in Germany. Blake showed
him the mystical diagrams of Raymond Lull and the Rosicruicans,
and this led to his giving Eliot countless old books to read that
contained complicated philosophical ideas about the universe.
Eliot was bored by the books, but enthralled by the apparatus.

During all this time, Blake continued to encourage Eliot to
experiment with his power and waited patiently for him to turn to
its further dimensions.

The inevitable finally happened in early September, two months
before the Annual Show. And when it happened, open warfare
finally broke out between the two lives of Eliot Appleman. The
painful, unstable equilibrium that had been established between his
opposing attractions to Max and Blake began to crumble. He knew
he had to choose between them, but he had not been able to. As
rehearsals started in earnest, Eliot wished he had stood up to Blake
and claimed the linking rings for his own act. He had had enough
of using the power under Blake's guidance. He had had enough
of winning money, cheating at school, intimidating teachers and
schoolmates. He had gotten his A's, he was the center of attention
everywhere. He had it all, and he was getting sick of it—for some
reason. Or so he thought. But still he went on with it, day after
day. He needed no protection from the power now. The skull ring
was unnecessary. He read minds at the drop of a hat, whenever he
wanted something. And he couldn't stop. No matter how strong
his work was with Max, no matter how much he saw of himself, he
went on using the power more and more in his everyday life.

*

Over the Labor Day weekend there was a wedding involving some
of the innumerable cousins on his father's side. Dressed in his
powder blue sport coat and his navy blue slacks and wearing his
new blue suede loafers, Eliot steeled himself for an afternoon of
boredom as he splashed handfuls of Old Spice on his face, wincing
as it bit into several major flesh wounds that he had inflicted on
himself while shaving. One right above his lips looked like it would

never stop bleeding, and he was forced to leave the house with a disgusting blood-soaked bit of toilet paper flapping under his nose. Apart from that, he looked pretty good to himself.

But for what? Musing in the family Chevrolet on the way to the synagogue, he could picture the boring brood of cousins, second cousins, uncles and aunts of cousins, sisters and brothers of uncles and aunts of cousins, children of uncles and brothers and aunts and whatnot, babies and tiny tots, business partners of someone or other, and the boring wedding ceremony followed by chopped liver, roast beef, melon balls or their moral equivalent, various species of fish all smoked to taste the same, Larry Something and his band playing boring music, much fruit and cake, *beaucoup de* whiskey, speeches on whistling microphones, gas pains, and decorated radishes.

All proceeded as anticipated until after the ceremony. The crowd of relatives jammed into the reception hall in the basement of the synagogue and took their assigned seats at the circular dining tables set up around the dancing area. Before Eliot there reposed an empty champagne glass and a small dish of the dreaded melon balls, and around his table there sat his mother and father and five relatives of unknown identity and uniform appearance. Eliot looked up from the melon balls and gazed absently into the space between the heads of two unnamed relatives, and whom should he see seated at one of the tables closest to the bandstand? None other than the beauteous Elaine Goldner, the only object of Eliot's romantic dreams who was not a movie star but a real live person, and a relative at that. There she was, wearing a dark red velvet dress, her long black hair flowing down her back, her lush lips parting to receive a melon ball as she bent forward, resting her sensational semi-bared breasts on the edge of the table.

Elaine, Elaine Goldner! They used to play together when Eliot was a small child visiting his grandmother's house on weekends. She was two years older than he was and often assumed the role of leader when a group of small kids went together to the Saturday matinees. Eliot had fallen in love with her when he was about five years old. During one Frankenstein move she had given him her sweater so that he could cover his head during one of the scary parts. The smell of that sweater lingered through the years.

She hit puberty far, far in advance of everyone else, and for years Eliot did not see her. When he did meet her again about a year ago at some other big family function, she was practically a stranger—distant, elegantly mannered, well-spoken. She was now living in New York studying music at Juilliard, inhabiting another world, better than his own. She had transcended Philadelphia.

She was gorgeous. She was intelligent. She was unapproachable. Yet there she was not more than ten yards away, an orb of radiant light and color in the gray world of relativeness. Eliot stared at her through the melon balls, the champagne toasts, and the boring speeches over the ear-splitting, shrieking microphones. She never looked his way. She talked and smiled and engaged in polite conversation with the relatives at her table. Eliot stared at her through the chopped liver, the roast beef, and the tapioca supreme. How could she be so interested in these relatives? My God, was she becoming a relative herself? Was she becoming one of them? Impossible. She stood out like a wild red bird among city pigeons, like a blossoming rose in a field of blown dandelions.

The band began playing. The dancing started, first the requisite Anniversary Waltz, then the requisite Yiddish music, *Bei mir bist du shane* and its progeny, and then gradually evolving into popular romantic tunes like "Too Young," "Tell Me Why," and "Again." Watching the dancers on the floor was like seeing a reverse time-lapse film of a crowd of older people turning young as the music changed from Yiddish to Tin Pan Alley and as the uncles and aunts on the dance floor gave way to the nephews and nieces.

Eliot sat in his chair feeling as though a long spike had been driven through him. He could neither stop staring at Elaine nor go up to ask her to dance. He was terrified of dancing. No matter how many times he had tried to learn, it never came out right, and the few occasions that he had attempted it with a real girl had been sheer humiliation, partly because of clumsy feet and partly because of his self-willed sexual organs. But even apart from the dancing, he was inexplicably incapable of initiating contact with Elaine Goldner.

These things had happened before, many times. Couldn't it be different, just this once? Was he condemned yet again to end the evening kicking himself for not having the guts just to approach a pretty girl? What was he afraid of? Sure, she wasn't looking at him. Did that mean she didn't want to talk to him? Of course not, logic told him. She was probably just as shy as he was. On the other hand, she was so much older, so goddamn mature. She probably had a boyfriend who was much older, maybe a college professor or something. She probably regarded Eliot as just a kid. Maybe she was engaged or some such goddamn thing. And he, Eliot—not only was he still a virgin, he had not even. . . .

Oh, what the hell. He looked down at his ring. What the hell. Why not? He turned on the power and in a flash he saw into her mind. "How cute he looks," said the mind of Elaine Goldner. "Why doesn't he ask me to dance?" it kept repeating. "Is my hair all right?" it asked itself.

Eliot shook his head in wonderment and dragged his body up from the chair. Why didn't it want to move? Didn't his body hear what his head now knew? Apparently not, because as he walked over toward Elaine, it—Eliot's body—moved him right past her, making it look as though he had gotten up to go to the bathroom or something.

Eliot found himself walking away from Elaine. In order not to appear too ridiculous, he went over to the bar and ordered a Canadian Club and soda. Then, in a flash of inspiration, he ordered another as well. How suave it would be if he went over with a drink for her and used it to start a conversation—something like, "We used to like the same kind of ice cream." Pretty darned good.

Incredibly, he sailed back toward her table and his body took him past her again.

And there he stood back at his own table, facing away from Elaine Goldner and into the uncomprehending eyes of his mother, who asked him, quite reasonably, "Why are you holding two drinks, Eliot?"

Instead of answering his mother, he quickly downed one drink and then the other. A warm flush immediately spread through him, and as he waited for the alcohol to bring him some courage, he noted, almost impassively, that the power was still operating. Elaine Goldner's mind was spread out before him, and he saw nothing in it to make him feel the least fear of her. On the contrary, *she* was afraid of *him*! What really struck Eliot, however, was the fact that knowing all this about her had absolutely no effect on his own behavior nor on his own feelings of fear. Using the power to read other people's minds no longer involved his feelings at all. So this was where Blake had been leading him!

The alcohol began to do its work. Eliot spun around and marched toward Elaine. His blood was roaring in his ears as he stopped in front of her.

"Hi," he said.

She pretended to be surprised and pretended to need a few seconds to recognize him.

"Eliot!" she said. "How wonderful to see you again!"

The band was playing "You Are," one of his favorites.

> You are
> The promised blush of springtime
> That makes the lonely winter seem long
> ... etc.

Sweet emotions began churning inside him as he stared down at Elaine's breasts and as the image of Robert Mitchum lent him added courage.

Looking back later, Eliot realized that his big mistake was trying to be like Robert Mitchum. He should have just pulled up a chair and chatted with Elaine instead of recklessly asking her to dance. But that was exactly what he did, and as she graciously excused herself from the table of relatives, Eliot noted with horror that he still had the toilet paper glued right under his nose! With a swift movement of the hand he pulled it off, but he could tell from the tingling sensation that the cut was not yet entirely healed. Would it start bleeding again or wouldn't it? And if it did, would he know? Gone was Robert Mitchum and there remained only poor Eliot Appleman stuck with a beautiful woman in his arms, his brain invaded by L'Heure Bleu perfume, his legs wobbling with social insecurity, his chest and loins aching from the sentimentality of the music, his ego driving in crazy circles around the possibility that at any moment he would start bleeding under the nose.

All went well for about ten seconds. He had managed to absorb the current of electricity that passed into him when he touched her soft bare back and her equally soft, warm bare arm. He absorbed the sight of her apple-red lips so close to him and the way she looked right into his eyes. But when she pressed herself against him, he knew he was defeated. The song's lyrics started spinning in his head:

> You are the angel glow
> That lights a star
> The dearest things I know
> Are what you are
> ... etc.

For a moment, Robert Mitchum returned, accompanied now by John Wayne and Cary Grant, but they were like voices from a distant shore. Not all the self-assured Hollywood images in the universe could weigh against the forces of tumescence between his legs. Embarrassed beyond measure, Eliot tried to put some distance between his lower body and Elaine's, while his legs clumped up and down in no discernible rhythm or pattern. To add to Eliot's confusion, as if that were possible, Elaine had started conversing about her viola studies—something about her summer work with the concertmaster of the Boston Symphony, whatever the hell a concertmaster was.

Then came the *coup de grâce*. As he tried to at least catch the gist of her cool, but rapid-fire chattering about quartets, trios, Schuberts, and Tanglewoods—whatever the hell a Tanglewood was—and as he lumbered around the dance floor trying to keep his stridently erect sexual organ from touching her body, without appearing to those around him as some kind of arthritic cripple, Elaine boldly squeezed her body against him, all the while conversing about chamber music in general and now Palestrina in particular.

Eliot's eyes bulged as he stared right into Elaine's face, which maintained its cool, detached expression while her lower body, as though it had a life and mind of its own, rotated against his sex. As an added shock, Eliot suddenly realized that he and Elaine were not actually dancing at all, but just standing there, rubbing. At that point, the music ended.

And then started up again. This time the song was another killer, "Long Ago and Far Away":

> Long ago and far away,
> I dreamed a dream one day
> And now
> That dream is here before me
> . . . etc.

Swimming in sexual agony and romantic longing, Eliot allowed his left hand gradually to slide down Elaine's back to the topmost rise of her rear end. As though from out of nowhere, her own hand grabbed his arm and brusquely jerked it upward. And when Eliot oh so tentatively suggested that they might perhaps sneak away for a little while, she pretended not to hear it at all. She had now moved on to other lofty topics such as the cultural life of New York, even as her thigh slid in between Eliot's legs.

Although still a virgin, Eliot was, like all of his contemporaries, extremely well-versed in the theoretical and hypothetical aspects of the sexual act. Surely, he thought, this was the moment in his life to finally lose his virginity, and this was the woman. But was she willing? What else could it mean that she was dancing like this? But then why was she resisting all his moves? Her thoughts were an open book to Eliot. How come it made no difference? He could see that she wanted to go off with him somewhere; he could even see the image she had in her mind of the two of them walking hand in hand by some pretty little lake. Where was this? New York? Central Park? But each time that she resisted his advances, he became paralyzed. He even saw that her talking was only a screen for feelings that she was afraid of. But it made no goddamn difference; seeing this had no goddamn effect on his behavior. Eliot was disgusted with himself and with his so-called "power."

Mercifully, the band stopped and took a break. But—shit! — what was that he was tasting? It was blood! His goddamn shaving cut had opened and it was bleeding down onto his lips. This was the last straw. Eliot felt like an absolute fool. Never in recorded history had anyone made such an asshole of himself. He could practically hear a chorus of Hollywood actors, such as Robert Mitchum, Humphrey Bogart, Clark Gable, and John Wayne, laughing at him from the sidelines.

He stood there helplessly with Elaine still in his arms. His embarrassment about the shaving cut took his attention away from his lower body, however, and that particular problem quickly became smaller. The dancers began leaving the floor.

Then, like the Lone Ranger galloping in from out of the pages of history, the words of Max Falkoner came to him, words which had once before helped him out of a jam: "When you make a mistake, really make it!" Eliot slowly, very, very slowly took his hand from around Elaine's waist, touched his cut, and gravely stared at the blood on his fingertips. Out of the corner of his eye, he noted that Elaine, who had suddenly stopped talking, was looking at him with an expression of puzzlement and the beginnings of concern. Good. Eliot remained in his place and began intentionally to breathe harder. He did not move a muscle, except for allowing a slight tremor to appear in the hand that was still clasping hers. He waited. They were now almost alone on the floor.

Finally, she said in a soft whisper. "Eliot, what is it? What's the matter?"

He had his story already made up. He had a bleeding disease—hemophilia. He had caught the disease a few months ago and now faced serious consequences with the slightest wound. He knew, of course, that hemophilia was not a contagious disease, but so what. Chances were Elaine knew nothing about it and besides, who said he had to explain anything at all? Hadn't Max once said, "Never apologize; never explain"?

Eliot disengaged his hand from Elaine's and slowly walked toward the exit door. Elaine followed close behind.

Outside, a spectacular sunset filled the air with a beautiful light. The drab row houses seemed to glow from within. A huge orange moon hung low at one end of the narrow street and a huge orange sun at the other. It was like a world with two suns, as in a fairy tale. For a strange moment, Eliot did not know which was the sun and which was the moon.

The late summer air was thick and balmy, but directly above, the clear, cloudless blue sky was autumnal; the first stars were just coming out. Eliot and Elaine slowly walked together without speaking. They walked for several blocks until the sky turned dark and the street lights came on, one by one. All during the walk, Eliot could think of only one thing—how to find a place where he could be alone with Elaine.

Finally, they came to Thirtieth Street. Across the broad, busy thoroughfare, atop a short, steep rise, sat the big Fairmount Park Reservoir. When the traffic light changed, he took her hand and led her hurriedly through the aisle of automobile headlights and up the grassy rise to the reservoir. There, behind the tall chain fence, the water stretched out before them, a shimmering surface reflecting the full low moon that now dominated the sky.

Scores of people were strolling along the gravel path that circled the huge reservoir, but Eliot remembered that at the southernmost end there was a little stone park guard house where they used to play when they were kids. He remembered that it was always unoccupied after sundown. If they kept walking, they would soon come to it.

Elaine had begun talking again, but Eliot was not listening to her. In the bright moonlight, she was even more beautiful, her naked shoulders and partially bared bosom plunging into red velvet even more inviting, her streaming black hair even more like a magical night forest. Her perfume contained them in a cloud of flowers that mingled with the pungent late summer smells of the oak and sycamore trees that lined the path. The sounds of the traffic down below merged in the air and hung still like the roar of a nearby waterfall. All about them, fireflies blinked on and off.

Eliot stopped at the park guard house. It was exactly as he remembered it from his childhood: a small cubical structure of concrete blocks covered with green moss and overhung by the heavy boughs of an enormous pine tree. Although the wooden door was locked at night, as children they had discovered that the top half of the rear window could be knocked down with a sharp blow and, by standing on the big rock that was set against the back wall, one could easily clamber through the window.

They both laughed as Eliot went through the exercise of climbing into the structure and opening the door from inside. Elaine stood at the doorway, and Eliot held out his hand to her.

Inside, it was also as Eliot remembered, a tiny space about eight feet square with a low ceiling, in the center of which was a wire-protected light socket that never had a bulb in it. Pine needles still blanketed the floor and were strewn over the narrow metal table against the rear wall. The same broken wooden swivel chair stood in the corner under an old metal telephone housing from which the telephone itself had long since been ripped away, leaving two pairs of blackened wire conduit tubes dangling like plucked flower stems. He had once cut his finger on those conduits.

The moonlight poured in through the open window. The air was musty and still hot from the day's exposure to sunlight, but the space was immediately filled with Elaine's perfume. She laughed nervously and said something about their childhood, which Eliot interpreted as an invitation to embrace her. But when he did so, she turned her head away and pushed against his chest.

Eliot stepped back and began to apologize, but she showed no signs of wanting to leave. Instead, she sat on top of the table where the moonlight caught her from behind, outlining her shape in a dusty gold light. To Eliot, she was the most beautiful, alluring woman he had ever seen, and he went up to her again and tried to kiss her. She shook her head again and started talking. He sat on the table next to her and put his arm around her; she moved it away, and then laughed—a girlish giggle. Again, he pulled her toward him and they both tilted backward against the wall.

He had not even been thinking of using the power, but it had never really turned off and he saw her imagining them kissing. So he went for her again and, to his amazement, he found himself tearing at her dress. She shrieked and tried to fight him off, but he went on. His head was filled with her smell and the sight of her breasts. He didn't know who he was. He had never behaved this way with a girl and . . . it wasn't so bad, it wasn't so difficult. It was a little like facing down Zero Zaretsky.

By now, he was boiling inside from touching her. He reached his hands everywhere and when she jumped from the table, he grabbed her and wrestled her down to the pine needles. And then, without, it seemed, even choosing to do so, he turned to the power that Blake had spoken about, the power to make other people think what one wanted them to think, and to do what one wanted them to do. He projected into her mind his own image of them lying naked on the floor and with all his strength willed that she comply. Suddenly, she started crying as Eliot removed her clothes and then pushed off his shoes and clumsily removed his pants and underwear.

She looked at him with a crazy light in her eyes and, for a moment, she seemed grotesque to him—her mouth wide open, tears streaming down her cheeks, the soft moonlight illuminating her breasts, thighs and dark, electric sex. He had never seen a naked woman before. He did not even know exactly—precisely—what to do. But he kept projecting the erotic image into her mind, and although she went on sobbing and shaking her head, she spread her legs wide open, her fingers scratching at the thick layer of pine needles under them.

He rolled on top of her, moaning her name, and closed his eyes. Before he could enter her, it was over. He opened his eyes and looked down at her. She seemed wasted; her features seemed strewn aimlessly around her face. She was quietly sobbing and shivering.

And the power was still on. For the first time in months, its after-effects shattered him—as strongly as they had done before his apprenticeship with Blake. He saw her in New York in a small dormitory room practicing her music late at night; he saw her kneeling by her bed praying to God that she succeed; he saw her riding in a car with another man, an older man who made advances to her, his hand on her thigh. She turned him away and he persisted. Eliot felt disgust for him. He saw Elaine at her desk writing letters to her father who worried about her all alone in New York; he saw her feeling lonely and frightened seated in an orchestra in a country setting on a summer night. He could feel her thoughts, of how she loved the music, the man conducting the orchestra. . . . He saw her standing naked in front of a mirror in the same country setting. He tried to turn away from that image, but it followed him and he found himself staying with it and growing excited again.

He pushed himself off of Elaine and hurriedly covered her with her clothes.

"I'm sorry," he said, sitting down next to her.

But the power was not finished with him, he knew that. He made a move to touch the skull ring, to protect himself, but he stopped in mid-air. He did not want to be protected. Who or what was he? He desperately wanted to understand what had happened. Using the new dimensions of the power, he had harmed someone. Why?

He felt compelled to stand, hastily put on his clothes, and then bent down to touch Elaine's forehead.

"I'll go outside," he said, "and let you get dressed."

He stood outside the guardhouse door while the effects of the power poured into him. He saw the face of another woman, older, serene. Yes . . . it was the face of Irene. But her voice was different than he remembered.

"You will never understand," it said, "until you choose. You want to understand before you choose. That is no longer possible."

PART 4

THE BOWL OF FIRE

THE ANNUAL SHOW

A cold November morning. The day of the Annual Show. Eliot awakened to darkness. Troubling dreams he could not remember hung over him like an oppressive cloud as he dressed.

No one else was awake yet. He made coffee and sat at the kitchen table staring out the window as he drank it. The sky was becoming gray, and he saw that it had begun to rain. Eliot thought back to the time, exactly a year ago, that he first met the Sorcerer's Apprentices. It had been a day just like this—a cold rain stripping the last brown leaves from the trees. But he felt like a different person now.

It wasn't only that he had just passed his sixteenth birthday. It was more than that; he felt that something down deep inside him had changed, and not even his nervousness about the show tonight could distract him from thinking about it. He had resigned himself to doing what Blake had ordered him to do in the show. The power would do the work for him as it always did. He would go along with it all. So, for the moment, he put that out of his mind. He sipped his coffee and continued to wonder what had happened to him.

The work with Max Falkoner had left him confident of his mastery of the linking rings, but it had also made him see how helpless he was in the face of everything life threw at him. He had taken up magic out of a dream of power, yet now he felt more powerless than ever. He knew that was the truth, and he didn't want to escape from it. He knew that with Max he had been touched by some elusive force that gave him hope when it was there. But he could not bring it about by himself when he was away from Max, and this depressed him.

He had felt this way ever since the experience with Elaine. It seemed that now he had something he had to pay for, to make up for. But he did not know with what coin. And it was getting heavier, this sense of accountability. He had used the new power a number of times since Elaine. Or, rather, he had been used by it, since it had always appeared without his intentionally choosing it. He felt oppressed by getting so many things he thought he wanted, by people suddenly doing what he wanted them to do. All this only increased his feelings of accountability. He knew that, by grasping the ring, he could ward off this sense of remorse. But he did not want to protect himself anymore. He sensed that somehow this painful feeling was his only link to reality.

When he had confessed to Max about Elaine, he had expected at the very least a reprimand of some kind, something that would accentuate his own sense of failure. Max had only looked at him with kind, impartial eyes and said, "I'm very glad, Eliot." Why? What was he glad about? And immediately he had put Eliot through a fiercely demanding session with the rings, which left Eliot feeling he was a beginner again. It now dawned on Eliot that Max favored anything that could bring him a sense of remorse about himself— not guilt, not regret, not passionate vows to do better next time, all of which Max dismissed in no uncertain terms. Only remorse about what he was, with no possibility of doing anything about it, but only feeling it more and more.

Blake, it was clear, had been taking him in an opposite direction. Eliot had not told Blake about Elaine or about anything important at all, not for a long time. And Blake did not require it of him. Eliot told himself he would see it all through, play the game, until the Annual Show and then quit the club and cut his ties to Blake. But now he feared he would not have the strength to do this. Although the automatic use of the power brought him only momentary pleasure followed by a feeling of hollowness, he could neither choose to turn away from it nor could he turn it toward himself, as happened sometimes under Max's guidance.

He did not understand what Blake really wanted. But now, having finished his coffee and feeling more alert, he turned his thoughts to the main thing that had been troubling him. Last night, at the final dress rehearsal, Blake showed his own act, which was sensational. And Blake's work with the linking rings was unbelievably good—even the Sorcerers were fooled by it. Eliot knew his own work was good, but it paled next to Blake's routine. And the concluding trick, the fire-bowl production, was breathtaking, awesome. Blake swirled the great scarlet scarf bearing the insignia of the Sorcerer's Apprentices, and out of thin air a blazing fire leapt high from a burnished copper bowl. Yes, that was the magic Eliot had dreamed of. Why did his own real magic seem so pale in comparison, so complicated with the sorrows and disappointments of ordinary life?

But it was not Blake's act or even his work with the linking rings that troubled Eliot most. He had expected it would be magnificent—had it not been the principal thing that had drawn him toward the Sorcerers at the last Annual Show? Then, Blake, costumed as a Hindu pasha, with a great bejeweled turban, had ended the show by drawing flowers and living birds from out of the air so that the curtain came down on a wondrous magically materialized garden with Blake, the smiling, radiant lord of this creation, bowing low to thundering applause. Eliot had sat in the back rows with his mouth agape.

No, what troubled him now was what Blake had asked of him just as the rehearsal was breaking up. He had taken Eliot aside, and full of light and laughter, he had expressed confidence in Eliot's ability to carry off his act. And then, very casually, almost as an aside, he said, "You must compel Max Falkoner to come on the stage during my finale and serve me. I want him to acknowledge me in front of everyone—*everyone!*" Blake held his gracefully clefted lips in a beneficent smile, but his eyes bored into Eliot's soul. In that look, Eliot saw that Blake knew about the work he had done with Max, and he saw that he, Eliot, was meant to be a pawn in Blake's rivalry with Max. With those words, Blake had turned aside and gone back to the others.

Eliot would have treated it as some kind of joke had it not been for the way Blake had looked at him. Of course, to obey Blake was out of the question, but now Eliot was troubled and afraid. He had seen that he really had no control over his power, especially not its new dimensions. He would rather die than be an instrument in the humiliation of Max or the exaltation of Blake over Max. His reason told him such a thing could not happen. But still he was afraid.

*

After breakfast, Eliot put on a warm sweater under a hooded poncho and spent the morning walking in the park, by the Wissahickon Creek, where it was most like a forest. He was glad to be away from people and from magic for a while.

He loved this part of the park. The creek was wide and strong, especially today with the rain falling. He was enthralled by the water as it rushed over and between the boulders strewn in the creek. He loved the bare branches of the trees shrouded in mist, the thick mat of wet leaves underfoot, the somber black-green of the dripping pines and fir trees, the brilliant white shafts of the birches.

What had become of him? What world was he living in? What had the world of people to do with this magnificence of nature? How was it that nature was always beautiful, always right, no matter what she did, and the world of people always wrong?

In the distance there was a flash of lightning and, after a pause, thunder. Then silence. Eliot stopped walking and stood listening. He listened to the rain, to the barking of a crow somewhere. He began to feel cold, but only on the skin; inside himself he was warm. He listened. He remembered the silence of the planetarium. This silence, so full of sounds, was even deeper.

He began to walk again, listening to the sounds his feet made as they fell on the leaves, breaking twigs. He listened to his own breathing. Again lightning and thunder, a little closer, a little louder. The rain was becoming heavier, stronger, louder. And yet the silence was growing, too.

Continuing in this inner state, Eliot walked toward where the Wissahickon broadened out before flowing into the Schuylkill River, and paused under the great span of the Henry Avenue Bridge.

Sheltered in the cold dank shadow of the bridge, he listened also to the automobile traffic far above. It seemed to him also part of nature.

Under the bridge, the sound of the Wissahickon became a roar, but somehow it only drew him further into himself, as though he were listening to his own blood moving through his body. He walked on muddy gravel to the edge of the creek, until the rushing water nearly touched his shoes. The water was very rapid, very clear, and black. He bent his head and watched it.

He wondered why Max had allowed him to go so far with Blake, why he hadn't ordered him to break his ties with Blake. Thinking this, but still listening to everything around him, he slowly removed the skull ring from his finger and held it over the water. He held his arm outstretched until he began to feel pain and to sense the kind of struggle in which Max had guided him. Minutes passed, five, ten minutes. He recalled Max saying, "Search for those special muscles, Eliot, search, search!"

He closed his eyes from the pain and weariness. His breathing was coming harder and then, suddenly it turned very quiet, very silent. He felt that he was being breathed by silence, and he sensed that special quality of light inside him. His attention was drawn toward the light, and all his large muscles relaxed. A fine sensation of energy welled up from his abdomen and spread evenly through his body. He let go of the ring. It fell into the water and glimmered once. He watched it tumble and roll as the rushing current pushed it downstream and quickly swallowed it. Eliot slowly lowered his arm and turned toward home.

*

The rain had fallen the whole day, but had begun to let up as Eliot arrived at Pennypack Hall. It was almost dark, and had turned quite cold. It might even snow, although it was only mid-November. Eliot entered the old, run-down theatre by the stage door and was glad to see that he was the first one there. It was only just five o'clock and the show was not scheduled to start until eight.

He found his way to the dressing room and switched on the bright bare overhead light. The room was tiny, with a large cracked mirror on one wall, dark yellow paint peeling everywhere.

There was one rickety hard-backed chair in the room and two red buckets labeled FIRE and filled with lumpy sand. He took off his wet trenchcoat, hung it up on a metal wall rack and carefully set his bag next to the buckets.

He looked at himself in the mirror. He was wearing his navy blue Jacob Reed three-piece gabardine suit and his favorite red, white, and blue striped tie. He then hunted for the stage, passing by numerous other buckets, coiled ropes, and barrels in the narrow, dimly-lit backstage area.

Eliot stood behind the heavy, threadbare curtain and looked up the long ropes at the sandbag weights near the top. His job during the first two acts would be to manage the curtain, and he studied the way the ropes were wound around the side posts. Everything smelled old, felt old, looked old. His hands got dirty touching everything.

He found a bathroom and washed his hands in the cold, rusty water that came choking out of the faucet. There were no towels. He went back to the stage and wiped his hands on the curtain.

When he stepped in front of the curtain, his heart started pounding. He looked at his watch. Two and a half hours to go. He stood in the center of the stage and picked out the seat he had occupied a year ago at the last Annual Show. "What is time?" he thought. He had the eerie feeling that he was still sitting out there and yet he was here, too, now one of the performers. He did not remember the theatre seats being so dilapidated.

The first Sorcerers to arrive were Edgar Wick and Gordon Bunche, who announced their presence with some raucous noise that Eliot could hear even before they entered from the back of the theatre. One of them had dropped something, and Gordon was yelling and coughing his terrifying spasmodic cough. They came down the aisle with the bulbous-nosed Gordon Bunche bent backwards carrying the orange-lacquered guillotine. Wick slithered behind wearing a black Chesterfield coat with a velvet collar and carrying a black leather suitcase that contained the black art props. Eliot stayed in his place at center stage as they noisily made their way backstage and began setting up.

Stillman Clipper, the president of the club, padded briskly down the aisle next, accompanied by the bearlike Don Papermaster, the mathematical whiz. Clipper greeted Eliot and placed his elegant attaché case on the piano that stood off to the side just below the proscenium. He opened the case and took out several stacks of programs and tickets. Before Eliot could go over to him, he came to Eliot and gave him a queer look as he matter-of-factly handed him a program. Eliot was surprised to see his name last with no mention of Blake. Apparently, Blake intended the "materializing" of his Egyptian priest persona to be some kind of big surprise for the audience. Sure, thought Eliot, why not? Good idea.

Next down the aisle came the "Monte Carlo Boys," Joe Ferrante and Kim Vogel, skipping merrily, their chests jutting out, their heads turning to either side like a pair of small, energetic birds. Ferrante, the chief clown of the two, had red paper streamers hanging out of his mouth like long worms. He jumped on the stage and knelt histrionically before Eliot, saying, "Hail, O Master!" and then pranced off backstage with Vogel.

Next came the escape artist, Sandy Hyman, sidling diagonally down the aisle carrying a heavy canvas sack filled with his chains and other escape apparatus. He wore a giant plaid overcoat two sizes too big for him and was sweating. His head was tilted back at its customary alarming angle. He was some kind of yappy puppy dog. He regarded Eliot sideways and chattered out some incomprehensible greeting. Then he moved on.

Next came Ben Schulweis, "Benngali" in person, charging down the aisle like a bull, followed closely by the frail, floating crane, Terry Laken, "The Great Lakini." After them, good old Wally Pound paced thoughtfully down the aisle, his fruity pipe giving off billows of blue smoke. He came to the stage, looked up at Eliot like a faithful steed and said, "How are you feeling? Nervous?" Eliot gazed down, feeling great love for him. He nodded his head, yes. Wally Pound trotted away.

Eliot sat on the edge of the stage while the other Sorcerers busied themselves with their apparatus. Much noise came from backstage, always punctuated by the howling, hyena-like cough of Gordon Bunche. Suddenly, Eliot felt a cold shiver. He looked down the still-darkened aisle and saw the eyes of Ronnie Pitkin. He was standing there, looking at him from out of the darkness. Slowly, gracefully, Ronnie emerged into the single spotlight, which was still the only illumination in the theatre. He glided like a great cat, his camel's hair coat, as always, dramatically draped over his shoulders, his silky blond hair falling handsomely to the side, partly covering his forehead. Eliot averted his glance from Ronnie's brilliant eyes, so full of hatred in a face of such extraordinary good looks. As Ronnie silently passed by, Eliot felt his vibration.

An hour and a half to go. Eliot sat on the stage going over in his mind the routine that Blake had planned for him. He heard a creaking sound and turned his head to see the curtain being drawn behind him. And there behind the curtain stood Blake, dressed in a gray suit with elegantly curved lapels, his cuffs glistening with the big silver masks of comedy and tragedy. His costume was draped over one arm. With his other hand he stroked his chin, while he looked upward examining the placement of the spotlights. Instinctively, Eliot concealed the bare fingers of his right hand. Blake glanced down at Eliot and smiled at him. It gave Eliot a strange sensation to see Blake now standing on a stage, as though he were only an actor in a play.

In and around the dressing room there was pandemonium. The box office had just opened and there was only an hour to go before the show began. The Sorcerers were changing clothes, stuffing body-loads, pouring liquids into plastic shells, checking latches, magnets, pins, and rubberbands on their varied apparatus, preparing decks of cards, ropes, and silk scarves, and setting up their tables. Each of the Sorcerers was playing his role: Ben Schulweis and the "Monte Carlo Boys" were horsing around, snapping wisecracks; Gordon Bunche and Edgar Wick were quarreling; Clipper was busy making order and smoothing things over; Don Papermaster was examining his complicated mechanical apparatus; Terry Laken was making flowing gestures with his silks; Sandy Hyman was jumping up and down, loudly complaining about everything.

Blake was not with them. He was somewhere else changing into his elaborate costume, but when he appeared in the dressing room, a hush fell over the whole assembly. Ronnie Pitkin appeared and leaned elegantly against the doorpost. Sandy Hyman's mouth fell open. The "Monte Carlo Boys" stood still. Bennie Schulweis said, "Wow!" Wally Pound puffed energetically on his unlit pipe. Bunche and Wick stopped squabbling.

Eliot was electrified by what he saw. It was not so much the robe and tunic and the jewelry Blake wore, spectacular though they were—shimmering white silk reaching down to the floor, bordered by an intricate olive and rust Egyptian pattern of interlocking lotus leaves upon which rested a huge, breathtaking inlaid breastplate representing the great eye of Horus held by an awesomely winged vulture. Nor was it the extraordinary white headdress curved in an elongated single bulb and starkly decorated with a black ibis. Truly, Blake appeared to be the incarnation of an ancient priest or pharaoh, especially as he stood tall and erect with the regal bearing of a great prince. No, it was not the costume that stunned Eliot; it was Blake's whitened face, rouged clefted lips and startling sharp black shadows painted under his eyes. It was the very face Eliot had seen in the vision on his first night at Blake's house—the second vision in which the power revealed Blake's ambitions and lies! But the face that vision revealed was of a man exposed and defeated; this, however, was the face of triumph and power.

"I only wanted to remind you all what we are aiming for," Blake began, as the Sorcerers gathered closer around him. "We are here to amaze and confound. The audience wants to be fooled, don't forget that. They are not your enemy; they are for you. They want you to succeed. Remember that! They will look where you want them to look; they will see what you want them to see—" here Blake gave Eliot an especially pointed glance "—and ultimately they will believe what you want them to believe. Don't imagine they have acute critical powers or insight into what you are concealing from them. They have nothing of the kind! They are fooled every day of their lives by the life they lead. They've come here to escape from their so-called reality. Make the most of it! You are all magicians in the making. You've practiced, worked hard. You know your techniques. Don't worry about that now. Pay attention to the audience, not to your technique. Woo them, romance them, let them laugh or gasp. Don't hesitate and don't be in a hurry. Let the timing unfold naturally. And remember, you're only beginning. There is much more I can teach you, much more! Do this well tonight and I promise you things you can't even imagine afterwards. I am proud of you all and I know Irene would be proud of you, proud of what she has transmitted to you through our club. Make us even prouder of you tonight! And . . . have fun, too!"

Blake laughed, and a loud cheer went up for him from the group. To his amazement, Eliot heard himself joining in the cheer! Immediately, however, Blake's face—or rather the face of the great priest—became gravely serious. Silence again, a thick, heavy silence. Blake stood there for a long minute without speaking while the Sorcerers remained frozen in their postures. Then, with great majesty and aplomb, Blake bowed deeply and, swirling his robe and tunic in a dazzling flourish, started out of the dressing room. He paused at the doorway, turned around and said to the hushed group, "You see? I romanced you. You see how easy it is?" And with that, he left.

*

The houselights had been turned on and, with about a half hour to go before the start of the show, Eliot took his post backstage by the curtain. Peering through the crack between the curtain and the wall, he saw that a scattering of people had already taken their seats. The theatre held about two hundred downstairs and another one hundred in the balcony, but tonight the balcony was closed. It hung so far forward that the audience could see things they weren't supposed to see, such as the contents of the black wells built into magician's tables, or the silks and artificial animals stuffed inside the hidden loads of the production boxes.

People were now filing in at a slow but steady pace—at first mainly mothers, fathers, brothers, and sisters. They occupied the first rows, and among them were Eliot's mother and father. But soon other people started coming in from the real outside world— strangers, genuine ticket buyers, who wanted something for their dollar. Eliot's heart started pounding again as he observed them taking their places. The theatre actually began to fill up.

There were many young people in the audience, but also a surprising number of adults. Eliot watched them carefully, studying their faces, even trying to hear their conversations. There seemed to be people of all kinds—well-dressed and not-so-well-dressed, elderly and middle-aged, Orientals, Negroes, some chattering animatedly, others silently studying the program. There were tall people and short people, attractive women and homely women, strong-looking men and clumsy-looking men. Over there, on the far aisle, were two very fat people, a man and a woman, squeezing into their seats in the fifth row. And there was a tall thin man in a soldier's uniform stepping over knees in the seventh or eighth row. And there was a woman carrying a sleeping baby in her arms.

Eliot could not make out the people occupying the darkened back rows, but what a turnout! It felt to him as though the whole world was in the audience.

Finally, Max Falkoner walked briskly down the aisle toward the seat reserved for him at the end of the third row. He eased his squat, solid body into the chair, crossed his legs and carefully examined the program. He seemed deadly serious. He looked up, swiveling his head to study the audience, and for an instant his strong dark eyes passed by the crack in the curtain where Eliot stood watching him. Eliot knew he had been seen. It gave him strength.

Bearlike Don Papermaster was standing next to him manning the lights, and behind him was Kim Vogel at the phonograph. Wally Pound, the first act, was standing stiff as a post a few feet away. Everyone was looking at their watches. Sandy Hyman came rushing toward them pointing at his watch, which he had taken off his wrist, for some obscure reason having to do with the urgency of the situation. Then Clipper, the president, appeared. "We're sold out!" he said in a loud whisper. He motioned Papermaster to dim the lights and signaled to Eliot. The curtain rose. The audience was hushed. The show began.

It was a good audience, a fine audience. Wally's first trick went wrong—he dropped one of his multiplying golf balls, which bounced off the stage, but he kept his aplomb and finished well. Eliot congratulated him as Sandy Hyman, breathing heavily and sweating profusely, stood by, tensely waiting to go on with his escape act. Curtain up—Sandy bounded on, had himself tangled up in loud clanging chains and managed to escape. Curtain down.

Curtain up, curtain down, curtain up. End of first segment. Generous applause. Ten minute break. Lights on, off. Next segment. Curtain up—Wick and Bunche pulled it off—although the audience did not realize until the end that the black art routine was not meant to be a comedy act. Chastened, the audience then failed to grasp right away that Ben Schulweis's all-my-tricks-go-wrong act *was* meant as comedy. All right, no problem, applause. Curtain up, down, up, down. The audience was great. Max applauded respectfully. End of second segment. Lights on. Ten minute break. Eliot was now trembling violently on the outside, strangely calm in his head. The heart within his breast walloped him like a jackhammer. The third segment was about to begin. Changing of the guard at the curtain. Eliot stepped aside to allow Ronnie Pitkin by.

Ronnie passed without looking at Eliot, and once again Eliot felt the vibrations of his hatred. But what was that on Ronnie's hand? How had he never noticed it before? Ronnie was wearing a gold skull ring! Suddenly, Eliot froze with a sense of fear that had nothing to do with his nervousness.

Watching Ronnie going through his mentalist routines, Eliot could not stop thinking about the ring on Ronnie's hand. What did it mean? Did Ronnie have the same special relationship to Blake as he, Eliot, did? Or perhaps—was Ronnie there before Eliot? Perhaps—perhaps—"My God," thought Eliot, "was Ronnie told the same things? Did Blake make him also believe that he was that 'special person'?"

Of course. It must be something like that. A cold shiver passed through Eliot, a sense that Blake's actions had a much broader scale than he had thought. This would explain why Ronnie hated him so much.

But then another thought, even more terrifying, occurred to him. What of Ronnie's coldness, his strange absence of feeling, almost like that of a zombie? He who seemed to have so much—such good looks, such aplomb, such success with women? Had Blake—how to say it—"sucked" something out of him?

Eliot's mind continued to race as Ronnie's act rolled on, coming to its conclusion—then, thought Eliot, then . . . where . . . what of the power? Where did it come from? Who or what gave it to him?

Who or what *was* Blake? What of the image he had seen in Ronnie's mind—that dead girl, that horrible cold pain in Ronnie's mind? Did Ronnie once also have the power, and did he go too far with it with some woman who was drawn to him? Didn't he have Max to help him? Or did he simply not *want* the kind of help Max offered?

Suddenly, as he watched Ronnie, Eliot saw again the image of the dead girl that Ronnie carried in his mind, but this time without being affected by Ronnie's fear. He saw that the girl was not dead at all! It was all a creation of Ronnie's fear. What had he done to her? Did he *want* her dead? Eliot saw Ronnie quivering and then running away from the girl, this woman who was older than he—he who was only a little older than Eliot himself, after all. Unsure of himself, after all!

Eliot remembered his second vision of Blake—the melting, dripping face. He remembered the recorded words of Irene—"even secrets are not what they seem," even the reality behind the appearances was only another appearance. Engulfed by confusion, he desperately peered again through the crack between the curtain and the wall. He needed to see Max, just to see him sitting there.

But Max's seat was now empty! And Ronnie's act had ended to great applause. Wally Pound had lowered the curtain. Eliot must now begin his own performance. As Ronnie walked by him, Eliot understood that what he had perceived as strength in Ronnie was only fear. He had the impulse to reach out and touch Ronnie. But Ronnie coldly passed by before he could act on it.

Just as Eliot prepared to go on stage, Blake, standing tall and majestic in his extraordinary costume, appeared beside him, as though from out of nowhere. His rouged, clefted lips were curved in a deep, V-shaped smile, and a musky, flowery scent surrounded him. He looked intently into Eliot's eyes, took hold of his right hand, and slipped another gold skull ring on his finger.

*

Eliot was now on stage. The curtain was rising and he was momentarily blinded by the proscenium lights. But even as his eyes adjusted, he saw no one; he was afraid to look at any faces. His thighs trembled, and as he started to speak, he heard his voice quivering. He didn't know where to look. He focused on a point in between him and the rows of faces in the audience.

"May I have a volunteer, please?" he said, too softly. He waited. No one stepped forward.

"A volunteer please!" he said in a louder, quivering voice.

A red-haired teen-age boy, about his own age, emerged from the audience and leaped athletically onto the stage, laughing back, to some comrades in the audience. Eliot was already reading his mind, without even intending to.

"This will be very simple," said Eliot, his voice growing calmer. "Very easy, very miraculous," he went on, improvising his patter. He positioned the boy directly to his side and looked at him. Out of the corner of his eye, he saw Blake standing in the wings watching carefully, his pharaonic face knotted in concentration. Eliot turned his eyes away from Blake and toward the audience. He now began to discern faces. Through the lights, he saw his mother and father smiling proudly in the first row.

Both boys were now facing the audience. Eliot saw the volunteer's name. *Wes.* An unusual name. Good.

"All right, Wes," he said, "—that *is* your name, isn't it?" And the moment he said that, Eliot saw the boy's full name: Wellesley McQuade. "Or, Mr. McQuade, do you prefer to be called Wellesley?"

The boy was visibly startled. He smiled in wonderment, first at Eliot and then out to his companions somewhere in the audience.

Eliot now felt stronger. He saw the names of the boy's friends. "Your friends Jamie, Danzy and Hank do call you Wes, don't they?"

The boy again dropped his jaw and nodded yes, looking out toward the audience and shrugging his shoulders in disbelief.

"All right, Wes, suppose we try our little experiment in thought transference." Gone from Eliot was every trace of fear and nervousness. He now felt very strong indeed. His body was charged with pleasurable excitement. He felt in complete control. He felt the attention of the whole audience—hundreds of people of all kinds looking at him with admiring anticipation. He felt he had them all in the palm of his hand.

Eliot went on. "I want you to think of something that only you could know about. Something that you have not told anyone, except perhaps your friends out there. . . ." The moment Eliot mentioned the boy's friends, he felt a strange sort of vertigo. It quickly passed and he remained calm.

He continued. "Yes . . . that's it. Your recent report card at school, Germantown High School, isn't it? Yes . . . that's it. I promise that I won't reveal anything to embarrass you, but I do think you ought to apply yourself to your algebra in the next few weeks. . . ." By now, the boy was completely transfixed. He had stopped looking out toward his friends. His eyes had lowered. "Of course, you deserve congratulations," said Eliot, "on your grades in gym and wood shop, and you are holding your own in English and history. But that recent algebra test was a real disaster and the upcoming French exam also has you pretty worried. Of course, track practice takes a lot of your time, but I'm sure the coach, Mr. Boegershausen—or Bogie, as you all call him—will understand your situation. After all, you did clear six feet, two inches in the high jump practice this afternoon, so I'm sure he has confidence in you. . . ."

From the way the boy stood there without making a single gesture and without even looking up, from the way he practically ran off the stage when Eliot dismissed him, there could be no doubt in the audience's mind that Eliot's performance had been genuine. No confederate would have behaved that way. Eliot now stood alone on the stage, and after a moment's silence, there was a veritable explosion of applause.

As the applause died down, Eliot began the next routine, exactly as Blake had prescribed. Before doing so, he looked again to see if Max had returned, but his seat was still empty. This troubled Eliot, but did not lessen the exhilaration he was feeling. He began the patter about the uniqueness of the next experiment—each member of the audience would be asked to write down a number and then to stand up, one by one, while the magician announced the number they had chosen.

While the audience was writing down their numbers, Eliot sat down on the single chair at the rear of the stage and histrionically feigned deep concentration. In fact, however, he was feeling that wave of vertigo again, as well as a little nausea. But it soon passed.

He stood, returned to center stage, and proceeded to unreel the numbers as each person stood: 4, 1287, 5,243,681, 00, 176–47–8810 (someone's Social Security number, apparently), 851–9974 (a phone number?), 5711 (the year according to the Jewish calendar), 99.99, and so on and on—men, women, kids, seat after seat, row after row.

With a brilliant stroke of showmanship, Eliot asked each member of the audience to remain standing after he had called out their numbers. He had now almost completed the "experiment." As the people in the last rows stood one by one, Eliot read off their numbers without being able to see them. The vertigo came and went now with increasing frequency. He had never entered so many minds—however superficially—in one short period, and it must be this, he guessed, that was having some kind of effect on him.

Suddenly, as he moved quickly from one person to the next, he stopped cold. His legs began to tremble and a big wave of vertigo washed over him. Instead of some number, he saw the intensely vivid image of a face—the face was old and ravaged, ugly and full of pain. Then he realized: it was his own face!

Struggling to keep from falling, he managed to get to the chair, sat down, and tried to compose himself. He tried to make what was happening seem like part of the act. As the vertigo receded, he stood again and carried the chair to the front of the stage, sat down on it and, while going on with the act, squinted into the darkness at the rear of the theatre and tried to see the person whose mind had had such an effect on him. He could see nothing. Not only was it too dark there, but the whole audience was on their feet, blocking any possibility of his seeing that far back.

He had now almost completed the "experiment." Feeling stronger, he rose from the chair and squinted again into the darkened back rows. Still nothing. At that point, he decided to make a gesture of reading the last numbers by standing on the chair so that he could see the back row, and what he saw there shook him so profoundly that he immediately jumped down and sat again. He was certain that the person in the back row was none other than Irene Angel!

Summoning every ounce of his strength, he bowed from his chair, signaling to the audience that he had completed the task of reading everyone's mind. The audience, all standing in their places, burst into a deafening applause, and with the applause roaring in his ears, Eliot tried quickly to assimilate what he had seen—the person he had glimpsed in the last row. Could he be mistaken? Could his eyes have been playing tricks on him?

But he had no time to think further. Having exposed himself to the minds of every member of the audience, the aftereffects of the power now came flooding in upon him to an extent and with a force that far, far exceeded anything he had yet experienced. At first there was an extremely rapid succession of unconnected images: an old woman dying in a hospital bed, a fat man and woman making love in a motel, a little boy opening a birthday present, an airplane crashing, another man and woman viciously quarreling, a soldier killing another soldier, an elegantly dressed older man receiving an award at a banquet, a baby crying from hunger, a dog being killed by a car, a woman falling or jumping from a window ledge, another woman in jail screaming for a drug, a man masturbating, two teen-age boys winning a bowling trophy, a mother caring for a sick child, a man and woman standing by a graveside, weeping . . . and on and on, hundreds, thousands of images one after the other came faster and faster, each one stabbing at Eliot's feeling and senses, as though he were receiving all the experiences of humanity in one brief spurt of time.

But that was just the beginning. He began to see different parts of the world, places he did not recognize. He saw night scenes, morning scenes, he saw dusk and blazing sunshine, storms, fires, earthquakes, ocean waves, he saw jungles and desert wastes, all with people in them, he saw great cities, he heard strange languages, and all the kinds of sounds human beings can make— screams, sighs, groans, laughter, shouting, pleading, whining; and then, superimposed on all that, he saw the image of the planet earth itself, which he saw as a kind of green viscous sphere with people crawling on it like bugs; he saw wars, famine, revolutions; he saw crowds chanting, mobs rioting; he heard music of every kind; monuments being erected and destroyed; he saw and heard bombs exploding, he saw blood flowing, and soon all his senses were involved; he smelled, tasted things he had never known and did not know now. And in the midst of all that, he saw the starry sky as though this were all being experienced within the silent space of a planetarium. Yet it was not a planetarium. And the silence that surrounded it all was not enough to buffer the sense of sorrow and anguish he felt for the whole of this humanity. He reeled from the perception of planetary sorrow, violence, fear, and desire. He held tightly to the seat of his chair and tried to clear his eyes. He could not bear what he felt. Then he remembered the ring that Blake had slipped on his finger. He needed to protect himself; he could not stand this anymore. But he did not want to go that way again. He didn't want to be under Blake. There was no other way, however. He knew he would faint if these perceptions continued. He was seeing man on earth, but it was not some abstraction; it was deep in his guts and it was intolerable! This could not be the whole truth! And yet it was what the power was bringing him.

Slowly, his left hand reached over across his knees toward the ring on his right hand, which still clutched the chair. He could not stop it. It trembled as it crossed his knees and came closer to the skull ring.

He knew Blake was standing in the wings watching him. He would not look that way. And then, from the other side of the stage, he heard the voice of Max Falkoner. "Appleman, cut the shit! Pull yourself together and do some honest work!"

Eliot turned toward the voice and saw Max standing in the wings opposite from Blake. A cigarette was dangling from his lips, which were curved in their typical ironic smile, and in his hands he held a set of linking rings!

Eliot felt like a sleeper tearing himself out of a nightmare. As though fighting against an immense gravitational pull, he rose out of the chair and walked toward Max. He could sense Blake's eyes on his back. He kept his gaze on Max and the linking rings.

In what seemed like an eternity—but all of this was taking place within the space of minutes—he reached Max and took the linking rings from him. As he did, Max whispered to him, "Work, Eliot, search, wish! Nothing is stronger than that!"

Eliot returned to center stage. The power continued to pour sorrow into him—more and more perceptions of mankind in its suffering and bewilderment. But now he knew that instead of touching the skull ring, he must summon his attention and consciously place it on the linking rings. He was pulled, drawn as by a gravitational force, to protect himself from the effects of the power by touching the ring. But he knew he must choose to give his attention to the eight large steel rings he now held in his left hand, and especially to the key ring—the ring with the gap cut in the circumference—which allowed the other seven to move in and out of each other with apparently miraculous effect.

He started the routine, again and again, moment by moment choosing to attend to it instead of touching the skull. The sorrow spread through his body as the routine proceeded. The sorrow, the pain, became an intense sensation penetrating every tissue of his body as the linking rings clanged and glistened before the enraptured audience until suddenly, in a moment more extraordinary than anything he until now had experienced, he no longer felt it was he who was aware of these impressions and images that coursed through him. Suddenly, he himself was one of these images. He was no longer seeing; he was seen. The sensation brought by the power became finer and lighter and, suddenly, it was sensed as *I*. It was simultaneously joy, weight, substance, warmth, light, and authority.

As the linking rings routine came to its triumphant conclusion, a big puff of white smoke blew onto the stage from the wings where Blake had been waiting to make his entrance. Seeing that Eliot had departed from the plan, Blake had ordered Clipper to blow the smoke from the bellows prepared for this purpose, and as the audience applauded Eliot, the tall, magnificently costumed Blake made his dramatic appearance holding his own set of rings all linked together in the same circular formation in which Eliot had arranged them for the climax of his routine.

As a piece of theatre, the transition worked beautifully, creating the impression of a great royal magician summoned to the stage from the distant past. As Blake appeared on stage, Eliot's inner state gently returned to its usual ordinary quality, and he obediently played his role, although not without noticing the expression of anger in Blake's heavily mascara'd eyes and the lines of tension in his whitened face. The crimson, clefted lips were stretched thin.

Eliot gracefully stepped round Blake and theatrically backed off the stage through the traces of smoke still hovering in the air.

Backstage, there was a sense of great excitement. The Sorcerers congratulated Eliot on his routines, but everyone's eyes were now on Blake as he went through his act. His "continuation" of the linking rings was spectacular. He seemed driven beyond himself and had the audience, already primed by Eliot's extraordinary performance, gasping at every move.

With the applause for his rings routine at its full, Blake abruptly silenced the audience with a regal upward gesture of his arms, his white robes and breastplate gleaming in the spotlights. Wally Pound started the record spinning that accompanied the Sands of the Desert routine, and all the boys watched breathlessly as Blake filled the glass bowl of water that was now in front of him with five colors of sand—black, red, blue, yellow, and green. The music, "In a Persian Marketplace," echoed through the theatre. But Eliot could see that Blake's face had retained its fury and tension. And, unbidden, the thought arose in him to get Max on the stage as Blake had wanted. It was more than a thought; it appeared in him as an actual impulse, and he found his mind picturing Max—who had now returned to his seat in the audience—coming up to the stage to serve Blake's act. And as he saw this in himself, he was aware of the power starting up again, but in its new dimensions—the power to force people's minds and actions. He felt fear, fear for Max.

But what of the woman in the back row? He had no room in his mind to think of that, try as he might. He could not let go of Blake's command to draw Max up to the stage.

Blake completed the wondrous Sands of the Desert effect. The audience was thrilled by it.

And now came the grand finale, the fire-bowl production. Wally Pound changed the record and started up the music again, this time the Khachaturian "Sabre Dance." Blake picked up the silk scarf from his table, crossed his arms over his chest, lowered his head, and slowly stepped toward the front of the stage into the spotlight that had been specially positioned for him.

Eliot tried to make out the outlines of the fire-bowl that he knew was concealed under Blake's tunic. It was held there vertically in a special holster under the armpit. The bowl contained lighter fluid in a specially constructed compartment and had a sparking device built in that ignited only when in the horizontal position. Even from the side, where Eliot was standing, the whole apparatus was very well concealed under Blake's loose white tunic.

Blake, his head still bent forward as though in deep meditation, now uncrossed his arms and opened the black, white and red silk scarf bearing the insignia of the Sorcerer's Apprentices on it—the large ringed skull with the seven keys hanging from the lower arc of the ring. He freely turned the scarf around so the audience could see that there was nothing concealed.

The "Sabre Dance" began to grow louder. Blake took his time, and then with a sudden grandiose gesture, extended his arms forward and, with his head still bowed—the gleaming, white, elongated headdress pointed diagonally forward—draped the scarf over his bent left arm.

Now came the move in which the magician reaches under his arm to bring out the fire-bowl, tilting it horizontally and simultaneously drawing away the silk scarf, creating the effect of a bowl of flames materializing out of thin air. Here the timing was of utmost importance. The smallest mistake or hesitation not only made for an ineffective trick, but ran the risk of the silk scarf catching fire.

Which was exactly what happened as Blake dramatically, and with great bravado, drew the scarf away from the fire-bowl. Eliot was not aware that he had willed or even wished for this shocking event to happen. He was as startled as everyone else when he saw the long tongues of yellow flames trailing menacingly at the corner of the scarf in Blake's hand. At the same time, somewhere in himself, he was not surprised at all. Suddenly, this whole incredible scene began to seem like something he had witnessed before, as though in another lifetime. Only much later, when it was all over, would he vaguely remember that just before the fire he was projecting his power not onto Max, as Blake had commanded him, but onto Blake himself.

Unaware of what was taking place, Blake proudly and majestically displayed the bowl of fire for all to see on the palm of his outstretched left hand. At just that moment, the flaming scarf touched the side curtain, which instantly caught fire. And all hell broke loose.

The stage was now filled with Sorcerers running and shouting, shouting and running. Flames were leaping up the curtain. Blake dropped the fire-bowl, and its blazing liquid splattered onto the stage and ignited the bottom of his robe. He looked down in disbelief, and his headpiece fell to the floor. Sorcerers, still shouting, appeared with buckets. Somewhere a bell went off. Somewhere else a hose was turned on and sprinkles of water started raining gently onto the stage. The fire on the curtain was roaring and crackling. Sorcerers with other buckets appeared. Giant gushers of water jumped out of the buckets and landed on the first two rows of the audience. Some water hit the burning curtain. No one seemed to notice or believe that Blake was on fire, not even Blake himself, who was caught in a still life posture like that of a policeman directing traffic as the flames shot up his costume. In an instant, Max Falkoner was on the stage heaving a bucket of water onto Blake and then grabbing another bucket and another until the fire on Blake's costume was out. Blake stood unmoving, water dripping from his head, his blackened costume clinging to his body. Buckets and more buckets appeared, water and more water flowed out onto the audience, hitting the curtain in passing. The fires were now out, but the Sorcerers were in a paroxysm of filling water buckets and hurling the water in the general direction of the audience. As for the audience, most of them realized this was not the intended finale of the show, but it all happened so quickly that the only members of the audience who had left their seats were the relatives in the first rows, more out of fear of drowning than of burning.

Gradually, like the winding down of carved dolls in a steeple clock, the Sorcerers moved slower and finally came to a halt. In this still life tableau, brilliantly spotlighted, Eliot, holding an empty bucket, found himself standing about six feet from Blake and Max, who were facing away from him. He watched Max gently drape his jacket around Blake's now sloping shoulders and, seeing this compassionate gesture of Max's toward Blake, Eliot suddenly felt choked with tears. Then Blake turned round to face him.

The tears then burst forth, and Eliot actually heard himself let out a loud cry when he saw Blake's face: it was precisely, to the very last detail, the melting face he had seen in the second vision on that night when he first visited Blake's house and was told of the prophecy of Irene! The water dripping down Blake's face, washing away the makeup and the black eyeshadow, was precisely the melting face he had then seen in his mind.

He could not tell what Blake was feeling. The rouge on Blake's lips had been blurred, erasing the contours and the natural cleft, making his mouth into a crazy smear of some kind—happy and grim at the same time, as though the masks of comedy and tragedy had been superimposed one upon the other. This impression of a mixing of two contradictory qualities was strengthened by the smeared eyeshadow, which made his eyes seem at the same time both mordantly dark and comically misshapen. The magnificent breastplate was blackened with soot; the regal priestly robe was in tatters and partly covered by Max's exceedingly ordinary sports jacket. And the water held by Blake's full head of hair kept dripping so that his face seemed continuously to melt, like a melting waxen mask.

Eliot simply could not understand Max's tender solicitude toward the defeated Blake, but his heart seemed to understand it very well, for now, the power descended from the back of his head and with great force penetrated his whole body, including the region within his chest. While he was weeping for the defeated Blake, the power was presenting him with a vision of himself as well. Eliot felt that the tears streaming down his own face were melting away his own mask. And suddenly, a great sensation of joy welled up in him. He felt he understood—Blake had also been a pupil of Max! He felt Blake as a brother.

Relatives in soaking clothes now milled around on stage, and the theatre began to empty out. Several bursts of good-natured laughter were heard from the audience as they left. It was clear that the audience had had a good evening.

Except for the subdued action on the stage, the theatre was now empty and quiet. Only one person remained. She was seated in the back row, obscured in the shadows of the balcony.

IRENE

Eliot watched Max lead Blake down from the stage and toward the back rows of the theatre. He was sure now that the woman really was Irene and that he was the only one of the Sorcerers who had seen her. At first he remained behind, but when he saw Max and Blake disappear into the shadows, he walked down the aisle after them. Seeing this, the Sorcerers in their turn, one by one, followed after Eliot as though in ritual procession. A great hush had settled over everything and everyone within the big, empty space of the theatre.

When Eliot caught up with Max and Blake, at first he could see only their backs, Max in his shirt-sleeves and Blake with Max's coat draped over his shoulders. They were standing in the row in front of Irene, blocking Eliot's view of her. He stopped a few yards from them, sensing that something private was being exchanged.

He stood there watching, not wanting to intrude and trying to overcome his fear of seeing Irene in the flesh. From the back, he saw Max gesticulating as he spoke to Irene, while Blake stood and listened with his head bowed. Then he heard her voice. Its deep resonance and clarity startled him. She said something about everyone seeing himself within his proper role, and as she said this, Blake slowly straightened his head.

Then Blake and Max stepped aside and Eliot saw her. She was looking right at him. Behind Eliot, the Sorcerers suddenly broke into subdued gasps and cries of disbelief as they backed away. It was as though they were seeing a ghost.

But Eliot stood his ground. He was overwhelmed by her looks—she was far more beautiful, or more *something*, than her photographs, and also considerably older. Her pale hair was the same, but it was now longer and intricately formed around the long oval of her face. As for her eyes, he had never seen eyes at once so quiet and strong. They emanated a light that seemed to include everything.

Max motioned Eliot to come forward, and Eliot nervously moved into the row where Max and Blake were standing, taking his place between them. Slowly, a few at a time, the other Sorcerers returned, like small, shy animals, and gathered in the rows behind Eliot. Eliot quickly turned to look at them and saw that now even the face of Ronnie Pitkin was open and full of wonder. The hatred was completely gone.

Eliot strongly felt the presence of Blake and Max on either side of him. Irene spoke directly to him, but seemed also to be speaking to all the Sorcerers standing behind him. He felt he was at another initiation, only this time far more real and serious.

"What do you want?" she asked him.

He felt she had the power to grant anything he wished. But to his dismay, he realized that he didn't know what to ask for. He was not surprised when she spoke again, having obviously read his thoughts.

"In fairy tales, you have three wishes," she said. "But in life you only get one wish. So, tell us, what do you want? Think carefully about it. Be sure of what you ask for."

Eliot's mind started racing. He wanted to know who she was. He wanted to know why Blake had lied about her being dead. He wanted to know about the difference between Max and Blake, how they seemed to stand for such different things and yet now had come together in her presence. He wanted to know about the power, where it came from, what it meant. Yes, that was closer to the mark—the power.

"It may help you," she said, "if you take the ring off your finger."

Eliot obeyed. She extended her arm, and he placed the ring in the palm of her hand.

More thoughts and questions came to him—about his own life, what he should do, what career to follow. But these things did not seem so important now, certainly not enough to waste his one wish on them. But then what *was* the most important thing in his life, really? He had seen that by using the power, under Blake, he had been able to get whatever he wanted—money, sex, honors— and that it still wasn't enough. Guided by Max, he had touched something entirely different, something he never could have imagined wanting, and it was enough, more than enough. Yet it always cost him so much. It was always bought with a price. And he knew that he had barely scratched the surface of what Max had to offer him.

Irene then spoke again. "Turn on your power, Eliot."

He did—or tried to—and experienced nothing. He waited, and still nothing came. He tried with renewed effort, but it simply wasn't there.

After another pause, Irene said, "Your power is gone, Eliot. It will come back only when you know what it is you want most out of life. For that to happen, you must now live without the power."

Eliot stood there, speechless. He looked toward Max and then Blake. But they said nothing. In a burst of panic, Eliot said, rapidly, "I know what I want. I want . . . I want . . ." But while he was stammering, thoughts came to him: Was it so bad if the power was really gone? He didn't want to use the power as Blake had directed, and with Max the power was not that important. With Max, he always had to search for something deep within himself, coming from his own struggle.

Irene interrupted his thoughts. "*That* can never be taken from you."

But Eliot kept on stammering even though, within himself, he was quite at peace about losing the power.

"I want . . . I want to know the truth, to help others . . . I want to know about the universe, about God, I want not to die, I want . . . I want . . ." His mouth went on, but inside he felt peacefully separated from everything "it" said. Again Irene interrupted him, gently. She said something that Eliot did not understand, or even remember, until many years later. She spoke of another power within him, a power far stronger than anything he had yet experienced. She told him that he would have to struggle for many years in the midst of his ordinary life to develop this power and that both Max and Blake could help him, if he wished.

Eliot again turned to look at Max and then at Blake. Both maintained their silence on each side of him.

"In choosing Max," she went on, "you chose well. But remember, it was Stephen Blake who first sent you to Max. Both are necessary. When you feel the truth of that, you will be ready to enter the brotherhood of adult magicians. Until then, take this back."

Irene handed him the skull ring, after cupping it in her hands for a few seconds.

"The skull is death," she said. "But what must die? Think carefully about that. There are two kinds of death: the death of the ego and death by the ego. You must either destroy the ego by confronting it, or it will destroy you."

Eliot accepted the ring from her. But still a question was bursting in him.

"But why did Blake lie to me about you?" he asked.

"No," said Irene, "you don't understand. It was we who deceived him. It was necessary for him."

So, Blake had only just now discovered that Irene was still alive. Realizing that, Eliot felt an impulse of tenderness toward him. He sensed that a mysterious and compassionate logic governed everything that had taken place.

"Very like a fairy tale," said Irene, "where everything obeys ironclad laws except for one single miracle, at the navel."

Eliot looked at her uncomprehendingly, even while nodding his head in assent. He felt he was already filled with more than he could assimilate, yet he also craved more from her.

For a long interval, she did not speak. She seemed to be gauging him, and at the same time she seemed herself to be searching for something in some subtle way that Eliot could not identify. He had the sense that she, even she, was turning somewhere for some kind of help. But how? And to what?

Finally, without taking her eyes from him, she continued. "Of all that you have experienced with us," she asked, "what has meant the most to you?"

There was no question about that in Eliot's mind. But ought he even to speak about it? It was when Max had watched him from behind the mirrored wall at the shop, when Eliot had stolen the secrets of the tricks; when he had then confessed his intention to rifle the files and had experienced such overwhelming shame that he felt himself unworthy to continue with the work that Max was giving him; and when Max then stunned him by accepting it all so quickly—as though Eliot had passed, rather than failed, some pre-established test; as though what he had experienced was the main purpose of all the work, all the struggle, all the practice with attention and the rings, and with Blake, and with everything else; as though, or almost as though, the experience of remorse in seeing himself was even the central aim in life itself.

Eliot tried, but was unable to speak about it, even to her.

"Try, Eliot, try. . . ." It was Max, standing to his left, whispering to him. Eliot could not speak. That experience was too . . . too emotional? No, not just that, but too intimate, too real. He simply couldn't speak about it. But Max continued to whisper to him, "Try, Eliot. Find the words. Only now can you speak truly. All other talk is lies."

Eliot could not. After a few seconds, Max whispered, very softly, "Let it go, then. For now."

"You understand," said Irene finally, "that what you feel is the sacredness of something. Sacred and secret are the same word. You must keep it secret from the part of you that profanes everything it touches—until you discover what true speech is.

"Can you understand," she continued, "that this remorse is what we have given to Stephen? He has seen the black magician in himself, the ego that is symbolized by the death's head on the ring you have been given. This death must die.

"It was necessary for Stephen to believe I was no longer alive. We gave him the gift of temptation, as Max gave it to you. This experience has been handed down through the ages in the traditions of real magic. To become a magician capable of serving, you must first confront yourself as you really are.

"A teacher of magic such as Max creates conditions so that the pupil can experience both the force of the spirit and the force of the ego within himself and bring them together in his own being. Only when you can bear to see good and evil struggling within you can the transforming fire of remorse appear. This brings the peace that passes understanding, the marriage of two mutually opposing forces. Only then can a human being strive to serve that which calls to us from Above. No power of mind or heart can exist for long except under the rule of conscience. . . ."

* * * * *

But surely, here the tale must end. We cannot speak further about what Eliot himself did not and could not yet understand. A tale has its own laws. Another tale could be told after Eliot goes back to his ordinary life without the power, after he falls in love and travels and finds his career, after loved ones die and friends betray him, after he tastes the depths of the joys and sorrows that mark the life we must all lead. Perhaps one day, long after the miraculous year that was given him, on a day when he begins to sense what man really must search for in this life, the power will return to him. He will find another Max and another Blake and eventually another mystical Lady to bring them together in himself.

May we all share his search for that which our own hidden power may truly serve. May you, dear reader, and I who have told this tale, find the real struggle and the real magic that was long ago prepared for us.

CPSIA information can be obtained at www.ICGtesting.com
Printed in the USA
LVOW11s0114141015

458015LV00002B/2/P